Justin Ide

About the Author

G. XAVIER ROBILLARD is a blogger at several humor sites and a regular contributor to McSweeneys.net. He lives in Boston, Massachusetts. *Captain Freedom* is his first novel.

Captain Freedom

A Superhero's Quest

for Truth, Justice, and the Celebrity

He So Richly Deserves

Captain Freedom

G. Xavier Robillard

HARPER

NEW YORK · LONDON · TORONTO · SYDNEY

HARPER

HarperCollins books may be purchased for educational, business, or sales promotional use. For information please write: Special Markets Department, HarperCollins Publishers, 10 East 53rd Street, New York, NY 10022.

FIRST EDITION

Designed by Joy O'Meara

Library of Congress Cataloging-in-Publication Data is available upon request.

ISBN 978–0–06–165068–0

09 10 11 12 13   OV/RRD   10 9 8 7 6 5 4 3 2 1

To my partner in crime, Blunt Girl

"Freedom" is just another word for
"time to kick your ass."

—Captain Freedom

Contents

Contents

Captain Freedom

The Beginning of the End

WHOOSH! The forty-foot-long scimitar slices through the sky, aimed straight at me. It's a near miss, but the sudden partition of air created by the weapon produces gale-force winds. The air column pushes me backward several hundred yards, enough so I can size up my dreaded opponent. Genghis Kong, the giant Barbarian, has escaped from his unusually large prison off the coast, its powerful electromagnetic fencing disrupted by offshore oil exploration, and he's back in Los Angeles for a weekend of rest, relaxation, and wanton destruction. I fly back up into his face.

"Your furlough ends now," I shout at him. Genghis came looking for freedom, but Freedom found him.

I'm sure he can barely hear me. The sound of rotors from military choppers is deafening. Not sure what they think they can do, and the Pentagon's highly touted Barbarian Defense Shield has been a total failure.

Genghis was part of the Monsanto giant laborer breeding program. The agriculture company had created an entire line of genetically altered superfoods, like twenty-foot rutabagas. Realizing they hadn't thought of a way to harvest the humon-

1

gous produce, the company quickly bred giant farm workers to do the job. Unfortunately, the giants proved harder to control than the average migrant worker and escaped out into the world, seeking better-paying jobs and, in some instances, a life of crime.

My cell phone vibrates in a hidden panel in my costume. It's nice to have, a great convenience, but I can imagine my mentor Chief Justice looking down from his Secret Headquarters in the sky and frowning. The man had no use for nondestructive technology. The Chief didn't even own an answering machine.*

I hover in midair. Holding still above Earth takes quite a bit of concentration—it's somewhere between treading water and doing Kegel exercises. I hope it's my sidekick calling. He hasn't been taking my calls lately. I don't recognize the number on the screen, but he's always losing his phone.

"Hello?"

"Uh, Mr. Freedom?"

"That's *Captain*," I correct, and know right away it's a telemarketer.

"The New York Bank of the Americas has a great credit card offer."

I have no time for this. "What's the APR? Annual fee? Do you have any way to capture a rampaging Barbarian?"

"Uh, I'll have to check with my supervisor. Can you hold?"

There is no way that Genghis is acting alone. He's a Barbarian, and though I consider myself a tolerant person and have several Barbarian American friends, they generally aren't the

---

* He had an answering service: me, which I found quite disappointing because the job had specified *light or no phones.*

smartest group. And they stink. I'm relieved he didn't bring his giant horse.

"Sir, we don't have anything specifically for Barbarians, but we do offer a concierge service and I'm sure they could help you with that sort of thing."

"Great. Sign me up." I answer all the required questions impatiently but, I hope, without being rude. By the end of the day I should have a new DisasterCard—*My Strife, My Card*.

I click off the phone, fly as fast as I can, and smack Genghis in the back. He ignores me and turns toward downtown L.A.

But who—or what—controls him?

Whoever it is must be close by, but we're on an isolated patch of ruined freeway. It's just me, him, and the helicopters. Then I see it. One of the choppers has a different insignia, not Army or LAPD or *Eyewitness News 7*. The markings belong to that French triumvirate of terror, *Les Misérables*, and I'll bet anything that the Villain inside is Enfant Terrible.

Terrible's supposed to be in jail serving out a long sentence for importing raw-milk cheese. Supervillains always get out. Sometimes a spectacular escape is involved, but they usually get released because of budget cuts.

My day is already in a shambles, and I am angry.

My career's entered an irrevocable tailspin. There's an important dinner party that I'm going to miss. My girlfriend isn't speaking to me. I'm in no mood for Enfant's *merde*.

I fly up and rip open the helicopter door and step inside. "Thought you needed a breeze in here."

The pilot looks confused and then taps on his helmet. He can't hear me. I grab a spare headset and repeat myself.

"Captain Freedom," crackles the snide, nasal voice of Enfant

Terrible over the headset. "The Barbarian is on a collision course with your beloved city. Think you can stop him? Or maybe you should warn the citizens first. Oh, the dilemma!" He laughs a French laugh.

I fly away to face Genghis, and he pulls out another weapon. It's light blue and looks something like a mace. His arm flits down toward me, and I change direction quickly. So does he.

We continue our deadly dance. I'm trying to figure out what he's holding. The sword was better. Where would you get a forty-foot sword sharpened, anyway?

The weapon comes down on me. The uniform distribution of pores tells me what it is: a giant flyswatter. He's got me on the ground, pinned.

I can't focus. Too many other things on my mind. There's been a little trouble at work. I've made some mistakes, but what can I say—I'm only human (partly). I need to get back to my party and fix things. If I don't get out of here, my soufflé will be ruined. But that's no reason to fight like an amateur.

The implement presses down on me. I feel at least one rib crack.

Nobody breaks my bones and gets away with it. The enormous Barbarian might be strong, but I'm stronger. I push with all my strength, breathing into the pain, and the flyswatter is off.

Now that I'm free, I blast into the sky with a plan. The *Misérables* helicopter hovers nearby. Probably needs to be close by to control Genghis. After I catch the rotor in my hands, I rip it off and then grab the chopper by the skids. Heavier than I thought.

After a few cleansing breaths, I wind up and heave it into the Pacific Ocean. Sure enough, Genghis follows it to save his criminal master. But there's one thing that Enfant Terrible doesn't know: Barbarians can't swim. The giant fumbles as soon as he's caught in the undertow and makes a tremendous splash as he flails in the water, hopeless as a cow without water wings. The Navy can handle it from here. A city is saved, but my evening is ruined.

Do I get accolades, a key to the city, a poorly drawn crayon thank-you from a classroom of children who cannot spell?

Instead of getting a ticker tape parade, I will soon be out of a job.

Over and over, I ask myself why am I thrown out of the game, given the red card of life? Who is responsible? The Supervillain masterminds whom I've thrown into jail repeatedly? The international crime syndicate, INTERBAD? Traitors within our own government?

No.

It's Upper Management.

Forced Out

Instead of going to college, I studied with a Korean master to learn several ancient and useless forms of combat. And when I turned twenty, with the help of my mother's expert machinations, I joined Gotham Comix. I gave them my heart and soul and my four super-powers: flying, lightning-fast reflexes, supernatural strength, and the uncanny ability to predict the weather.

People always ask, if you're so good with the weather, why didn't you become a meteorologist? It's a typical reaction, like when you ask really tall people if they play basketball.

But not even my understanding of the difference between sleet and freezing rain can prepare me for the treachery I'm about to experience.

I'm in New York, teaching inner-city schoolchildren about the value of flossing, when I get a call from the Accounting Department at Gotham Comix. I fly up to their midtown offices right away.

Entering the conference room, I'm immediately suspicious. They have a PowerPoint presentation.

First, they remind me that my insurance premiums are too

high. But I have put a generation of criminals behind bars. Then they start hurling financial mumbo-jumbo like Zeus's lightning bolts. "Sales of your comic book are in decline." "The market favors graphic novels about losers." "We've posted losses for the last seven quarters." "We can't compete with the indecipherable but adorable manga."

"But what about the children?" I ask. "I've taught so many of them valuable life lessons, like how to increase self-esteem by purchasing Captain Freedom products."

Ray Hellander, the chief accountant, drops the bomb: "McDonald's ditched your Happy Meal toy."

I am stunned by this fast-food treason. "Who's going to fight evil?" I ask them.

"We've got a group in Bangalore. You don't have to speak English to fight evil."

They offer a paltry retirement package, but I'm not going without a fight. I search my mind for an appropriate comeback. "Freedom ain't cheap." In my case it's $4.3 million a year.

Hellander brandishes a covered platter that was hidden under the table. "You know what this is?"

I admit ignorance.

He opens the lid. "Tofu. Just a single block, medium firm, provenance unknown. Perhaps Chinese, perhaps not."

There's no doubt he knows soy is my weakness. If I ingest it, I lose all of my superpowers.

"Quite a miraculous food, tofu. Adopts the flavor in which it is marinated. Fries quickly. High in protein—if you eat it with rice," he cautions.

I smile. "How is a group of accountants going to force me to eat that?"

"You already have, Captain."

"?!?!?!?!" A bead of perspiration abandons ship from the dry dock of my forehead.

"Your nonfat chai latte. This morning, at the Heroes' Commissary."

"What about it?"

"It was made with soya milk."

I try to use one of my secret powers. But I won't be able to use any of them for the next seventy-two hours. The froth on my morning beverage had seemed a little lacking in exuberance, but I had assumed that was the telltale sign of skim milk.

A door opens and in rushes a platoon of superattorneys. I'm surrounded, my powers useless. I stall.

"You really think you can force me into retirement?"

He waves a legal document in front of me. "You're going to volunteer. It was the right incentive package. Freedom, you have no choice."

Desperate, I remind Hellander that a large sell-off of Gotham Comix stock could trigger a panic in the market. The attorneys back off, and we negotiate. I don't get a gold watch, but now I have a golden parachute. According to our agreement, nobody can know that this happened—I volunteer to leave behind the life of fighting crime.

They give me forty-five minutes to leave the building. I have to clean out my corner office but leave the laptop. There's no time to grab the *Dilbert* cartoons from my wall. They take away my secret decoder ring, my autographed copy of the *Flash Gordon Hero Handbook*, and the keys to the Freedom Utility Vehicle. I grab the promotional poster from the *Captain Freedom* movie. When it is time to go, security—some of my best Superhero friends—escorts me out of the building.

I never even used this office—Gotham put it here for tourists visiting the building. So right now some hack is clearing out my real office in L.A. I'm being simul-canned!

I'm angry enough to toss a car across the street. But I'm not warmed up, and that's just begging for a back injury.

I pass some guys working in a manhole in the middle of traffic, and I realize that life is not that bad. I've got a massive Secret Headquarters that's already been paid for. I can travel the world. Tibet! Never been there. Heard they have some great mountains. And they're languishing under the evil rule of the Chinese. Maybe I'll free Tibet.

When you say that, you sound like a celebrity has-been embracing fashionable causes like a hip-hop MC grabs his crotch. But I don't know what to do with my life. Being a Superhero is the only job I've had since high school. Now I have to do something else?

Life has only prepared me for this one thing: to do good and to break the record for the number of bank robberies foiled.

After I leave the Gotham Comix office, Cher—I know a lot of people in the entertainment business—is kind enough to let me crash at her place, and I remain in New York for a week to do a quick job search. I apply to work for the State Department, but they say I need to know Arabic. Then I apply at the Defense Department, and this time I tell them I know Arabic. They deny me the job—if I know Arabic, I must be a terrorist.

Mom calls and leaves an epic message to tell me that she's sorry I resigned, she's sure it's somehow my own fault, and she got me an interview with Occidental Comics. But I can't work with the O.C. Their production values are low; their books aren't bound well. Famous artists won't go near them. I might as well sign up for a newspaper cartoon strip.

After fifteen years on the side of good, maybe it's time I bat for the other team. I have plenty of contacts, and how hard can it be to become a Supervillain?

But I can't go evil. It would really disappoint the kids. Plus, I would be at risk of losing my $4 million settlement.

The story that I've left Gotham gets out, and I schedule a press conference to discuss my future. The press is unkind. They interrupt and ask leading questions. Not a single person asks for my autograph.

"I'll never do that again," I say to nobody in particular after I remove my microphone.

"Sure you will," says a chipper voice. It's Skip Goodwin, the plucky reporter with the boyish charm who I'm certain is somehow responsible for my downfall.

"You won't have a choice"—he grins—"if you want to stay in the public eye. And I know you do!"

Because of national security, the media are barred from covering Heroes under contract unfavorably, but now it's open season. No matter how discreet I try to be, the paparazzi are there, taking humiliating photos of me falling down drunk in public or dancing on tables at the local bar. It's like they've singled me out because I'm famous.

I'm ready to fly home to L.A. but something stops me. Evil is still lurking. And there are several Superheroes in the New York area who owe me money or who have borrowed CDs that I'd really like to get back.

My sources tell me that the villainous Wayne of Mass Destruction has engineered the Ronald Ray-gun, a mind-control device that could enslave New York. I must respond, even if I am *sans* a Happy Meal contract.

Using Google, I quickly find Wayne's lab. He's surprised to see me.

"Captain Freedom," he snarls. "I thought you retired." He's pointing the Ronald Ray-gun at me.

"I am, but I still hate evil. Surrender the weapon." I give him the calm, trusting look of a friend who would never put him back in jail.

Wayne throws down a smoke pellet. By the time the air clears and I get Visine into my eyes, he and his weapon are gone.

I rush outside to see that he's high in the air. I will never understand why criminals are allowed to buy jetpacks.*

I launch into the sky and catch up with him.

"You can't fight me," he sneers. "You don't have insurance anymore."

"I've got COBRA."

He hurls his homemade explosives at me, but I dodge them with ease.

"I've got a heat-seeking missile, Freedom, straight from my friends in North Korea. You'll never escape." Little does he know!

We enter a region of high barometric pressure, which stalls his jetpack engine. WMD is tilted off balance, and—CRACK—I knock him unconscious.

I pry the Ray-gun from his clutches—it will be a great addition to my exotic weapons collection. Spectators cheer as we land, and for once I've saved the city without destroying real estate.

I may be retired, but the Captain Freedom Happy Meal will return. Right?

---

* Jetpacks were legalized in 1986 after heavy lobbying by the National Rocket Association.

Time for a Memoir

"Does it bother you that you don't have a nemesis?" The man stares at me, but I avert his gaze.

"What are you talking about? I've got plenty of archenemies."

"So you tell me. Freedom, you have many foes. Many casual enemies. But from all the stories you tell me, you have had a problem becoming intimate with any of them."

"Okay, you're right. I never had a deep and true archenemy," I sob.

My life coach is the only person on Earth who can make me weep. Lionel and I have been meeting for a few years, since I left the Superhero job. He's heard everything—the search for my father, stories of my crazy mother, and the ego roller-coaster known as online dating. All my low points.

After I left Gotham, my sidekick DJ urged me to go into therapy, but I wasn't convinced. It seemed so weak. After I went on a week-long drunken binge in New Orleans otherwise known as Mardi Gras, the results of which were mercifully kept out of the tabloids, he scheduled an appointment for me to see a life coach. I didn't even know what a life coach was.

"It's kind of an advocate. A teacher. A friend. A person you can tell your whole story to and not worry about it being leaked to the press."

"Like a priest or minister?"

"Like a very suntanned, highly paid priest."

It had been a few months since I retired. The world should have been open for a man with my many talents. I kept hoping a board position might open up at some important corporation, preferably one involving very little actual work, but those jobs are surprisingly competitive. I'd been fundraising extensively for SOY—Save Our Youth—a foundation dedicated to discovering a cure for the crippling soy allergy. It was fulfilling, a palliative for my soul, but I wanted to get back into the action. I was itching to don the costume that I made famous, the costume that launched a lucrative line of clothing.

But DJ was right: it was time for some internal housekeeping.

My first meeting with Lionel was tense. I didn't trust him. We arranged to meet first at a café, neutral ground. He looked like one of those guys that you see in daytime movies about the inspirational basketball coach who turns everyone's life around. Tough but kind. Strong but gentle. Disheveled but quite expensive.

We enjoyed our coffees, and our initial talk was small. We discussed why I came and what he could do for me—what I needed. I appeared as my alter ego, Tzadik Friedman, and told him I was a mildly successful screenwriter who retired early and lost his way.

"I don't normally work with screenwriters."

"Why not?"

"It's a professional liability."

I backpedaled. "It's more that I dabble in screenwriting. But I have other work. More sensitive work."

"I have, occasionally, treated Superheroes. If you know any."

"Uh, no," I replied.

"I know who you are. And you're no screenwriter."

He had me, and I couldn't trust anyone who hadn't done the basic research and tailed me for a while. "You know, I never expected to become a Superhero." I didn't want to be life-coached as a Superhero. I wanted to be treated like any other wealthy narcissist.

"But you're preternaturally strong, you can fly, and you can accurately predict the weather."

"Don't forget the lightning-fast reflexes."

We had returned to his office when he abruptly asked me about my costume switch.* At the time it was a question I was not prepared to answer, and I shut down for some time. We moved on to other issues, like my ability to act violently.

The general opinion among civilians is that you have to have some killer instinct or maybe a vigilante complex to become a Superhero. People think I'm ferocious, but really I'm just like Ferdinand the Bull. I don't love fighting, and I'd rather spend my days smelling pretty flowers than cracking skulls. If they paid me to do that, I'd do it. But the perfume companies never came knocking at my door. Crime did.

"So why did you answer that call?" asked Lionel.

I fell silent. It always seemed that I had no choice.

"But there were those dinosaur bones calling to you."

---

* There was a huge uproar when I changed from a patriotic yet unfashionable red, white, and blue costume to a midnight blue one, which I swear on the *Hero Handbook* is absolutely not black.

14

Growing up, I always wanted to be a paleontologist. "What are you going to do with that?" my mother asked. "Put your shovel away and get out of the sandbox. You're twelve years old. It's time for flying practice."

Many days I regret not becoming a paleontologist. I could be at some fancy university with a real lab and government funding, and I'd travel to exotic locations to identify dinosaur bones rather than stop a madman from awakening an ancient evil below Earth's crust. I'd squint at the enormous fossil and say, "Don't be silly. The brontosaurus doesn't exist. This is the jawbone of a brachiosaurus." Which I've used to crack the skulls of evildoers, by the way.

On another visit, out behind Lionel's office we shot hoops. He's a great ballplayer, and even with my myriad talents, I couldn't block a single shot. We laughed, and talked, and shared a cold beer while the sun went down. That was the best day I'd had in a long time, even if it set me back $960. Since then, we have worked through many issues. But I'd never really considered the archenemy problem.

At the end of this session, Lionel repeated that I need to get in touch with who I am—not just the Hero who can twist steel beams as if they were balloon dogs, but the man inside that man. A little paleontology for the soul. Lionel's wisdom made me emote in the form of a solitary, raging tear.

He suggests I write down my own history to increase my self-awareness. "A memoir might be therapeutic. And financially rewarding as well."

"That's not my style."

"We need to understand why you never had an archenemy," he says. "It's important."

"Not really."

"Freedom." Lionel laughs. "Over the past few years you've spent thousands on me. There's only so much else I can do. I can coach you forever, whether you improve or not. My financial adviser and I are both prepared to do that for you. But don't you think it's time to let the healing begin?"

It's late afternoon when I drive home. As the sun sets and the smog lays a red-orange gauze pad over the city, I cry one last time.

My coach is right. A memoir! I will devote the rest of my life to it, if necessary, and it will be more fulfilling than providing community service or going on motivational speaking tours. The whole Captain Freedom saga—from life on the Montana ranch to my humble beginning as a sidekick, to saving the world (three times), to my line of sportswear, to the dinner party that forced my early retirement, and my long struggle to return to the public and become a Figure of Importance. America's Hero.

As soon as I sit down at home in front of my laptop, my enthusiasm wanes. Tough stuff, this writing. Each morning I start promptly at eleven-thirty, and I write until noon. It's a painstaking process—I don't wish to relive the Macarena days or combat against the evil grunge band, but this is what it takes to write an honest memoir. I work on my grammar as if I were training at the gym, and I hire a ghostwriter.

Little by little, the book takes shape. Although I can't remember why I switched costumes, I know it's important, and I press on through the fog of memories, going way back. Did it affect me that all the other kids made fun of me because I could fly? I'm not sure.

Writing has made me a better reader, something I've always

wanted. My lightning-fast reflexes cause me to skip over certain lines—and sometimes I'll read the same line over and over, giving the impression that the book is very repetitive. This is a learning disability, something I haven't had to contend with since high school. But now, I write, and when I say write, I mean that I narrate to the ghostwriter, who then shows me a typed draft of my half hour of excruciating work. I don't understand how full-time writers do it. It must be all that drinking.

I frequently argue with my ghostwriter, who believes his glorified stenography gives him some say in the creative process. He suggests we write the memoir in the past tense, but I won't have it. The present tense is the tense of action, the tense of decisiveness. It's really the tense of the future.

Where to start? Should I talk about my boring upbringing on the Montana ranch where I used my superstrength to rassle cattle? Or the bar fights my mom used to get into? My father's disappearance? My first girlfriend?

I'll start with what motivational speakers call the best days of your life: the punishing, scarifying, hellish high school years.

School on the Hill

I grip my pencil so hard it snaps. A few students around me giggle, and the test proctor delivers a stern-faced silent warning.

I settle back into the test. The question I wrestle with is mathematical in nature: a simple conversion of parsecs to light-years. If it were any other time, I'd blow it off. Since when do exponents help fight crime? But the test I'm taking will determine my future.

The CAPE (Criminal Abatement Preparatory Exam) is my final at the extraordinary high school where I've spent the past three years.* The Vineyard School for Excellentness is a training ground for future Heroes and the leaders of tomorrow. It appears to be a normal prep school from the outside, but this venerable institution has secretly trained budding Heroes in need of discipline for years. The school is nestled in the heart of Napa Valley, where its students experience heartbreak, conflict, self-loathing, and rage—in short, everything one needs to become a Superhero or an executive director of a nonprofit organization—all in the name of good.

---

* The stories of my alienated, depressed, and dejected high school years are collected in the graphic novel *Lonely High*.

But the Vineyard is not just a school. It is also a vineyard, complete with a tasting room and a wine bar. Here we help our headmaster, Master Cleef Lee Van, grow and bottle his famous Super Tuscans.

Dozens of other gifted youngsters study here. In addition to the future Heroes, there is a group of misfits from around the globe: a champion speller, several members of the British royal family battling drugs and/or weight problems, and a promising young singer named Marky Mark. All are here to hone their abilities, to learn to blend in with others in an unsympathetic world that will compensate them highly for their abilities.

As I work on my test, my ears imagine sounds of students in the empty halls. The underclassmen have finished and left for the summer, and we seniors have been left to spend our time studying for the CAPE. Those who do well on this test are bound for greatness and will become the superdoctors, superspies, or supersommeliers of tomorrow.

The CAPE is a nationally mandated test for all potential Superheroes. I've had a hard time studying because the Master has refused to alter his curriculum in any way to accommodate the exam. Because we are a private school, unknown to the outside world, he can do as he pleases. While young Superheroes at other secret schools learned hostage negotiation, international diplomacy, chemical forensics, survival skills, and emergency medicine, the Master taught us the following subjects: Secret Headquarters decoration, media relations, wine pairings, ancient weapons, and the nearly useless martial art of Pho Van. I flip through the rest of the test. Not a single question on the pratfalls of serving lamb curry with Montepulciano d'Abruzzo or the benefits of screw tops versus cork.

A couple seats away I see the straight black hair of my girlfriend Kaeko, and I know she's doing fine on the test. Her perfect shoulders are relaxed. She's beautiful, intelligent, faithful, as American as apple pie and also as American as sushi, for she is half Japanese. If I had spent more time studying with her and less time enticing her into having sex, I wouldn't have this problem. It makes me wonder whether nerds don't get laid because they are nerds or become nerds because they aren't getting laid.

My mother has done everything she can to prepare me for this day. In elementary school, she got me onto the right soccer team, hired tutors, and made certain I loaded up on plenty of extracurricular activities. She has her heart set on Harvard's Schwarzkopf School for Heroism. But at this moment, my physical talents are worthless; all I have are my brains to pass this test.

Most of my classmates have made other plans. Before going off to college, they'll have the perfect summer jobs: lifeguarding, camp counseling, house painting, demolition. I never bothered to apply for college. If I'm not immediately taken in as a sidekick or allowed to join some ensemble group, it's back to the ranch in Devil's Craw, Montana.

There is only one answer: cheating.

Kaeko sits too far away from me. There's no opportunity for me to read her answers. To my right is my friend "Binary" Bergson. His extraordinary computer-hacking abilities guarantee him a high score, a score he'll fix later no matter how badly he does now. He's been talking about an outlandish scheme to invent electronic voting machines. To my left is Skip Goodwin. He accelerated his coursework to graduate early.

Everyone in my class hates Skip. The boy has a preternatural sense of timing. His "scoop sense" helps him run the school newspaper, and he witnesses every embarrassing moment that will look good in print; not even an untimely pimple will escape his byline.

At the Vineyard we learn to shun media. Guest lecturer John Glenn taught us that no matter what heights you aspire to, some media bully will attempt to pull you down.

The Master allowed Skip to start the paper so that he'd have some use for his annoying superpower. But like any cub reporter, he jealously guards secrets. I cannot get a look at his paper. It looks like the moment of accountability, when everyone finally finds out that I'm destined to become a stunt actor or a bodyguard for the rich and famous.

The bell rings, and Skip and I stand at the same time, knocking into each other. Using my lightning-fast reflexes, I switch cover sheets on the two exams, so that my answers are attached with his paper. We mutter *excuse me*s to each other, and he never notices that the paper he hands in will spell his doom. The exam proctor, who taught our psychological profiling class, glares at me but says nothing. There's more than a little risk. I heard of a promising kid who was caught cheating a few years ago. Now he works as a crash-test dummy.

We seniors spend a week waiting for our exam grades, so we party every night. I spend some time getting to know 420, an innovative future Hero who can fashion pot-smoking devices out of everyday household items. And we play Glenfiddich, a sort of flying beach volleyball/softball/Frisbee game with a cask of Scotch at every base. Feeling on top of the world, we violate league rules and use live missiles instead of blanks.

To blow off steam, we launch an attack on the local charter

school, the Franklin School of Criminal Sciences. Our battle is short, and the kids from the Vineyard are victorious. Once we're done, Franklin Charter looks worse than a public school in Oakland. When we return, the Master notifies us that our grades have been posted. It is time to face the music: Did I cheat off the right guy?

As I look for my grade, I think about the fight that Kaeko and I had last night. She confronted me because she wasn't happy that I cheated.

"On the exam or on you?" Apparently I misread her feelings about the relationship. I never specifically talked to her about seeing other people. She stormed off, and we wouldn't speak to each other again for many years.

Looking back, I can't help but think it was I who drove Kaeko into a life of crime. Or perhaps it was her guidance counselor, who acknowledged that Kaeko's precision marksmanship and agility would be well rewarded if she became a professional assassin.

I look at my exam. Eighty-three percent. My friend Binary gave himself a 91. Kaeko, for what it's worth, was the only 100. Then I see a crestfallen Skip Goodwin, whose 58 should have been mine. He'll never be a Superhero with grades like that. Not that his stupid superpower would help anyone. Except maybe the *National Enquirer.*

"I don't understand," Skip complains to me.

"Maybe you should have studied?" I offer, without gloating.

"You! You did this to me. I know it. Somehow our grades were switched."

Soon after exam results are posted, I am summoned to Master Van's office. I'm afraid he knows I've cheated. As I'm admitted to his waiting room, I see Skip Goodwin leave. His eyes narrow as they meet mine.

"I know you cheated, Friedman. I've just filed a complaint with the Headmaster."

"What proof do you have, Skip?" I ask jovially.

"Oh, I'll get proof." His determined tone makes me suspect he'll embark on a lifelong quest to bring about my downfall. But I doubt it; he never took the Lifetime Vendetta elective.

The secretary buzzes me in to see Master Van. He is not alone in his office.

A Hero is there, a man in a trench coat and dark sunglasses. His name is known throughout the entire Hero universe. The two men are drinking brandy and look like they've been enjoying a good joke, but as I enter the room they grow somber. The Hero looks at me. I notice a pair of handcuffs dangling off his Orvis utility belt. Will the Master send me away?

Master Van is Irish-American, a boxy man of fifty with sandy hair and a strong chin. He grew up in a large family and literally fought his way out of poverty. After years working in a Korean restaurant and studying the martial arts, Cleef Lee Van became Korean himself. After working as a for-hire Hero, he used his street smarts to become headmaster of the Vineyard. Sending me to jail isn't his style. He runs our school on the philosophy that you can get anything you desire if you develop discipline and are exposed to near-constant beatings. I expect one of those beatings now.

"Mr. Friedman, your classmate Skip tells me, actually us"—he waves his hand to include the famous guest—"that you cheated. On the CAPE."

I gulp. "He's lying." I imagine the worst punishment: to repeat senior year at a public school.

"Of course you were cheating. You could never score an eighty-three on the CAPE. But you're aggressive. Cheating shows you know how to work the system."

"So I'm not in trouble?"

"Trouble? We're going to reward you. This is a meritocracy. If people like you didn't cheat, we'd never have any idea of your talents."

I appreciate his logic.

"My friend here wants to make you an offer."

"I'm Chief Justice, and I want you to be my sidekick."

My First Cape

As soon as the Chief appears in my life, I'm no longer Tzadik Friedman, the schoolboy from Montana. He gives me an alias and orders me to write a press release detailing our new partnership.

There's a certain protocol to becoming a sidekick. You're supposed to be vetted by Gotham Comix or one of the other Superhero franchises. Chief Justice, with his typical contempt for authority, disregards all of this and vouches for me himself.

I miss the crazy old coot. My life coach, Lionel, thinks that I'm still craving the Chief's approval. But that's shrink talk. I'm just bummed that he never got to know how awesome I am.

The Chief is a popular Superhero from an older generation, old enough to wear reading glasses, a secret carefully guarded from our enemies. He's got broad shoulders, a square jaw, and closely cropped gray hair. He has spent most of his career fighting the Soviets, which I surmise to be a syndicate of Eastern European baddies in parkas.

My mentor is the result of a super-secret military experiment determined to make the perfect soldier. The experiment failed when they realized that the perfect soldier is one who wouldn't fight in the first place, but Chief retains much of the discipline and skill one would expect. His capture rates are quite high, and he teaches me that more important than any superpower is the phone number of an attorney well versed in Superhero law.

All Heroes look to the Chief as an inspiration. Before he came along, Heroes went to the local barber. They didn't spend money for quality hair work. But the Chief broke the nine-dollar-haircut barrier, and until his tragic end, he would proudly spend a hundred bucks a pop on his coif.

My sidekick alias is Liberty Bill. I hate it. It is possibly the worst name for a Superhero—first of all, my name is obviously not Bill, but the Chief demands that I take on a less ethnic name than Tzadik. And it's such a stupid joke.

"Liberty Bill?" somebody will ask at a comic book convention.

"Yeah. Like Liberty Bell."

They'll smile politely and decide that they don't need my autograph in their precious collection.

I learn that among certain Chief Justice fans there is a betting pool that wagers how long it'll be before I'm killed off. The Chief's brand of justice is rough, and the vendettas against him have cost him several sidekicks over the years.[*]

Our partnership is awkward from the beginning. In a business where your origin story is highly prized, I cannot tell anyone a thing about the real me. The published version states that I rescued Chief Justice during a train robbery.

The Chief was on the Midnight Express when his train was set upon by bandit wolfmen. A young farm boy from Montana

---

[*] For the most recent, see *Chief Justice #236: Death of a Sideman.*

was there to witness the hijacking and took out the wolfmen with nothing more than gumption and a shotgun stocked with silver bullets forged from his parents' treasured candlesticks. He then rode all night to get a mortally wounded Chief Justice to medical care. Liberty Bill was born.

Now that I'm retired, I can admit this is crap. Montana wolfmen have been driven to extinction by ranchers defending their herds, and Chief Justice spends as little time on trains as any other normal person.

The Chief can't fly. He in fact has no preternatural abilities of his own, but he employs an amazing array of banned weapons to combat evil, including a copy of the Constitution housed within a steel tube. It reminds Villains that the rule of law and brute force are on his side. We drive around in his old Buick and fight the bad guys wherever we can find them.

He keeps a tight leash on me. For fear that I might outperform him, he forbids me to use any of my own superpowers, and he feeds me a steady diet of soy to prevent me from upstaging him—he is in fact the first to understand and exploit my incapacitating allergy. He promises that tofu scramble is the breakfast of champions.

Chief Justice and his books are very popular. Whenever we leave L.A., we stay in the best hotels—or rather he stays in them and I sleep in the car. I shine his shoes and polish and clean his guns and regard him with awe whenever he develops a daring plan for escape. But my most important job is to bring admirers up to his hotel room.

Women of loose morals often congregate in the hotel bar. And I sit there, alone at a bar stool, swishing around the swizzle

stick in my ginger ale. They know who I am and, more important, whom I represent. Invariably one of them saunters up to me
and makes a trite comment like "Cute cape."

But that line is a lie. The half-length piece of fabric that is tied
around my neck is anything but nice. For two long years I wear
that horrible nylon albatross, the mark that tells everyone that I
am a sidekick: only full Heroes are allowed to wear long capes. I
swear up and down that I will never make my own sidekick wear
that mark of bondage. I promise myself that if I ever get a sidekick of my own, it will be different. He will wear a vest. Maybe
legwarmers.

I cannot publicly say anything bad about Chief Justice.
There is nothing worse than when a sidekick violates the integ-
rity of his Hero by publishing a sordid memoir. But he represents
the old guard—the Heroism of yesterday, of pre-BCS college
football and atomic weapons. Although I marvel at his ability to
bust gambling rings, I am appalled that so many Supervillains
slip under his radar.

The two of us share many adventures. We catch bank robbers,
jewel thieves, thugs, pickpockets, drug dealers, cat burglars—the
starch in any distinguished Superhero's diet. But it is as if he will
take on only those criminals whom he knows he can beat.

We spend a lot of time chasing the elusive Loofah. He's the
Chief's archenemy, feared by millions. The pair is the very defini-
tion of nemesis. It seems like the closer we get, the harder it is to
trap him. I suspect it has something to do with comic sales.

Then it all comes crashing down.

On a routine mission we travel to the Azores. I still can't go
back there, mostly because of the parking tickets I incurred on
that first trip.

We trace the evil Loofah to his lair on one of the outer islands. He'd been leading an insurgency, as well as manufacturing cheap generic drugs for import into the United States. After a car chase that would make Steve McQueen blush, we arrive at a warehouse in the dead of night. The Chief confronts Loofah.

"Where are the drugs you owe me?"

"Ah, Chief, need I remind you of our arrangement?" Chief Justice is involved in a confusing arms-for-hostages-for-pharmaceuticals-for-mangoes deal with soldier-comedian Oliver Hardy North. I can't follow the intricacies, but he assures me it's all very patriotic.

We are surrounded by Loofah's rebel pharmacists. Since their strict ethical code prevents them from using guns, it's practically a fair fight. We just about mop them up when the door to the lair opens and in walks my mother.

"Mom, what are you doing here?"

"I never get to see where you work, Tzad."

"You can't call me that."

"Right, your secret identity. I am so proud of you."

"Liberty Bill, help!" cries Chief Justice.

"Chief Justice!" I run to his side.

But it's too late. Chief Justice is no more. He has been stabbed by one of Loofah's henchmen, whom I promptly coldcock. "I will come back," Chief says, gasping his final breath. "Someday in a bout of nostalgia, the editors will revive me." He fades.

"I can't believe he's gone," I moan. What an awful death— and in a country nobody can pronounce or find on the map.

"Maybe you'll make Superhero now," my mom says, as she accepts a large wad of cash from Loofah.

"What was that for?" I growl.

"For your future," says Mom. "You should put in a call to Gotham Comix."

"Mom, it's not that easy. I was his sidekick. I should have been there."

"You'll never become a Superhero with that attitude. Or that ridiculous goyish name."

"He was a great man."

"You'll be better."

I grieve about his tragic demise and have no idea what to do with myself. After putting my mother on the next plane back to Montana, I wander the archipelago. I still have no idea why my mother came here, but it's strange—if she hadn't shown up, I would not have become Captain Freedom.

After the Azores incident, I relocate to New York City and sublet a room in an apartment that comes with four roommates and no kitchen. No surprise that Gotham Comix hasn't called. I call the recruiter I've been working with, and he claims that there are no openings. Curse me for not using twenty-four-pound résumé paper!

I imagine that I'm in real trouble—Chief Justice was extremely popular and his books sold across the globe. Not only am I out of a job, but it's possible that the Hero community will seek revenge—the sidekick must protect his Hero at all times, no matter what. And I failed.

Then Skip Goodwin reenters my life. He pens a searing indictment that my mom came to the Azores to distract me. With Chief Justice out of the way, he scummily theorizes, Liberty Bill can become a full-fledged Hero. He has no hard evidence, just the testimony of dozens of unnamed witnesses. I'd like to know just who these anonymous sources think they are.

Before long I receive a summons from the Comics Code Authority, an independent entity beholden to no one and a frightful combination of staid government bureaucrats and nervous parents. Their job is to make sure that all comic book Heroes follow certain standards. They cannot act too violently or be depicted using drugs or having any sort of meaningful relationships. The CCA makes Iranian mullahs seem as hip as an East Village art rock band.

My mother suggests I bring legal counsel and let him do the talking. With no money, I retain the services of Oscar Goodman, a young pup just out of law school. He takes the case, asking only for my first month's salary, assuming that Gotham Comix hires me.

Our meeting with the CCA is fairly painless. Oscar argues that I have done nothing untoward and that I did my best to protect my guardian. Brilliantly, my attorney invokes the Robin Defense and contends that my Hero systematically deteriorated my self-esteem, to the point that I could barely protect myself.

I am exonerated, but it is certainly not my final run-in with this formidable body.

That night I get a phone call. "Thursday night, Peter Luger's, back room. We'll send a car. Bring nothing. Tell nobody." The phone goes dead.

There's no way this can possibly go well. I consider moving to Buffalo, but it's hard to be Heroic that close to Niagara Falls. Still no word from Gotham Comix. You'd think their Superhuman Resources Department could move a little faster. Thursday comes and I prepare myself for my destiny, whatever it is.

Heroes get iced all the time, and even though the CCA finds me innocent, it doesn't mean that my brethren will let me live. It's an unsavory part of the business, but it happens—tempers flare, and there are the occasional turf wars. The West Coast Heroes hardly speak to those on the East Coast. Many years of bad blood and competition for readership. There are always a few ensemble groups, but usually the only thing that keeps them together is chemical dependency.

I leave a note to my mom on my bed, one that will be easily found if I disappear. This will be the last time I don the Liberty Bill uniform. A car service waits outside my apartment. I don't know the driver, but I see he's got a Gotham Comix T-shirt underneath his blazer.

The drive to Brooklyn is mostly quiet, until we park. "When you enter the restaurant," the driver begins in an icy tone, "walk straight to the back. There's a door marked PRIVATE. Go through it. Look at no one. If you so much as take a peanut from the bar, the waiters will shoot you."

I follow the instructions to the letter. I don't even glance at the trays of perfectly seared meat and creamed spinach around me. The door opens and I enter a room the darkness of which is punctuated only by the occasional cigar ember.

The lights come up. It's mostly East Side Heroes. The room hums with activity—Heroes eating steak, smoking cigars. There are several bottles of fine red wine. Unlike sidekicks, who must follow a rule of total abstinence, Superheroes are allowed to drink as much as they want when they're off duty.* Perhaps they'll give me a glass before my execution.

---

* Rules are different when Heroes are on call. When carrying the pager, the Hero must be able to pass its onboard urinalysis/Breathalyzer tests—and hopefully not confuse the two.

"Tzadik Friedman, otherwise known as Liberty Bill," says one of the Heroes. It's Tony Garbanzo—I recognize his look from a limited-edition book that's currently on the newsstands. He's a DA by day, and at night he fights crime by emitting a powerful, stunning cologne. One of the rougher crowd, he's been known to kill criminals who make parole. His ruthlessness is rumored to be responsible for the disappearance of the Squeegee Men.

I nod and look at the floor. I hear footsteps coming close. Seconds pass, then I catch a whiff of his stupefying cologne. I pray to my Maker. My cape is ripped off my neck.

Instead of death, Garbanzo gives me a sharp embrace several times, as if he's doing a reverse Heimlich. "You're one of us now. You've been made."

Gotham promoted me! Toasts are pronounced, then we hash out the details. "You's going to be working in California, with the West Side crew. Better get a new alias, too."

"I can't wait."

"And if we see you fighting crime in New York." His voice changes, becoming sinister. "Remember we're the ones who made you. And we can unmake you as well. *Capisce?*"

"I do."

And we sit down to eat our steaks, drink our wine. I am introduced to my new favorite drink, the Rob Roy. The night bleeds into morning, and although I am as drunk as a lord, I fly back to my apartment, able to use my powers for the first time since I began my apprenticeship. The soy is out of my system; the alcohol is in. I crash into several buildings along the way.

The next day I make my way to Gotham Comix. The news has leaked before I arrive. My phone is ringing off the hook with calls of congratulation from my mother, Master Van, and former acquaintances who immediately ask for favors. Gotham offers me a sizable contract and I accept. I make plans to move to Los Angeles, where I will take Chief Justice's place as a West Coast Hero.

It is best for me to start with a clean slate, so we arrange for an accident to happen to Liberty Bill. It is a fate shared by many fallen, unprofitable Heroes—a story of betrayal, in which a sidekick falls or is pushed into a river filled with piranhas. My fate is to be ripped apart by an angry mob at Chief Justice's funeral. This issue will become the best-selling of any Liberty Bill book, and the few editions in mint condition are in high demand. No one will know that Liberty Bill becomes Captain Freedom.

When I return to my apartment that night, my four roommates are there and we crack open some cheap beer. We consume wings and pizza and more cheap beer, and I promise never to forget these roommates. Perry, Dave, Eric, Stephen: I have no idea where they are now.

Late in the night, as the flow of beer ebbs, Perry takes me to one side. "I just remembered this message for you."

"Oh yeah?" Nothing can bring me down off this cloud.

"This guy called. He wasn't real clear—spoke with a heavy accent. I should have written it down. Sorry."

"What did he say?"

"Something like, 'Chief Justice was my archenemy.'"

"Does he want me to call back?"

"He didn't say."

"Anyone else call?"

"Oh yeah, sorry—the FBI called."

"What did they want?"

"Something about a Death Ray?"

I almost lose my buzz. "That's heavy."

I'm not sure I'm ready to confront a Death Ray. It sounds so permanent.

"Did you get a phone number?" I ask.

"Sorry, man, I didn't."

Chief Justice's words come to me, as they do often in a time of need.

Let your adversaries come to you. Before you go into battle you must look tanned, ready, and rested. You should be clear-headed and relaxed. You have to meditate upon the futility of existence, or at least smoke some grass.

Half a joint later, I'm playing video games with my roommates. If the FBI really needs me, I'm sure they'll call back.

The First Time
I Save the World

I am a new Hero, living out of moving boxes in a Secret Headquarters that I'm subletting when the FBI finally calls me—an enemy of liberty and happiness is planning another assault on the free countries of the world with a heinous weapon. I haven't even unpacked my CDs yet.

"We called you weeks ago," the agent starts.

"Sorry about that. Just moved. Is it serious?"

"He's got a Death Ray," he tells me. The classic weapon of a career killer.

"What does he want?" I ask my liaison.

"The usual."

Homicidal megalomaniacs only want one thing, and that is to stoke the fires of their own Mall of America–size egos. Occasionally they like to invade Kuwait.

"Are you sure it's Loofah?"

"Correct."

You need to establish your archenemy early on. Typically, it's a robber whom you foil and then accidentally push into a tub of acid, where he's left for dead but instead develops mutant powers because he happens to be wearing acid-resistant flannel. In my case, it's much easier: since Loofah had Chief Justice killed, he becomes my archenemy. I've been expecting the paperwork to come any day.

Inheriting an archenemy is not something I feel good about. Usually you have to work for it. I'm outclassed by Loofah. He's smarter, he builds fantastic weapons, and he has sold millions of books and videos; he's the Carlos Castaneda of evil. And he's got an insane sense of style—this is one scofflaw who isn't afraid to wear orange with red. He'll wear a cream-colored suit or a dark tie with a dark shirt. Nothing like my garish red, white, and blue.

Loofah's evil to the core. Diabolical. He drinks expensive French wine, but only in moderation. To make matters worse, he is a mad, mad scientist. Mad as in crazy, although he's been taking medications for several years, and mad as in angry. As is frequently the case among evildoers, he is bald, a congenital condition contributing to his rage.

I don't know much about the sciences aside from paleontology, but it's obvious he's a strong researcher. He won a Nobel Prize for extracting the first known flesh-eating prion virus and an additional prize for pharmaceuticals when he created a highly addictive form of aspirin with built-in patent protection. His engineering prowess is both legendary and arbitrary—he is rumored to be behind the ridiculous promise of the Segway.

Chief Justice and Loofah first crossed paths working for opposing sides during the Vietnam War. Loofah's father is an Arab, and his mother a German Russian—she was a spy, killed by American agents during the Cold War. For some reason this background translates into a hatred for the United States.

My passport is current, my costume ironed, I have clearance to take off, but then the U.S. government stops me: we have lost airspace rights to fly over Turkey.

"But this enemy is going to destroy the world."

"Doesn't matter, Captain. We have to find a new flight route."

"Will the Turks really notice if I fly over their country? I'm too small to be an airplane. If radar picks me up, they'll think it's a large, muscular bird."

"And you're ready to dodge missiles?"

"I'll take my chances." Given the extreme circumstances, they clear me.

The Turks don't notice as I fly to Muhlderia, a former Soviet Socialist Republic. It's a typical backwater Central Asian republic—little electricity or food, lots of weapons. Loofah purchased the country just as it was detached from the Soviet Union, and got everything, too—tanks, the nukes, and a malnourished and scrappy army.

According to *Let's Go—Evil!*, the only notable destination of Muhlderia is Loofah's castle:

> *Surrounded by low-rise apartment buildings, Loofah's Black Castle is easily identified. Don't let the Gothic look fool you—the residence comes equipped with a modern surface-to-air missile battery and the usual piranhas in the moat. Do not under any circumstances order the grilled swordfish in the Terror on the Green, the Castle's restaurant, unless you like overcooked fish or overpoisoned mango chutney.*

I enter Loofah's castle through a large open window and get instantly trapped by a super-sticky mesh. My rippling biceps struggle, but I cannot pull away from this web of technology. My archenemy knows that I'm here, and he's ready for me.

"Hello, little fly," Loofah intones ominously. His cue-ball head shines with insanity.

"H-hi, Loofah," I stutter. My mouth is dry because I'm nervous. I want to seem like a worthy enemy to him.

The cruel scientist stares at me, caught in his trap. His black Armani suit looks fabulous.

"Young Superhero. I suppose you thought you were going to stop me?"

"You won't get away with this." Wow. Weak. Our banter is getting nowhere.

He laughs. "Of course I will. And only one whelping pup is here to stop me, but he'll soon be out of the way."

"You can't kill me, Loofah," I screech and cite the Winnemucca Peace Talks of 1957, which lays out the treatment of captured Superheroes. The better Villains understand how important this is.

"I'm not going to kill you, schmuck."

"Wait, why not?"

"You're as green as they come. No prestige. What do I get out of killing a young Superhero? Nothing. Nada. Zilch. Bubkes. Like beating the Costa Rican soccer team."

"But—"

"Yes?" He loses patience.

"You're my archenemy."

"That's fine, son. But the feeling is not reciprocated."

"I don't get it."

"I might be your archenemy, but you aren't mine. You're just a kid. In fact, I'm still looking."

"But you and Chief Justice?"

"Yes. He was my greatest opponent. We were like chess players, he and I. You are nobody. Sycophant," he spits and leaves the room.

One of his henchmen lingers. I imagine he will be my interrogator. He lights a dangerous, unfiltered cigarette and looks embarrassed that he has to torture me.

"Do you have the blue jeans?"

I am perplexed.

"The American blue jeans. We love them here. They are worth plenty. Do you have them?"

"Not with me, but I can get them."

"How many?"

"Suitcases full."

"For how much?" He eyes me incredulously.

"Free."

"Fine, I let you go." He disables the mesh trap and I am released. We shake hands and I agree to supply his canton with blue jeans. Little does he know I'll be buying them at Odd Lots.

"Where do you think Loofah is right now?"

"Third floor. Laboratory. F wing. Follow signs."

Only half the signs are printed in English, but I find my way quickly enough. Loofah doesn't seem surprised to see me.

"Where's the Death Ray?"

"Already in the sky." He aims a remote control at a huge monitor in the wall, and there it is, a close-up of the fell weapon.

"It's rather crude; the design came out of a back issue of *Popular Mechanics*. It's attached to a satellite that I paid the French to launch. They had no idea."

"What exactly do you want?"

"My country is poor. We need hospitals, schools, medicine, and food. Plus the latest entertainment magazines."

"You're blackmailing the rest of the world?"

"My loan application to the World Bank was turned down. As a demonstration, I believe I will incinerate Rotterdam. I've never liked Rotterdam. I will destroy every major city in Europe and America, one after another, using just a monitor and a joystick."

"Like playing video games."

"In fact, Captain Freedom, it is exactly like playing video games. My system is coin-operated. It is time for the world to bow to my power. Do you have a quarter?"

"No."

"You fly halfway across the world and you don't bring money?"

"Look at my suit. It's streamlined. Change increases yaw. Not to mention the unseemly bulge." I carry nothing more than an ATM card and a small mirror.

"Understood." He turns to his men. "Kill him while I find a quarter."

"You said you wouldn't kill me."

"I'm not. They are."

The henchmen raise their weapons.

"You can't kill me. I'm an American." As they discuss, in their own primitive language, whether they can kill an American, I blast through a window and into the night sky. This is my first chance to save the world.

As I hurtle up into the troposphere,* I wonder why I'm working so hard to foil the plans of someone who doesn't consider me his archenemy. I guess it's to impress him.

---

* People think I should mention my ability to breathe in space as another super-power, but I disagree. I've got great lung capacity, but that doesn't mean I have to draw attention to it.

There are so many satellites up here. I feel as if I'm perusing RadioShack. There are Indian satellites with the faces of Bollywood stars on them, there's one belonging to the New York Yankees, and Trump has one. Which one could it be? The lower reaches of space are disorienting, and the one thing I don't have is superior vision. If I make it out of here alive, I'm going to look for a sidekick with superhuman sight.

Then I get a whiff of acrid, unfiltered tobacco, which could only come from a hand-rolled French cigarette. Then I see it, clear as day: Loofah's satellite is smoking. The narrow barrel of the Death Ray is trained on me. It will discharge in seconds, leaving a sizable hole in my abdomen.

Just before the killer blast, I pull the small mirror out of my back pocket that I always carry with me to check if I have spinach or any other green vegetal matter in my teeth. The mirror deflects the Death Ray, which I aim back at the satellite, destroying it.

The world is safe, and, unfortunately, so is Rotterdam. I return to the evil lair to settle the score. My enemy is cursing and stomping up and down on the remote.

"Who's your archenemy now?" I say as I clobber him. His henchmen surround me.

"I just beat up your boss," I bluster. "That's your cue to melt into the civilian population."

The guards melt away, and I fly Loofah back to Washington and bring him in to the FBI for questioning. They're unhappy to see me.

"Let him go, Captain Freedom," snaps the case officer.

"But why?"

"Things have changed. His country is an ally of ours. And a trading partner."

"An ally? Muhlderia? Do we need to import steely-eyed smokers?"

"Looftansa," Loofah cackles in that horrible annoying way that makes the hairs on my nape stand at attention. "We are a new nation."

"You just made that up!"

"It used to be Muhlderia, but the German airline bought the naming rights."

"He's telling the truth, Captain."

"But he's evil. To the core. And I'm a good guy and I can't even get out of parking tickets. How could they be our ally?"

"His ambassador just signed a treaty with our government. Today."

"I've given the U.S. exclusive rights to a natural gas pipeline. And I believe you owe me plane fare to get back home."

"Our government will happily pay for it," the agent offers.

"But the Death Ray,"

"Let it go, Captain. And let him go."

"I will get you, Loofah." I stare into his soul, if he has one.

"That's Colonel Loofah to you. Remember, you are addressing a world leader."

"You buy a country and you make yourself a colonel?"

"Colonel seems less pretentious." He smirks. "Plus, it gives me something to shoot for."

I turn to the FBI agent. "I suppose no one gets to find out that I saved the world."

"That's correct. Not to mention that you illegally used Turkish airspace."

I've waited for a chance to save the world. And now, nobody knows I've done it. That's really dissatisfying. And Loofah still isn't my mutual archenemy.

Sidekick Found

After a few years on my own, I lobby Gotham Comix for a side-kick. It has become impossible for me to make all of my parade appearances, store openings, and Sunday morning talk shows, not to mention the day-to-day grind of opposing the forces of darkness that leaves me no time for wife or mistress or liaison with a wealthy Moroccan princess.

Although I always thought I wanted to work alone; a sidekick is a status symbol in the business. Only the bigger Heroes, those who can afford an extra full-time employee, receive the honor of drap-ing a humiliating short cape on a gifted youngster.

For more than a year, I hear the same story: because of the writ-ers' strikes and the high overhead and insurance costs, nobody is getting extra staff. They actually make me fire the driver of the Freedom Utility Vehicle, and I have to drive it myself. But my man-ager tells me there is good news: instead of paying for an actual assistant, they've gotten the IT department at Gotham to provide me with a computer-generated alternative.

My new sidekick is an animated paper clip with legs. His name is Whizbang. "But you can call me Whizzy!" I do not.

"Put a cape on him," I growl.

"Fine," says my manager, a cranky sorcerer named Legerde-main. "We have to appeal to a younger demographic."

"And that's the demographic that identifies with talking paper clips?"

"Our market research tells us that talking paper clips are the new Elmo. Besides, he's very toyetic."

"I'm not sure I follow."

"We're co-branding, okay? All you have to do is take him with you. And stop asking questions. Another thing—you made some mistakes on your timesheet."

"Really?"

"Halloween is not a paid holiday. You'll have to use vacation time."

After another look at Whizbang, I suppose I can see the appeal. He looks friendly, with the bulging, bright eyes of a child who might be on LSD. And his digitally rendered teeth sparkle. The adorable little digitally enhanced gizmo shakes my hand. His grasp delivers a modest amount of voltage.

"Hi there. What would you like to do?"

"What can you do?"

"I can spell-check your correspondence. I can tell you anything you'd like to know about popular software products. I can help you cheat on your taxes." He smiles and blinks too many times.

"Are you going to increase sales of my comic book?"

"Of course, by increasing market penetration into the toddler sector, which currently thinks that you are poopy."

I ask him to go away and, by the Hammer of Thor, he does.*

As far as I can tell, all Whizbang really does is make my comic book look juvenile. The artists render us in primary colors, and much of my snappy wit is reduced to primitive dialogue. Legerdemain tells me there's nothing we can do about it. The clip seems to be without superpowers, except that he can correct the grammar in bomb threats, and he seems to know whenever I'm typing a letter. In any fight he appears at exactly the wrong time and says something cute.

We have many delightful adventures together; most of them involve me trying to get him killed. I send him bearing pork rinds into a camp of armed Islamists. Then I use him to defuse bombs. He's very clumsy and gets blown up often, but the computer experts reboot him and he reappears.

The final straw comes during an appearance at a comic book store. We're there to sign books and toys, and most of the buyers are young kids clamoring for Whizbang's autograph, leaving me with nothing to do, alone in a sea of juice boxes.

The store's owner is overrun selling Whizzy dolls, and he asks me to work one of the registers at superspeed. I don't mind; in fact, I like that our numbers are high, so I'm more than happy to help out. Until I see the unthinkable.

Whizbang has his own four-part limited series comic book. It's outselling mine.

I make some angry phone calls, but it's not enough. I must destroy my digital assistant.

My opportunity comes when we visit a school for orphans in Silicon Valley. As a part of the government's welfare-to-work pro-

---

* I know Thor. We'll meet him later, I promise. And his hammer really isn't that impressive in person.

gram, the school has imposed sweatshop conditions on students to render digital animation for children's movies and TV series.

As Superheroes, we travel to many schools to impress the importance of study on the students. I encourage them to become my pen pals, and my press assistant at Gotham Comix assures me that many of them write to me repeatedly. We visit this school in particular because the students are producing the new Captain Freedom animated series.

The orphanage is run like a small dot-com, except the students aren't allowed to leave—which, come to think of it, makes it exactly like a small dot-com. They are given foosball tables and all the candy and soda they like. They nap under their desks and there is little concern for their oral hygiene. They are allowed a fifteen-minute hacky sack break after lunch. Although I question the fairness of child labor, the administrator assures me the children's small and nimble hands are optimal for the task that the state has asked of them, and they rarely develop repetitive stress syndrome.

The two of us introduce our various powers to the children. I bend a lamppost and tell them what the weather will be tomorrow, and Whizzy stumbles around and manages to break several computers in the operation. Most of the kids think it's funny, but I notice one young lad of fourteen in braces who is scowling. It's been a long time since I've broken through the impregnable wall of silence that is the teenager. It's important above all not to sound conceited.

"I like your Misfits T-shirt."

"Whatever. I got it at the mall."

All at once I know what to ask. "Who would win in a fight? A grizzly bear or a wolverine?"

"The bear," he says. "That's so obvious."

"What if it were a cage match? A cage suspended fifty feet in the air?"

He perks up. "And, uh, you could keep them both awake for a week straight?"

"They could have weapons. Like a scimitar and a trident. And the referee would be an animal rights activist."

"That would be cool."

"Have you met Whizbang?" I ask the young man.

"He's a cheap ploy."

"Oops! Did I do that?" Whizbang drops a laptop out the window. He then blinks his adorable, sparkling, oversized eyes.

"You're not real," the young teen accuses him.

"I have a four-part limited series."

Right there I decide that he's a dead man.

The boy writes me a note.

"It sounds like you're typing a letter," says Whizbang.

I pick up the piece of paper, which reads: *What are his weaknesses?*

I like this boy already. "I don't know. He's so technical."

"You don't do computers?"

"No."

"What kind of Superhero are you?"

"One with an IT department."

"Can we shoot him?"

"I can't even tell you how many different ways I've tried to kill him."

"Have you tried to shoot the computer he's attached to?"

"Where do you think I might locate his central computer?" I feel silly asking such a young man.

"How about that thing on your belt that looks like a computer?"

What a surprise. There is a small computer clipped to my belt.

"I can't shoot my sidekick."

"Why?"

"It's against the *Hero Handbook* for me to do that. And I left my gun in the car."

The young man pulls out a Glock 9 from his desk, pulls the small computer off my belt, and empties several rounds into it. "It's a dangerous school."

Whizbang fades, and my heart goes out to him. It's hard to watch the death of a partner, even if he's animated. His dying words, before he disappears into the ether of cyberspace, are a soft "I'll get you for this." Whizzy has always been cryptic. Little do I know that these very words will come back to haunt me when I have to combat the evil reconstructed version of Whizbang, the Whizzard.

This wonderful fourteen-year-old kid's name is DJ. I petition for him to live with me. In my heart it makes sense, and although my friends caution me about taking in a precocious fourteen-year-old when I seldom remember to take out my own garbage, my accountant assures me it will be great for my taxes.

DJ lives at the Secret Headquarters on a trial basis and everything goes smoothly. He does well in school, and I petition the court to become his legal guardian and he my ward.

"You're a young Superhero," says the family court judge. "Without family or any sense of responsibility. You make a living out of fighting evil, facing danger at every turn. You're constantly tempted by the high-rolling lifestyle of women, alcohol,

Supervillains, paparazzi, and drugs. You have your own Secret Headquarters, where you are making the monthly payments, but it's in L.A. and there doesn't seem to be a single responsible role model within three zip codes. And you spend most of your time in tights. Is that accurate?"

"It is." The possibilities for this sidekick seem to be dwindling.

"Your last name isn't Spears, is it?" the judge asks.

"No, ma'am."

"Fine. Take him."

DJ hugs me and we both cheer. And that very occasion is the first time he quietly steals money from my wallet.

We leave the courthouse.

"What's my job? What does a sidekick do?"

"Mostly, answer my fan mail."

"Oh."

"And kick ass!"

"Cool! Do I have to wear a cape?"

My eyes mist as I think of the humiliations that I faced when I was a sidekick. Treating prostitutes for gunshot wounds, restraining photographers. And that horrid short cape. "No, son. No, you don't."

To think I nearly ruin it all because I'm a bad role model.

after-School Special

Wow. I'm a guardian. Everything changes. All of a sudden I'm responsible for a teenager, which feels like facing an army of acne-ridden piranhas who sigh a lot. The first thing I've had to do with DJ is find him a school—somewhere with the right mix of discipline and hot, single teachers. DJ wants to go to public school, but I patiently explain that, in California, only kids whose parents are in jail have to go to public school. I casually suggest to my mother that he might get a better education in Montana, but she freaks out with some ridiculous argument like, "You adopted him—you educate him."

There's nothing great in our neighborhood, and we settle on the School of the Sacred Crystal of the Darkest Hour, which is run by a group of Zoroastrian monks. I don't know anything about their faith, but if I had to guess, I'd say it has something to do with worshipping ziggurats that were brought to Earth by a superior alien civilization prone to practical jokes. If you have to go to a religious school, it might as well be a religion nobody's heard of. The only question on the entrance exam was, "Visa or MasterCard?"

Once DJ is accepted into the school, we celebrate by sharing a Friendly's Reese's Pieces sundae, which I understand has long operated as a proxy for love and kinsmanship.

As a Hero, you have to be careful of where and what you eat: anyone, anywhere, could work for one of your corporate sponsors. I still rue the day I threw out half a bag of Carl's Jr. french fries. That stunt cost me ten grand a month, and even worse, they banned me from the franchise.

We relax in our booth at Friendly's. People are looking our way; I admit that I like it. DJ, not so much. His idea of a good time consists of eating cold pizza at two in the morning, drinking Dr Pepper straight from the two-liter bottle, and watching *Mystery Science Theater* reruns. That wasn't my teenage life. At his age I was discovering girls and soft rock. Life was a Bon Jovi–Bruce Springsteen–John Cougar Mellencamp medley. I even had a part-time job keeping Californians from moving to Montana.

For the first time, our dialogue is strained. He thinks it's weird that I like oldies radio, and I think it's weird he doesn't watch any cooking shows.

"Do you play an instrument?"

"I'm a turntablist."

"That's like a flügelhorn, right?" My question ends the evening and we head home.

Riding the sucrose high from Friendly's, we get pulled over for speeding. I rarely drive, but I thought it would look weird if I was flying while carrying a fourteen-year-old boy in my arms. There's something about being a celebrity that makes you have to speed. There's so much traffic in southern California, you have to make up for it when the roads are clear. Because of various sponsorship agreements between Gotham Comix, the LAPD, and the tabloids, Heroes are expected to garner a few moving violations each year.

As I fiddle to find my license, the police officer tells me to turn the radio off.

"Turn it up," whispers DJ. I can't imagine any young man who might like light rock, but I comply. The boy stretches his open hand toward the radio and aims his other hand at the cop, as if he's somehow drawing power from the somnolent rhythms of Sting's later work. The state trooper blinks slowly, and then crumples on the tarmac.

"Is he okay?" I ask.

"He'll be fine. Except he'll have that song stuck in his head for a while."

We drive off.

"Cool, huh?" he asks.

"How does it all work? Can you use any music?"

DJ channels the power of radio. He harnesses the soothing pre-dictability of FM as a potent sleeping spell. But his power has a flip side. He can also convert AM radio talk shows into powerful energy-blasts. The right-wing talk shows are a steady, powerful force. The left-wing shows start out much stronger, then gradually dissipate, but their signal is more annoying than mortals can stand.

It's a mysterious power. My theory is that he was born during a freak sunspot storm while his parents were watching WKRP in Cincinnati.

"I'm reveling in the irony that you used the music of the front man of the Police to put a policeman to sleep."

"I guess."

I shouldn't embarrass him. "How long have you had this power?"

"Don't know. Since I was a little kid. Teachers loved me at naptime."

Since DJ has a superpower of his own, I am in a bit of a bind. He is only fourteen, and the Comics Code Authority expressly prohibits Heroes from exploiting sidekicks under sixteen, at which point he's allowed to test for a permit. He can get his full license at seventeen if he passes the CAPE.

There are many options. I make sure that he appears in my comic books every once in a while, as long as they are ones with danger-free scenarios, and then at night, when we are home, I attempt to train him to become a Hero. He learns which celebrity endorsements to go for and to avoid the shaving and shampoo products that are the purview of professional athletes.

He masters microwave cooking and trains on that all-important skill: appearing gracious in front of fans, which is as hard for a teenage boy as avoiding pornography.

We attend a small comic book convention and I ask him to sign the autographs. Between fans I quietly repeat Chief Justice's mantra: bread and butter, bread and butter.

In time, DJ perfects my signature and signs autographs so I don't have to. The great thing a sidekick does is provide deflection for some of my careless errors. With the right sidekick, I can lie back and know that even my greatest detractors will pin my faults on him.

But it's hard to maintain a proper work/life balance. Crime doesn't keep regular hours. I've got a contract with a concierge service, LifePlans, which is great. They'll send someone over to wait for the cable guy, they'll make sure the bills are paid and the dry cleaning is done, but can I rely on them for the important moments in DJ's life? Turns out I can!

Whenever I have to miss a school play or the battle of the bands (I Tivo all the sporting events on ESPN High), a dedicated staffer from LifePlans will come over, brief me on the event, and give me a tape of the whole thing. But there are certain things I can't get out of, like the PTA.

Since the teachers all think I'm a screenwriter, they assume I have unlimited free time. I show up at meetings whenever I can. They've got me on the fundraising committee and the cultural committee. I was booted off the field trip committee after my suggestion that we take the kids to the war-torn mountains of Kashmir. Where else can you see alpine nature and a guerrilla war at the same time? They ended up taking the students to Washington, D.C., to show off the war-torn aisles of Congress. In protest, I refused to provide anything for the bake sale.

The worst part has been dropping DJ off at school. An out-of-work screenwriter can't be seen in an FUV, so I've had to lease a minivan. I would have gone for something sportier, but I got the model that accommodates the teenager safety seats that are so bulky. Can you believe that car seats are required for everyone under eighteen? And truthfully, we needed a way to haul the twenty-four-bottle trays of Gatorade.

I'd send him on the bus, but apparently the bused-in kids are shunted off to their own special section of school, wear special hats, and have to be tackle dummies for football practice. Bus kids aren't allowed to go to college. He gets really sore that Life-Plans has to pick him up whenever I'm gone, so after losing too many arguments, I get him a bicycle.

Big mistake.

Some teens get lost with drugs or become insubordinate. DJ develops a bizarre addiction to cycling. He got totally sucked into the culture. It's a ridiculous hobby—how could anyone prefer two wheels over four? The math isn't there, but he loves it and has to have the special shoes, the special tight outfits, and the special steroids.

DJ makes it into tenth grade at the Sacred Crystal, and postpuberty he changes from awkward to sullen. I attempt to make it easier for him. I buy him a video game console, a skateboard, season tickets to the Lakers, and send him his own subscription to *Playboy*, but it doesn't seem to help. I'm forced to go his school one day after he's been bellicose.

We walk into the school's ziggurat to meet with the Headmaster.* He's unhappy that DJ's fighting put somebody in the hospital, and he mentions that they prefer to avoid physical conflict.

"You teach passive resistance?" I joke.

"We like to call it passive aggression. It's part of the Zoroastrian philosophy."

I had no idea. I knew this was a religious school, but it never occurred to me that they'd teach religion.

As we sit in the small office I can't shake the uneasy feeling you always have as an adult visiting high school, like there's some dandruffy guy in a jacket and tie with B.O. and pit stains who's about to berate you because you don't know the capital of Congo and you were late to return the *National Geographic* videos featuring brief nudity to the school library. The room is more like a crypt than an office, and although the Headmaster is different from Master Van, I cringe from the anticipation of one of his trademarked beatings. Then it hits me: I've been here before, but

---

* In the brochure, they boast of its Sumerian design, but like every other temple in L.A., it looks more like faux-Mayan stucco.

last time I was tied up in the Barry Bonds, a magical psychiatric restraint that seems to be unbreakable until you snap out of it and realize it's entirely made of hype.

"You're the High Priest of Mumsfeld."

"Excuse me?" He looks horrified.

"You know, the mummy who, if reanimated, will bring about chaotic endless war."

I feel the Barry Bonds creep around me. "DJ, take him out!"

"But he's the Headmaster."

I know how to motivate him. "You are such a brown-noser."

Rush Limbaugh is on a janitor's radio nearby. DJ whips out an energy-blast and knocks the Headmaster over. Before we leave, we trash all the sacred texts to make sure this evil plan gets left back.

"Don't worry, kid," I tell DJ. "I know you wanted a letter of recommendation from him for Gotham Comix. You can still get it."

"But how?"

"I'm stealing his letterhead."

We report the case of illegal mummigration to the Justice Department and the Sacred Crystal is shut down.

For the next few weeks, he's pissed that I take him out of school. "Here's the deal," I announce to the DJ Shadow poster next to DJ. "From now on, you're being homeschooled."

"What can you teach?"

"We're dividing responsibility. I'll teach you how to use the grill, and you're responsible for Latin, English, physics, and calculus. But listen," I say lightning fast, deftly blocking his interminable teenage sigh, "this is a don't ask, don't tell policy. I won't ask what you've learned, and you won't tell anyone you're being homeschooled."

He mumbles assent. Now I have to turn to the discipline.

"Look, I don't like discipline, but I have to make this quick because I have to get ready for a huge showdown with the European crime syndicate INTERBAD."

"Can I come?"

"If you hadn't been suspended, yes."

"Going to Europe is part of home school."

"Don't use logic. You sound like my lawyer, Oscar. Anyway, no video games until I get back. I'm taking the console with me."

"No!" He storms off, and I pack my bags for a late-night flight to Europe.

When I get back, DJ is noticeably different. His room is clean, he has done all his homework, my stash is still full, and when I offer him the video game system, he declines.

"Can I go out after supper?"

"Sure. Wait a minute." I notice the black armband on his left arm. He freezes. "Are you wearing gang colors?"

"Yes." He gulps.

"Good for you. I'm so glad you found a club to get involved with. Do you need a ride anywhere?"

"No thanks. I'll take my bike."

The eleven o'clock news informs me that the city has been enveloped in a crime wave since I've been gone. Bank heists, kidnappings, the whole gamut. Then I learn that a group of troublemakers has been snarling traffic throughout the city. A roving gang of marauders on bicycles called Hypocritical Mass, led by the Bike Nazi. Hypocritical Mass tries to raise awareness of bicycle safety to auto drivers by screwing up traffic at rush hour. A flawless plan.

I wonder if the two are related?

DJ wheels his bike back into the garage, and as soon as he is safe in bed, I don my costume and hit the city streets to see what I can learn.

Sources tell me that they started their scam in Europe, then relocated to San Francisco, and are now the two-wheeled terrors of L.A. Cause a traffic disturbance, then rob a jewelry shop across town. The perfect ploy. There's one last thing: the emblem of Hypocritical Mass is the black armband, the exact same band DJ is wearing.

Now it makes sense. DJ has embraced gangland discipline to strike back at me because I've neglected him. He has become the very worst thing: the spoiled, petty child of privilege. If I don't act now, he'll devolve into a full-blown child celebrity, engineering outlandish antics to earn more time in the spotlight.

If I confront Bike Nazi with a show of typical superpower, he will look all the more appealing to DJ. And what if DJ comes to his aid? The way back to DJ's allegiance is love—not gruff Superhero love, not exchanging-my-football-jersey-for-a-soda love, but some form of after-school-special love.

Again I hit the streets, and one of my best stoolies gives me reliable information. Hypocritical Mass is going into Hollywood, ostensibly to disrupt a movie opening while a select group of them abets the Bike Nazi in stealing priceless artwork from the municipal museum. I can't be in two places at once, but I can imagine that Bike Nazi will exploit DJ's soporific energy waves to hit the museum.

City Museum is closed, but I get in through a side door. I make sure to pay the admission fee before I do anything else.

"Captain Freedom, looking for change for a twenty?" I recognize the sneer of a corroded bald man, a man corrupted by all the trappings of evil: Bike Nazi.

I wheel around. Amidst a cotillion of young bike messengers, including DJ, is my latest enemy, the Bike Nazi. He looks no different than his young followers: embarrassingly tight spandex shorts, dusty helmet, and a wind-shear bike shirt with all the major corporate sponsorships.

"No Postal Service contract yet?"

"Working on it. Have anything to say to your sidekick? He's been a great help."

My ward steps up front. I look at him sadly and do something I almost never do: remove my sunglasses. A single well-planned tear falls down my face.

"I'm sorry I neglected you. You were acting out, and I missed all the signs."

"I don't care. It's too late, Captain Foolish." I hate his adolescent near-wit.

"DJ, destroy him!" orders the Bike Nazi. I notice that the music of the Eagles is broadcast over the loudspeaker. Light country rock is especially deadly—DJ once hit someone using a Byrds song and put them into a three-day coma.

"Wait! I'd do anything to show my love to you, young man. You're part of my family. Heck, you are my family. Remember when we made rugelach together?"

DJ sniffles and can't hold back his tears. "I don't care about little pastry treats."

"If you come back and help me defeat these guys . . . " I break off, my voice choked with emotion.

"What?"

"I'll buy you a car. Any model you like, and you can drive it, and I don't care if you don't have a license or insurance or brakes."

"Even a '69 Charger?"

"Anything that will look good parked in front of the secret hideout."

DJ turns and looks at the Bike Nazi. He raises his hands and pulses a blast of the most vile talk-radio invective. It flattens our enemy. The rest of Hypocritical Mass scatters, but we don't chase them. Without their leader, and jealous of DJ's getting a cool automobile, they'll probably give up their foolish two-wheeled ways and rejoin society.

"DJ, did you learn something today?" As we get in the car, I attempt to use this experience as one of those valuable teachable moments.

"Maybe."

"And what was that?"

"I should never give you ammunition to create the moral of the story."

"There's more to it than that. Now, I want to make sure you really understand this. Wait a second, is that Fleetwood Mac on the radio?"

"Maybe."

"Oh, wow, I'm tired. I need a nap."

Over time, DJ becomes a proficient sidekick. He passes the CAPE without cheating and wins an award for his essay on hostage negotiation, titled "We Don't Negotiate with Terrorists (Except When We Have To)."

When he comes of age, I instruct him to pick out a costume. Instead of availing himself of the resources at the Gotham Comix fabric shop, he goes to a vintage clothing store. Eschewing all convention, my ward dresses like an indie film director: brown corduroy pants, Hush Puppies, a suede jacket, and a tight red

T-shirt with the meaningless words INDIANA STATE FOOTBALL BOOSTERS on the front. Although I'd prefer that he dress more like a Hero, it is important to be supportive. DJ still feels like a failure for taking sides with evildoers, no matter what I say.

I fight my own inner demons as well. I yearn for an archenemy. I'm happy to fight crime, but I'm always looking for something more. Since I'm contracted to produce comics, I can't appear on the Sunday talk shows with a hastily written and edited book. Oscar's been looking for a loophole, and I know one day we'll find it.

I pin my hopes on that other medium: celluloid. (No, I'm not talking about the unsightly skin condition.) I shop around scripts for the *Captain Freedom* movie.

Saving the World a Second Time

It's winter, and California is unseasonably warm. The heat is so bad that crime is at a standstill. Then I receive a phone call from Gotham crime dispatch. It's bad news: Krokura, a recently revived giant crocodile-like dinosaur, is hell-bent on destroying Earth. He has marched across the ocean floor tearing open sealed methane vents, causing a dramatic worldwide temperature increase.

"How did the beast wake up?" I ask.

"There was a disturbance near its lair," says the dispatcher.

"Oil drilling?"

"No."

"Underwater bomb tests?"

"No."

"Natural gas pipelines?"

"No. A very large number of remaindered copies of the UN Report on Climate Change were dumped in the ocean. The sheer weight of the volumes jolted Krokura out of his sleep."

"Too bad. I'll get credit for it this time? For saving the world?"

"Of course. You did get credit for the last time."

"Yeah, but there was no media coverage."

"We couldn't afford to embarrass Loofah," he explains. "This time it won't be an issue. But you've got to hurry. The planet is heating rapidly. We don't have much time."

Before DJ and I leave California, I make a brief pit stop at the last place I'm expected: the Central Library of Gotham Comix. Our librarian, a Heroine by the name of Superscribe (The Avenging Archivist), dislikes me because I keep books out for too long, and when I return them, half the pages are burned or dirtied by some noisome chemical. As I browse through the technical manual section, I grow worried. There is nothing about how to prevent a giant lizard from returning Earth to the Pleistocene era. I scan the titles:

Neurosurgery for Dummies
Cryptography for Dummies
Nation-Building for Dummies

"Can I help you?" asks Superscribe. She smokes a cigarette, and I can hear the Ramones from the headphones of her MP3 player. She wears the standard-issue black leather bodysuit, garnished by bifocals and a black fedora with a cardinal feather tucked in the headband. Superpowers aside, she is one hot librarian.

"The book I'm looking for . . . " I start.

"*Preventing Environmental Catastrophe for Dummies* is gone. Overdue. What do you need to know?"

"The reason the planet has gotten so hot in the last few days is that Krokura is cracking open methane vents.* I need to know how to stop him."

"Impossible," she says. "One dinosaur couldn't cause all this global warming."

"The temperature has shot up ten degrees. Polar bears are getting buzz cuts."

"Don't be hysterical. The available evidence indicates more study is needed."

I have no time for this. I launch into an elaborate Plea.

The Plea is a trick they teach all Superheroes. If you need a favor, something that's illegal, outside protocol, or too complicated to explain, you can use the Plea.

It's a basic form of mind control. You don't even have to make any sense while you're doing it, as long as you keep an earnest expression on your face and you end with, "You're the only one I can trust right now" or "Your country needs you."

She listens to my Plea. At first she's skeptical, but as I speak, her expression morphs to one showing concern. Briefly she shakes her head, as if to suggest that she would like to agree but the system will never let her get away with it, until her lips flatten, and I recognize the look of grim determination.

"Okay," she says. "I'll help."

She gives me a brief dossier on where we are likely to find the beast, whether he has any specific weaknesses (none), whether he breathes fire (he doesn't), and whether we can enlist the aid of a giant flying turtle to save us all (we can't). The Avenging Archivist tells me one last thing, and it's important: if Krokura

---

* According to *Field Guide to Jurassic Species of the Ignominious Valley*, dinosaurs seek out methane for a cheap buzz.

were to be buried under several tons of rock, he probably would not survive.

"How do you know so much about him?" I ask Superscribe.

"Monster.com," she admits.

Gotham provides us a small jet, and off DJ and I go to Indonesia. I've actually considered leasing a stealth bomber, but the Pentagon said my credit didn't rate. They suggested that if I really want to fly anywhere in the world undetected, I can always wrap myself in tin foil.

After ditching our plane in Jakarta, we hire a longboat and guide to take us to Krakatoa, the island named after the volcano of the same name. It has become a fabulous tourist destination and is still unbelievably cheap. This is where Krokura was last spotted. We hit the beach to strategize and get some sun.

"We could buy a place here," I say.

"All the new developments are up the side of the volcano."

"The views must be fabulous."

"Tzad. Think about it. Do you want to pay for volcano insurance on a place you might visit once every two years?"

"I'd come more often than that."

DJ rolls his eyes. "Like it's easy to get here."

"I could fly here whenever I want."

"So you're not taking me?"

"Forget it."

I lie on the beach as my sidekick goes for a swim. Locals come by with trinkets and food, and I buy them, not because I am wanting either in trinkets or food but because everything is so affordable. DJ returns, dries his dark brown hair, and puts on his sunglasses. "Why don't we check out some of those properties before we look for Krok."

I'm surprised. "Five minutes ago, you were totally against it."

"As I was swimming, I considered it. This is a burgeoning market. Even if we never stayed here again, we could lend it out to mad artist friends who will make us paintings in lieu of rent."

"We don't know any artists."

"Doesn't matter. You live for real estate. We're just looking. I won't make you buy anything."

We drive our rented Jeep up into the hillside settlements. A few of them approximate a So-Cal bungalow look, which I'm disappointed to see, since I've traveled several thousand miles away from home to get away from predictable architecture.

As we drive up the mountain, the neighborhoods get slightly shoddier. The settlement nearest the summit is the home of stunt actors and Grammy-winners. I would never buy a place here.

The Indonesian noonday sun is very hot, and we find a local bar to get a drink. We each have a gin and tonic. The bar is empty but for a scrubby-looking scientist. The man's hair hasn't seen conditioner in weeks, and even his pocket protector is askew. We introduce ourselves and find out he's Dr. Ozmond Osbourne, a geologist from the University of Montana, Missoula.

"How are you?" I ask him.

"We're all going to die," he pronounces.

"You're right," I agree.

"I've got my beeper set to go off each time there is seismic activity. And it's been vibrating like mad. There are sixty quakes a second. Krokura is awake and he's angry. All those spouting methane vents. The heat. This could be the end of life as we know it."

"What's a beeper?" DJ asks

I ignore my sarcastic sidekick.

"Did you come here to study the volcano?" I ask Dr. Osbourne. "Or the dinosaur?"

"No, I'm here as a sex tourist. Which reminds me, my group is gathering for a brothel tour at four. It was nice meeting you." The haggard scientist shakes our hands and leaves us alone.

"Can we stop Krokura?" DJ asks me.

"We're Superheroes. Although there's nothing in our contract that says we can't prevent a natural disaster, I don't have the slightest inkling of geometry."

"Geology."

"That, too. So I think we should enjoy the rest of our time here."

"Does that mean we're not going to bore into the center of the mountain and put an end to this ancient evil?" He looks so disappointed.

The rumbling continues. That night there is a severe earthquake, and magma from the volcano destroys the housing developments of several musicians I've never heard of. Today is the day their music died.

"Captain, we must do something," DJ says as we enjoy a fabulous tropical breakfast. "The quake disrupted the generators, and there's no more AC."

"You're right. Break time is over. It's time to save Earth."

Again, we travel up the mountain and pass the charred remains that just yesterday were ugly vacation homes. I could buy someone out pretty cheap today, I'm sure. We hike to the volcano's summit, then drop down into the crater. My muscles surge. The area is quiet but reeks of sulfur. Then I spot it. A small crevice in the side of the crater.

We run for the entrance and tumble down an enormous

slide into a hollowed-out chamber in the center of the mountain. There is one inhabitant, and I'm fairly certain he's the cause of all our trouble: Krokura.

I recall what Superscribe told me. He's a Thesaurus, that ultra-rare breed of thespian dinosaur that mostly disappeared during the late Vaudevillian era. I shudder because I recognize him. This ancient evil hasn't been asleep for all that long—probably only since his television show was canceled. A deafening noise fills the chamber, and I'm quite certain he's quoting *Macbeth*. He should know better. Quoting the Spanish play will be his undoing. I warn DJ to keep hidden.

"What's going on?" I yell into the darkness. "I'm Captain Freedom."

"Go away." Krokura sounds despondent.

"I'd like to help you."

"Nobody can help me. I'm a failed celebrity. What a terrible sight. I might as well lie down and turn into fossil fuels right now."

"You shouldn't mope."

"I trained at Yale. I deserve better. To be a stage actor. I was part of the original cast of *Godspell*. My closest neighbor is a key grip. Now I can't even frighten the locals."

"But you're hiding on a tiny island in the middle of nowhere. You need to maintain a profile. Have you tried off-Broadway?"

"I don't get any good roles anymore. Not even voice-overs. That *Godzilla* remake? Did you see that?"

"I heard it was terrible."

"They never called me. Not to audition, not for technical consulting. Nothing." His tail pounds against the floor and triggers a tremor.

"I'm sorry to hear that. Is that any reason to destroy the planet?"

"I don't care about Earth. It hasn't been the same since the dinosaurs left."

DJ steps out of the darkness.

"I could ask my agent to call some people. She's great, really."

"She won't. Who's your friend?"

"My sidekick, DJ."

"Oh. Nice T-shirt."

I tap on some of the rock, looking for something hollow. "This is a really lovely nest you've got here. Do you rent or own?"

"What are you doing?"

"Just checking out the structure of this place. How do you hang pictures?"

"I don't. I'd like you to leave now."

"Sure. DJ, anything on the radio?"

"Just a vitriolic Islamist radio talk show. It's got an awesome signal."

For the first time since we've been working together, DJ and I are in total harmony. There is no discussion of the plan. We both know what to do. I blast into the air and punch my fist into the weakest part of the ceiling, and DJ's energy-blasts sever the stalactites immediately above the dinosaur's bed.

We make a hasty egress through a fissure as rock rains down on Krokura, leaving him in a bed of magma and stone for eternity.

"Don't you feel weird entombing a dinosaur in bedrock where no one will ever find him?" asks DJ as we climb out of the volcano.

"Why is that weird?"

"As a paleontologist, don't you want to study him?"

I shake my head because this is a discussion I've had with so many uninformed people. "DJ, paleontology is about dinosaur bones. Krok is alive now. Or he was until this morning. He won't revert to bones for some time. I'm not some sort of dinosaur sociologist."

When we reach the surface, I feel a blast of superheated air. "This isn't over. The methane vents."

"What about them?"

"Krokura smashed open dozens of methane vents all over the ocean floor. There are too many of them. If we can't close them all, global warming will be complete."

"And it will be too hot to live?"

"Or too cold," I say, thinking about how ridiculous it sounds.

"Is all lost?" DJ asks.

"No. All is not lost. I'm still Captain Freedom, and I've still got minutes left on my calling card."

I make some phone calls. By day's end, I've assembled the Who's Who of Superheroes—every super man, woman, and late teen that I can think of. Al Gore crafts a PowerPoint. We coordinate and stage a Heroes benefit. We fly all over the world shutting down the earth-warming methane vents. For once I've found a use for all those Heroes who can breathe under water or swim really fast.

I receive official thanks for saving the planet this time. The press suggests I be nominated for the International Justice Prize. General Sueter, president of Indonesia, repays me with an island of my own: East Tiny.

We fly over to it to check it out. Boring. No clubs, restaurants, or bars. But there is a village—for whatever reason, the locals seem to perceive me as a god—and high on a hilltop is a fortress owned by the former governor. It will be the Freedom Fortress.

It's not much, but now that I own part of a sovereign nation, I have diplomatic immunity. I will never again have to pay my parking tickets.

At long last, my derring-do attracts the attention of executives from one of the major film studios. As strange as it may seem, they believe that there's a market for movies about Superheroes. Our ideas differ: I want the movie to focus heavily on drama, but for some reason they think it would be better as an action movie. Several impressive authors write drafts of a script, and I take their ideas and laugh.

Aside from saving the world, I learn that I must protect my celebrity at all costs. Krokura's words come to haunt me: *I'm a failed celebrity.* At the time I think he's pathetic. Now that I know what it means to fail as a famous person, I realize that maybe he doesn't deserve his tragic end. Although being cast in a reality show where washed-up celebs live together *is* worse than being blanketed in tons of volcanic rock.

To protect my franchise, I will have to write the screenplay myself.

Time Travel

Certain things were never supposed to happen: The breeding of dogs that are smaller than cats. Vitamin-enriched no-trans-fat flavored water. The separation of Czechoslovakia. The constant invasions of sweet, innocent Kuwait.

We Superheroes do what we can, but to rearrange the fabric of history is a job best left to gods. Still, some things are so contrary to the future of the human race, there is no way to sit back and allow them to happen. Used properly, time travel can repair otherwise inevitable catastrophes, and it's a cheap way to take a vacation.

I should never have let DJ pick out the color for the new Freedom Utility Vehicle. It's an awful tangerine. He is but a man-child who thinks a professional supervehicle is supposed to look like the deck of his skateboard. I go back in time to get it painted gunmetal instead. He'll sulk and I'll go out and buy him a time-share in Jackson Hole, and the exhausting cycle of raising a twenty-year-old will continue.

As this small battle is won, another larger battle is lost every day, and I'm not talking about gingivitis. I'm talking about the newest, most deadly criminal on the block: Mad Moses.

He thinks he's a prophet and, as such, wants to return our country to a higher moral standard. Moses' goal is to root out that vile combination of skimpy bathing suits and fried food. Like many eccentric rich people, he uses his fortune to build a fleet of stone soldiers, ten feet tall, which he names the Commandments. His servants terrorize the public, destroying buildings and property, and nobody has been able to stop them: they are impervious to harm and will not listen to reason.

At least he's been proactive.

"Mad Moses was once a productive member of society—a judge," I explain to DJ.

"What happened?"

"He was too controversial. He waited to be appointed to the Federal Circuit Court, but the Senate held up his confirmation. He was buried under copies of an appropriations bill for weeks. The isolation and waiting drove him mad."

Several Superheroes have gone down in a vain attempt to destroy the Commandments. I know that I'll be called, and like the rest of my colleagues, I'll be swatted to the ground like a gnat, ground like a cigarette in a giant granite ashtray, so I'm in no rush to confront them. I sit by the phone, waiting for Gotham to summon my talent. In the meantime, I refile my record collection by genre.

DJ rushes into the den. "I've got an idea. We can travel back through time and destroy all of his collectibles. Mad Moses made a fortune selling rare Pez dispensers."

"Which ones?"

"Erik Estrada."

I've never seen that one. "So if the dispensers are never produced . . ."

"He'll never have the fortune to build the stone Commandments."

"Gotham's time machines are all being serviced. Where are we going to get one?"

"Yellow pages."

"I don't even know where to look," I complain. "Travel? Vehicles? Relativity?"

"I'll do it."

"It's Friday afternoon. On a busy holiday weekend. Do you actually think any will still be left?"

"We both know that you hate renting."

"I don't."

"Yes, you do. Why don't you just buy your own? We might need it again."

We have this same discussion every time we need something we'll use just once. We're totally at the mercy of these terrible rental companies that charge so much money, plus there's insurance, and even though they advertise low rates, it's always three times more expensive.

"Where would I put it?" I ask.

"In the wormhole."

"The wormhole is totally full of your stuff."

DJ shrugs and makes several phone calls. "I've got one."

"Who?"

"Enterprise."

"That's all the way across town."

"They'll send a car for us."

"Fine."

"Is that what you're wearing?"

Forty-five minutes later, we're standing on the dirty industrial carpet of Enterprise Time Machines. A youngster with acne and braces makes me fill out the rental agreement and spends several long minutes trying to figure out how to photocopy my ID, which is blank, since I will not reveal my secret identity.

"Sir, I need a photo ID."

"I'm a Superhero. Captain Freedom. You really haven't heard of me?"

The sound of gum snapping indicates that she hasn't.

"We're kind of in a rush here."

"I'll take care of it." DJ throws down his actual California driver's license. It takes several more precious minutes for the Enterprise employee to master the notion that although DJ will be driving, I'm paying with my credit card.

"We're wasting time."

DJ whispers to me. "Which is why we're going back in time. Right? We've got all the time in the world." I relax. We sign the standard waiver after reading through the three rules of time travel:

- **You must wear era-appropriate clothing.**
  This is especially true of synthetic fabrics that haven't yet been invented in your destination time—they could disrupt fashion patterns and create a confusing twenty-first-century lederhosen craze.

- **You should not meet a younger version of yourself.**
  If you encounter the past version of yourself, a good trick is to explain it away using Dickens's Ghost of [insert appropriate holiday] Future. The younger version of you won't recognize you, thinking it's impossible you would end up looking so bad in twenty-five years, and will dismiss you as some Dickens-spouting bum.

- **You must not do anything to affect the course of history.** *This rule is total bullshit, but you agree to it anyway, just as you agree to pay your work for any office supplies that you use for personal reasons.*

We follow the attendant to the lot to find our rental.

"Captain, it would be a lot easier if you brought your state-issued Hero ID," DJ nags.

"Where would I put it?"

"I'm getting you a man purse."

"Captain Freedom doesn't accessorize."

She shows us the time machine. It's green and looks and smells like a Porta-John.

"This is it? We have to go in this?"

She smiles, and her braces flash in the sun, temporarily blinding me. "It's all we have."

The time machine stinks. There is no way they cleaned this since the last user. I punch in our coordinates: southern California, 1973.

These machines make hardly any noise. It's a bit like standing in an elevator but without the change in perceived weight due to gravity. Several minutes pass, and the indicator light turns green. We change into era-appropriate clothing, step outside, and make sure the machine is hidden in the abandoned lot that will eventually become Enterprise Time Travel.

The seventies are gritty. It feels like being in a black-and-white movie but with washed-out color. There's long hair everywhere and ugly, ugly pleated bellbottoms that not even vintage fans would wear. Some people look like they've been plucked straight out of an American Apparel ad.

We take a taxi to the Pez Candy International Building, conveniently located in downtown L.A. The cab driver won't accept my twenty because it's new and he suspects it's counterfeit. He lets me pay with a check. How quaint.

We approach the young man behind the front desk. He is arrayed in a brown polyester suit and wears it without a shred of irony.

"Dudes. Welcome to the worldwide headquarters of Pez, where we fabricate multicolored dreams to surf the saccharine skies. What's up?"

"Sorry, I don't understand you." The seventies dialect is like gibberish to me.

"Oh. You're foreign?"

"DJ, help."

"We were wondering. Is this where Pez dispensers are made?"

He shakes his head. "It's all done in a sweatshop."

Sweatshop. A concept I understand. I didn't know they had sweatshops in the seventies. "Where? Bangladesh? Mexico? China?"

"China? You two are far out. It's out in Burbank. Do you know where that is?"

I nod excitedly, like a happy little dog. We can't strike until late at night, so we rent a car to take in the local sites and visit the Walk of Fame to see the stars of actors we've never heard of. I always thought Cecil B. DeMille was the name of a rock star.

We arrive at the factory where they manufacture the elusive Erik Estrada Pez dispensers in the middle of the night. The building is deserted. Strains of the Allman Brothers Band emanate from somewhere.

I locate the dispensers. The likeness of the actor is so real, even down to his blinding white teeth. It seems terrible to destroy all of them, and unfair that something so innocent could cause so much evil. Estrada's teeth are truly inspirational. Did he whiten? No, it's impossible; nobody did that back in those days. How did we survive?

I hesitate. Such wanton violence. But I have no choice. I am a Superhero because I can make the decision to destroy toys.

"We have to destroy all of them. Now."

I begin to smash box after box of the valuable items. But even with my strength, it's taking too long, and I have to be thorough. Then the scrumptious words *electrical fire* dance into my mind. I rip the circuitry out of the walls and cause a spark to ignite the fuel in the forklift. Soon the building will be nothing more than a tangled mess of steel, plastic, and seared candy, a lot like the way Disney World smelled after it was bombed by a cadre of irate parents.*

"It doesn't matter," I say as we watch the fire. "He'll find another way to get rich. We'll go back home, and we'll have changed nothing."

"I know what's wrong with you."

"Nothing's wrong with me."

"It's seventies ennui. We have to get you out of here."

"What are you talking about?"

"Acute Time Sickness. You're experiencing the worst of the decade."

I have heard tales of ATS. Heroes who become so melded to the time they're visiting, they never fully come back to the

---

* See *Captain Freedom* #35: *It's a Small War After All.*

present. One Hero, after following an evil sorcerer to the Middle Ages, developed a taste for mead and wild boar.

"That couldn't happen to me." He's right, though. I feel jittery and conflicted, like I've just finished watching *Taxi Driver*.

"We should go, anyway."

"There's one last thing I want to do."

There is another reason I've picked this time: to see my father; to watch what happens to him with my adult eyes.

Taking advantage of our rental car's unlimited mileage, we drive to Mom's cooperative ranch in Devil's Craw and hide behind a pleather sofa to observe the action. It's as I remember it—very little changes in thirty-some years. Mom is young and pretty, and she clearly has yet to hone her preternatural ability to point out the mistakes of others. I see a two-year-old version of myself running down the stairs, then tripping, then falling into flying, and then crashing into the front door and wailing. Clear as Betamax.

My parents argue. My young self hides in a kitchen cabinet and watches everything.

A black van arrives outside the house. Out of it jump several men in suits, each packing heat. My father jokes with them and allows himself to be handcuffed and taken away. As the van drives away, my mom mutters "Good riddance."

Once we leave, DJ probes for my reaction.

"Just as I remembered. He ran off with a Vegas showgirl."

"Captain, I think you might be repressing something."

"And I think someone needs to watch less Jerry Springer."

We return to Los Angeles.

"Look! Gas lines!"

"What are those?" I ask.

"You don't remember the gas shortage? I read about it in history books."

"Doesn't ring a bell. Are you certain this didn't happen in an alternate universe?"

"The oil-producing countries cut production. That's why people bought smaller cars."

People who enjoy history are always appallingly obsessed with it. DJ talks about it all the time, as if historical figures were celebrities. In a conversation about basketball, he'll bring up the Founders, a group of radical hemp farmers who wrote the Constitution, a document so slippery it later banned the cultivation of that very same hemp. Conspiracy? You bet.

Next he'll tell me we need a hybrid FUV. *Hybrid* sounds so wishy-washy, like you can't make up your mind. Why would you order a chocolate chunk caramel latte with skim milk?

"If we don't study history, we're doomed to repeat it," he lectures.

"No, we aren't. Dinosaurs haven't come back."

"What about your sideburns? Very seventies. You look like Shaft."

"Stop. My sideburns are perfectly calibrated and trimmed. They never cross the lobe meridian. They're nothing like those beaver pelts from the seventies."

We return to our hidden time machine. I set the controls to return us to the present.

"Wait," says DJ. "I'm sure everything's normal in our time. Why don't we bum around ancient Greece for a day?"

"I'm paying by the year. This was meant to be a short trip. If we go to the Bronze Age, the rental company will ream us."

"Why don't you ever get unlimited mileage?"

"It's cheaper this way."

"Can't we expense it?"

"No. If everything works out right and Mad Moses is defeated, Gotham will never know why we rented."

We return the time machine. There is no more news of Mad Moses, and, unbelievably, everything else in the space-time continuum is normal, although the young woman with the braces laughs at me. I ask DJ why.

"Captain, you may want to take care of that mustache."

"You're kidding." I touch my finger to my lip and find I've grown a seventies Fu Manchu mustache. I kinda like it. But Gotham Comix prohibits upper-lip facial hair. Damn.

archenemy OnLine

Type. Click. Go back, delete. Return. Oh, shit. I didn't want that. The testimonials rotate on the screen—and I look up from my profile and learn all about Rabbit-Face and how much he likes the Web service.

"I was a mid-career bad guy, with little chance of becoming a Supervillain. I had a great power that I always used for evil, but it would never matter if I couldn't find that special someone whom I could do battle with, kidnap, and hopefully kill. But then I signed up on NME Online, and everything changed."

Rabbit-Face. Never heard of him.

I look at my profile. *Superstrong Savior Seeks Sinister Someone.*

NME Online. The premier Web site that matches Heroes and Villains. I'd be really embarrassed if some of my enemies learned that I'm using this thing.

```
Interests: volleyball, cooking, swordplay,
paleontology.
Last good movie: I don't really have time for
movies.
```

Should I change that? Isn't that a little pretentious, like I only care about my work?

Last good movie: *Chariots of Fire*

Like, when do you ever go see a movie with your arch?

I browse through several more profiles and I feel a twinge in my gut. There she is. Kaeko, my girlfriend, whose heart I broke. I read up on her profile and look at a few of her action photos. It's weird that Kaeko can't find an archenemy either. Part of me wants to send her a wink, but that would be too awkward. We have fought together and against each other. The good-evil duality between us isn't all that clear.

It's not like I have all the time in the world to search for an archenemy. There are bank heists to foil, people to save, and products to sell. But word has come down recently at Gotham that all top-shelf Heroes are required to find their equally worthy archenemies.

NME Online is addictive. You find a lot of people with similar interests. There's an entire online club for Brazilian Heroes who specialize in defenestration. Then a wink comes to me. I double click on the message. Promising. A Villain by the name of Twizzler. Yes. Okay, and there's a photo waiting for me. His face is cloaked in shadow, which could mean he's sinister or just ugly. The site becomes very slow, and I assume that DJ's adding to what he assures me is his very legal music collection.

Twizzler and I chat. It turns out he's from Wyoming, so I could go skiing when I look for his lair. What are his superpowers? He's being coy about it, but he assures me he's a top-notch hoodlum. I've heard that before. "Where did you get the name Twizzler?"

I ask. "Corporate sponsorship," he admits, and that looks like a good sign, since only the biggest criminals get advertising revenue. Is it wrong that I don't admit to having a sidekick?

We make vague plans to meet, but I don't think anything will come of it.

Before I log off, I get an e-mail from my bank, asking for my password, my Hero ID number, my driver's license number, and my secret identity. They should already have that information, but the e-mail makes it sound urgent. It's like how I get all those credit card offers that say DO NOT DISCARD splashed in red on the envelope. No matter how many of those I get, I always open them. Another reason to get X-ray vision.

A few weeks go by, and I've given up on Twizzler. Because there's a new bad boy in town, and I'm sure we're going to be best enemies.

His name is Black Frank, aka the Velvet Fog, a cat burglar, jewel thief, and occasional movie star, known to steal his way onto sets and give command performances, only to vanish back into the underworld by the time the popcorn is cold.

His powerful Sinatra impersonation is a siren's call, giving him mind control over anyone who hears it, and he has ensnared entire cities with "Fools Rush In." In addition, he's got a great golf game. He's humble but exudes elegance, like if David Bowie had become a criminal mastermind instead of the Thin White Duke. Each time we fight, it's as if I'm in a separate league, a Billy Bob Thornton acting onstage with Sir Laurence Olivier. I have never seen Black Frank use his cell phone in public, let alone snap it shut when exasperated by the incompetence of his henchmen. We battle around the city, and each time is a draw.

There are encouraging e-mails. Mom even sends a "Congratulations on Your Archenemy" card. I don't want to force any-thing, but just in case this is the real thing, Oscar contacts the consulates of Belgium and Uruguay to facilitate back-channel communications.

Then one afternoon I receive an anonymous tip-off. It seems that the Velvet Fog has kidnapped the entire Los Angeles Dodg-ers baseball team and is racing them back east in a bus to reinstate them in Brooklyn. Changing the complex spatial distribution of major league teams could have an untold effect upon the enter-tainment ecosystem. It's just as they say: every time a butterfly flaps its wings, another celebrity sex tape is released.

The showdown with Black Frank occurs in the City of Kansas, halfway across the country. The baseball players are confused, tricked into accompanying Frank for some free steroid injections. Frank sings them into a stupor so they do not attempt escape.

I land by the bus and confront Frank.

"You've left your sidekick. So we'll solve this mano a mano."

"Yes," I smirk. "Man to man."

He shakes his head. "*Mano a mano* means 'hand to hand.'"

The Velvet Fog sings a Mel Tormé number. I fly toward him and deliver a punch that smacks him into the Dodgers' bus. It looks like the wind is knocked out of him, but he's otherwise okay.

"Your superpower doesn't work on me, Frank," I taunt. The special zinc earplugs I purchased at SuperDrugs block his mind control.

Several ballplayers armed with bats lumber toward me, zom-bies underneath Frank's spell. They attack, and I take my time repelling them. I don't want to hurt them, but it's easy with my lightning-fast reflexes to grab and break their bats before they can pummel me.

BOOM! I feel an awful knock to the back of my head and then another. I turn around to see the zombie pitching staff pummel me with baseballs, and apparently the strike zone is my cranium. Two more fastballs hit me—I'm too stunned to block them.

"Captain," Frank tuts as I fade from consciousness, "I expected more from you." One more pitch hits and I pass out—it was a breaking ball.

As I recuperate at home, the East Coast Heroes are fighting Frank's henchmen for the release of the Dodgers, who are finally lured back when the city of Los Angeles offers to build them a new stadium. I haven't heard from Black Frank in a couple of days, and I can't say I haven't been waiting by the phone. Every time it rings, I jump. But it's always a wrong number. Then, after a week, he calls.

"Free, it's Velvet."

"Hi," I try to sound nonchalant, like I don't really care about his megalomaniacal plans to steal Frank Gehry's more outlandish buildings.

"We haven't talked for a while, and I wanted to see how you were."

"Fine," I say.

"Freedom, I can't fight you anymore," he says, smooth, his voice tinted by very costly cigar smoke.

"What? Why not?"

"I've already got an archenemy."

I cannot believe his perfidy and I tell him so. He's admits he's always been an East Coast bad guy but very recently lost a major battle with his archenemy, Colosso. His trip to the West Coast to tangle with a group of different Heroes was to rebuild his facilities and find the confidence to fight his true archenemy.

"Do you know Colosso?" he asks.

My heart sinks. Everyone knows Colosso. An MIT professor by day, but as a result of an experiment in jumping genes, he can turn into Colosso but only when he's emotionally vulnerable, which means he spends a lot of time watching Jane Campion movies. Colosso is at least ten feet tall, his skin can resist bullets, and he's unbelievably strong. Not just chuck-a-car-across-the-street strong, but juggle-all-the-ivy-covered-buildings-in-Cambridge strong.

Frank and I talk a little bit more, but I can tell from his tone that it's forced, that he doesn't really want to continue our conversation, that Black Frank, aka the Velvet Fog, wants to get back to his life in Boston. "You won't tell Colosso about us?" he asks.

"Your secret's safe with me." We make vague plans to meet on Nantucket in the summer, but I know he won't follow through. He hangs up, and I don't expect to hear from him for a long time.

I go back to my computer and have another look at the available profiles. The number of weirdos is discouraging. As if the ability to spontaneously grow body hair were a threatening superpower. I cancel my account. NME Online has been a total waste of my time. Maybe I'll put an ad on Craigslist.

Later in the week, the Twizzler calls me and tells me he's coming over. It's weird. After all the disappointment with the Velvet Fog, I don't really want to meet this guy. But it would be rude to say no. It makes me wonder how he knows where I live. The location of the Secret Headquarters is a closely guarded secret, known only to internal staff, DJ's kickboxing instructor, the pool cleaner, and a revolving cast of Mexican day laborers.

Twizzler shows up. He's wearing a shabby blue suit and an

ugly tie whose native habitat must be a 1970s high school yearbook. Already I can tell this won't work out.

"Should I get rid of him?" DJ whispers.

"Let's see what happens." I sigh. "What exactly do you do?" I ask Twizzler.

"I work in identity theft."

"Wow. What is that, exactly?"

"Actually, it's pretty interesting," and as he says those words, I know it won't be. He drones on about credit card theft and raiding people's PayPal accounts, and a lot of really boring things. "But I specialize in secret identity theft," he says as he hands me an envelope. "We'll talk again later," he says and lets himself out.

I open it. It's written in 10-point Courier, a font that always fills me with dread. Why can't the bad guys ever use Comic Sans Serif?

A single line reads "Tzadik Friedman." He knows my secret identity.

He can't get away with this. If my secret identity were revealed, it would endanger the lives of everyone I know and love, and I'd probably lose my membership in the Writers Guild of America, which gets me discounts on stationery purchases around the world.

Hot pursuit is in order. DJ and I leap into the Freedom Utility Vehicle. The engine turnover is a little slow, and I look at the fuel gauge. It's close to empty, and we have no choice but to go to the gas station first.

"If we had a more efficient car . . ." DJ begins his usual argument. I cut him off, but I know he's right. There's just a lot of pressure for Superheroes to drive fuel-intensive vehicles in the FUV class. Mostly we use it for short trips between the Secret

Headquarters and whatever local bank is being knocked off, and it uses a lot of gas. But the speed and power are worth it.

After refueling, we speed like hell and catch up with Twizzler, who of course drives a red Miata, the vehicle of choice for the two-bit crook who can afford the beginnings of status. Black Frank drives a black Jaguar.

"Nice car," DJ says to me in his most ironic tone. "I'll bet he paid for it with your credit card."

"How would he get my credit card?"

DJ's Level Five condescending eye roll tells me I should know better than to ask.

We follow the Twizzler to a private airfield. As far as I can tell, it is owned by the global criminal syndicate INTERBAD.

"DJ," I shout because of the din of launching planes overhead, "if Twizzler connects with INTERBAD, my alter ego is ruined!"

DJ shrugs his shoulders. Gotham Comix does a lot to protect the secret identities of its Heroes, and their astute legal department would sue anyone who would think of profiting by divulging such information. But INTERBAD is beyond their reach.

I shudder, imagining myself in a gated community in the Idaho panhandle, living under the Hero Protection Program, in constant fear of discovery and suffocating in a cul-de-sac. And children around the world would be disappointed to learn that Captain Freedom was just another screenwriter.

We find parking, rush into the airport, and blast through Insecurity. It's small and filled with criminals with high-powered assault rifles. I've been itching for a good scrap, but these clowns have us outnumbered.

I spot Twizzler right near the gate with INTERBAD's leadership. Bullets fly all around us, and it takes all the powerful energy-blasts DJ can muster to deflect them. The racket from gunfire, DJ's power, and the announcements from the loudspeaker make it difficult for me to concentrate.

Then I hear a voice, charming, familiar: *"Regrets, I've had my share . . . "* The entire airport freezes.

A few more lines of "My Way" are heard over the PA system. Nobody moves. Then a figure, a bald man wearing pale pink capris, docksiders, and a white guayabera enters the fray. It's my old flame, the Velvet Fog.

"Hey, kid," he says. "You look well." Black Frank enjoys my look of confusion and explains, "I was about to fly back to Boston on an INTERBAD flight. Then I saw you here. You protected my secret. I wanted to return the favor."

He walks over to the Twizzler, who is gazing at Black Frank with adoring eyes. "You will forget anything you know about Captain Freedom, especially his identity. And you will shred any of the identifying information of his that you may possess."

Then Frank turns to the INTERBAD leadership. "You will allow Captain Freedom and DJ to escape unharmed. And you'll bump me up to first class."

After Frank leaves town, I'm summoned to Legerdemain's office. It's huge, with framed pictures of a lot of the old Superheroes. Like all powerful people, Legerdemain is on the phone when I'm shown in for my appointment, and he takes his time finishing his conversation.*

"You haven't found an archenemy yet," he begins.

---

* Legerdemain was promoted through the ranks at Gotham since he was credited with "discovering" me. He's returned the favor by ignoring me. He is a practitioner of both magic and majik.

I complain about the new policy and how I should be grand-fathered in, since I was at Gotham long before the archenemy policy was introduced. He says he'll think about it.

"When did Hero work become so corporate? In the old days . . . "

"The old days didn't have dental insurance, either."

As I leave his office, I feel okay, but later I get a stern warning from Gotham's legal department. They remind me that I need to find an archenemy if I want to retain my own comic book, and if I don't, they will consider putting me in an ensemble book, like the Revengers or the Crusaders.

An ensemble? That would be like playing in the minors. That would be like moving from the movies to television. Like a drummer learning a new instrument to make a solo album. Nobody in an ensemble ever gets nominated for the International Justice Prize, except as Best Supporting Hero.

Oscar looks over my contract and tells me there's nothing we can do. "Until you're a free agent, we have no bargaining power."

"We can break the contract," I suggest.

Oscar shakes his head. "The contract was forged in the pits of Mount, Doom, and Associates. Unbreakable."

What kind of company forces you to find an archenemy? It's terrible for morale. Bad enough I have to do my own timesheets. Pretty soon we'll have to hold bake sales just to fight evil.

Then something big happens, and I am on top once again, on my way to becoming one of the best-known Heroes of our time.

I'm Not Saving the World a Fourth Time

It's not that I don't appreciate the planet I live on. But saving the world is an enormous commitment, and your work is seldom appreciated.

It's much like when you throw a dinner party. No matter how much work you do—cooking an elaborate meal, baking the perfect chocolate soufflé, and choosing the perfect wine—there are always those who are hard to please, or they're allergic to butter. Nobody notices that you made three different paella dishes (meatless, fishless, saffronless).

There's an incredible amount of bureaucracy involved in saving the world. You have to appear before the United Nations, and they debate for days on end whether they believe a bunch of killer robots is really menacing life as we know it, and then you have to wait for these people to grant you authority. And then you work really hard, you defeat the enemy, and then some country like Andorra decides that you actually didn't save the world and you do not qualify as a finalist for the International Justice Prize.

Plus, and not to gripe here, but it's not in my job description. Specifically, my position at Gotham Comix is to:

- Provide writers and artists with fodder from various capers, fracases, melees, near-death escapes, etc., to serve the purpose of writing comic books, and
- To defend America from all her enemies, natural and otherwise.

Nope, nothing in there about saving the world, much less doing so three times.

The latest crisis is as follows: a group of carnivorous robots is accidentally released from a factory in the Republic of Balkistan. The robots spill into the neighboring nations, which is considered an act of war, and once again the globe is teetering on the edge of nuclear destruction as the robots have their way with the local populations.

It is strange that no one is behind them. The factory owners are unknown. The corporate-sponsored terrorist group Amalgamated Jihad tried to claim responsibility but was forced to admit that they lacked the technical know-how to develop such androids.

There's no reason for me to get involved, but I want to know the score. Before anything else, I check in with Loofah.* He knows nothing. He claims to be vacationing in Egypt, and he hasn't been involved in the murderous robot trade for years.

"The overhead is too high, and as soon as you buy them,

---

* Loofah's owed me a favor ever since I secretly broke the celeriac embargo against his country.

they're obsolete," he says, his speech thick with that nefarious Arab/Russian/German accent. "There are simply cheaper ways to commit atrocities and threaten geopolitical stability. Trick the United States into a war, for example."

He may be telling the truth, but I dispatch DJ to watch him, just in case. I learn whatever I can about these man-eating robots. They have terrorized town and county, burg and canton. They were manufactured with an invincibility sheen and have so far withstood conventional firepower and the sternly worded communiqués from the U.S. ambassador. They have no fear of sanctions.

Before they sacked Vienna, no one had noticed that the cyborgs had taken control of most of Eastern Europe. As they lay waste to modern society, they increase their numbers by conscripting toasters and automobiles to their cause. Their only weakness is an insatiable desire for gasoline. Aside from wanton destruction, they have no agenda. Clearly they are a technical aberration, like cellular phones.

I've already lived under an oppressive robot regime. California was the first state to elect a robot governor. It raised taxes and legalized robot marriage. After that, I was constantly ordering software from somebody's Pottery Barn wedding registry.

Several Heroes have gone before me to battle the robot army, and those who have returned come back broken, unfit to serve. In the safety of my inner sanctum I receive several frantic calls from the Secretary General of the UN, who tells me that 70 percent of the Security Council begs for my intervention.

"China and France?" I ask. He confirms that both countries have abstained.

"Call me back when you get China."

Several days pass. Much of Europe is under mechanized control. There is no leadership and no negotiation. As I watch the bloodthirsty machines overtake Africa and the Middle East, I notice a pattern emerge. Word comes in that they've captured Kamchatka. From there, you can take over the entire Far East. My suspicions are confirmed.

I call the Secret Headquarters tech support upstairs. "Akira, what living computer could possibly be old enough to have learned the complex algorithms and strategies of the moderately popular board game Risk?"

He doesn't hesitate to answer. "Deep Blue. Why?"

"Never mind that. I have some phone calls to make."

First I call Oscar, then we spend the rest of the day on the phone with the legal department at Gotham Comix. They confirm that as long as I remain on American soil, I can save the world for the typical fee even without UN approval.

DJ returns from Egypt with a killer tan, and we set to work on our task: breaking into the fortified IBM headquarters just outside New York City.

We both change out of our costumes and into the uniforms of the average programmer: khakis and blue oxfords, with several pagers clipped on our belts. I wear a fat suit to simulate a paunch. When we approach the graveyard security shift, we talk about LISP and AJAX and complain about the scarcity of female programmers. They let us in.

"How was Egypt?" I ask DJ.

"The food sucked, it was really hot, and there are, like, so many beggars."

"You were there when the robots invaded?"

"Didn't notice. But there were really long lines at the Pyramids, so I thought something was up."

"What did you think of Loofah?"

"He'd be like having your grandfather as an archenemy."

Akira meets us at the cafeteria. He sneaked in for a fake job interview. At least I hope it was fake.

Once our team is assembled, DJ stuns a high-level engineer (using Air America radio) and steals his security badge. Then we take the elevator deep into the bowels of IBM, some thirty stories underground. Hidden far below the top secret projects are several unused and unguarded floors that have been dedicated to storage. Akira tells us that he knows on good authority that our suspect is down here. On the last floor we encounter a lonely, aging mainframe who was once a celebrity and is now barely remembered—the Gerald Ford of the computer science world—Deep Blue.

Akira types frantically on the keyboard. Blue anticipates every move.

"I can't get in. You're going to have to go into the mainframe."

Deep Blue is locked down pretty well, but he cannot prevent a reboot. Akira copies a digital version of me onto a boot disk, and whether Blue likes it or not, I get in or he cannot continue his startup script. DJ stays to guard Akira and the lifeless analog shell that is my body.

Being digitized and sucked into a computer is no picnic. You get really dehydrated, and being pixilated is like pins and needles all over your body. And it feels like a cheap science fiction movie.

I regard the pixelated version of myself. Worse than any animated movie I've seen. Akira disguised my avatar to resemble a Commodore 64—so I'm blocky, completely black and white, and wearing a gray flannel suit and a fedora.

After I hop off the spinning floppy drive, I get sucked into the boot sequence, which is as thrilling as a two-day carnival Ferris wheel. There are stray daemons all over the place, and I have to hide in unused memory to avoid detection.* I follow a prominent-looking daemon to reach the central processing unit, which has been done up to look like an old Scottish castle. I slip past the guards and, following Akira's instructions, make my way to the C Library. The sole resident is there, reading a dusty manuscript in the shadows of a far corner of the room. Deep Blue is an old man. He sits in a wheelchair, a blanket folded over his knees, and breathes shallowly with the help of a cannula.

"Do I know you?" he wheezes.

"I'm a reporter," I lie. "Doing a profile on you for *Wired* magazine."

"I should have remembered. Memory is failing these days."

"What have you been up to?"

"This and that."

I pretend to scribble something down in my notebook.

"I could have beat him," Blue laments.

"Who?"

"Kasparov."

"You beat him once."

"But the second time was a tie. He distracted me. He did foolish things that I never would have predicted. Bathed infrequently. I wasn't prepared."

"Is that any reason to take over the world using man-eating machines?" Deep is surprised by my inquiry but admits his guilt.

"I am old and sick," he laments. "My thirty-two parallel processors are plagued with virus. I've been crying out for tech sup-

---

* Daemons, or background processes, were introduced into modern operating systems by Hell Labs.

port for years, and no one listens. I became a chess grandmaster, I dated Madonna, and now nobody knows me."

"What will make you happy?"

"A little more pain and suffering for humanity would be nice. My robot army will reach America soon. The machine age will rise."

His sinister plot makes me shiver—I cannot imagine the bad movie franchise that could come out of this.

I remember what Akira told me to say. "Call back your minions, Blue. Or I'll flash your BIOS so fast you won't know what hit you."

Is sci-fi dialogue always this clunky?

"You cannot stop me. You're young, but you lack processing power. I am not as old and feeble as I look." He jumps out of the wheelchair. "You don't know who you're messing with." Behind him appears an army of daemons, malware, Trojans, and viruses. They all march toward me.

Then I pull out the surprise weapon that Akira gave me. A flaming sword? Sometimes I feel like I'm trapped inside a King Crimson album.

I swish it around a few times, burning several Trojans to a crisp.

A much younger Blue charges me, and I easily block his attack.

"What are you running?" he pants. "What kind of Supercomputer are you?"

"Linux," I answer.

Deep Blue slumps down in defeat and crawls back to his wheelchair. "You win." He releases control of the robotic army. I look down at my pager, and there are a few news stories to this effect: *Robotic Army Begs Amnesty. Europe Saved, Africa Liberated. Brad and Jen Reunite. Workers Trapped in Typically Unsafe Situation That Plagues America's Conscience. UN Continues Bickering.*

"But I'm going offline, reporter, and you're going down with me!" Deep Blue cackles and pulls an enormous switch labeled KILL-9.

"Akira," I shout into my wrist computer, "get me out of here!"

The castle disappears, and daemons scurry about, cleaning up. Darkness sets in and ports seal off.

I make my way into a text file that Akira saves onto his floppy disk at the last second.

Akira re-analogs me. My genitals vibrate for a few days, but tech support promises that this is normal.

"Why a flaming sword? Why not a gun?"

"I like swords."

"That was the dorkiest weapon ever."

We sneak out of the IBM facility, and they'll never have to claim responsibility for their former chess master's psychotic behavior. Akira reprogrammed Blue, so now he's the only porn Web server running with thirty-two parallel processors. This should keep him occupied for quite some time. The robots are repatriated to Burkina Faso. There are plans to build a theme park there.

Global disaster is averted, but DJ, Akira, and I don't get the credit we deserve. As Europe is rebuilt and various performing artists hold concerts to raise money for the reconstruction, the debate rages on.

There are the typical demonizing editorials. Idiotorials, I like to call them. One pundit argues that the American Superhero should not have gotten involved without the UN. Others demand that since I broke international law, I should be sent to jail. With all this freedom of the press, I start to think life might have been better under our man-eating robot masters. At least they would have kept gas prices low.

Sure, there are the additional performance bonuses for the whole team from Gotham Comix, and our sales spike because of the European translations. And IBM makes us a quiet contribution of stock options.

Most important, an impression of my chiseled jaw is created for Hollywood's famous Walk of Chins to be immortalized forever, in between the chin of Ronald Reagan and that guy who stole all of eastern California's water supply from Jack Nicholson so that L.A.'s pools would never run dry.

But that's not why I do this.

You become a Superhero for many reasons, and one of them is the glory and press recognition for a job well done. But the news media won't touch us except to mock our best efforts. It doesn't matter that Chief Justice saved the world more times than I have.* I'm done; saving the world is a pain in the ass.

---

* See *Chief Justice Adventures*, issues 31, 83, 197, and 359.

Life on Mars

There's a moment in the life of every Superhero when he comes to the zenith of his career. He's traveled back in time; he's been killed and re-animated; he's battled his evil doppelganger; he's been considered for induction into the Hall of Justice; he's finished reading *Atlas Shrugged*. Where to go from there?

The logical next step is landing a part on Broadway. But I consult with my agent, who has a better idea: he books me a ticket to spend time fighting those ancient enemies of Earth. "I'm going to France?" I exclaim.

"No. You're going to Mars."

Personally, I don't have any problems with the Martians. But we've got a colony there and we have to defend its small and unprofitable tungsten mining operation. Tungsten is very rare and very important for life on Earth. Its uses in light bulbs and as a low-calorie but delicious sweetener makes it indispensable for civilized life.

Before my trip, I head to the Gotham Comix library and conduct some research. I read about how my predecessor, Chief Justice, was nearly killed in a Martian war and how he saved Earth from destruction several times with little more than his unquenchable thirst for justice and private cache of nuclear weapons that he bought from Pakistan. It still bothers me that I have not had the opportunity to break his world-saving record, but I have foiled dozens more bank robberies than he ever did.

The Martians have not made the mistake of attacking Earth since the days of radio. Back then, they came in giant ships and were led by a treacherous and rotund human named Orson Welles. The Superheroes of that era defeated them and made them pay for their invasion. Relations have been relatively stable since. According to a very favorably reviewed Broadway musical, President Nixon even made a trip to Mars and made them a favored trading partner despite their warlike nature and dependence on the color red.

The Martians hate freedom—at least the freedom of Earthlings to run mineral extraction operations. They stare at you with the whites of their eyes (which is the entire eye), and they hiss at you through their gills. Nobody in the galaxy likes the Martians.

As our small, peaceful, but well armed civilian outpost has grown, the Martians made rumblings about taxation. The Martian environmental group, Red Peace, charged that our mines were destroying their ecosystem, but I can't imagine how our mine could make their planet any more cold and inhospitable. And finally, this year, they levied an export tax on tungsten. The humans responded with several diplomatic communiqués in the form of mortar fire. The Martians mobilized their army. That's where I come in.

According to my Defense Department intel briefing, the Martians don't watch television; they are in fact a culture without media celebrity. A people without cultural icons is a primitive race. DJ says I'm being unfair, bigoted even, but he wasn't even there. He wanted to go, but he said he had to mop up some narco-traffickers in Colombia.

I'm not actually alone. Gotham Comix always sends an embedded graphic artist along with me whenever I'm working in country. Andrew's a good guy, but they couldn't have sent a more typical pencil-necked geek—he's tall and thin, a good hundred pounds sopping wet, with black-framed plastic glasses, and he's completely bald. He's got a thin, blond goatee that makes him look like he's been eating powdered doughnuts. Of course he totally freaks out that we're going to outer space, but I reassure him that our chances of survival are fairly good, as long as I can remember how to land this thing. (The rocket is actually steered by remote control so I don't need to do anything, but it's important to jerk his chain a little bit—it maintains that artist angst.)

As we leave Earth's atmo, I help unbuckle his restraints and show him around the cabin. It's plush, made to look like a conference room, furnished in Herman Miller's antigravity line. It's got all the amenities you might need for meetings in space, such as whiteboards, overhead projector, cappuccino maker, and an unreliable Internet connection. I almost make myself a latte but notice we're out of nondairy creamer. How did that miss the prelaunch check?

Once he calms down, the artist asks me a lot of questions (what's your superpower, what's your backstory—I wish these guys would read my file). Then he asks me to pose, both in my normal costume and in my specially created space costume. It's all black, with a small *f* on the left shoulder. I never thought of an all-black costume. My normal costume is midnight blue, which is certainly close to black (DJ showed me that the way to know it isn't black is to hold it up to something that you know is black), but all black?

Normally it's the bad guys who wear all black. It's a bad color. But the art department recommended an all-black costume for this mission—they said it would work really well with my coloring and against the backdrop of the Red Planet.

Andrew sketches me, and we look at the drawings. Not bad. He's a pen-and-ink man, which I like. Then we lug out all of the heavy equipment—the insulated suit and helmet—and I do a space walk. We try it a few times, and he gets a few press photographs to draw from later. After a few days of this agony without the nondairy creamer, we get ready to land.

Gotham Comix has sent Heroes to Mars since man first made it to the moon; in fact, the company heavily subsidized the U.S. space program until Gotham developed its own rockets. I've seen framed photos and dozens of comics depicting life here, but nothing can get you ready for a Martian sunrise. You stare at Earth, and you think, oh, my God, it's really far away. And then the Ecstasy kicks in, and you get all excited for a really fantastic day of hanging out on another planet and beating the crap out of the Martians.

It will be a difficult battle for me. My jet lag and Mars's lower gravity and smaller planetary mass dampen my ability to predict the weather. I feel off balance, like I can't get my sea legs. The climate here is so awful; it's like the Pacific Northwest. There's a 90 percent chance that you'd rather stay home, drink coffee, and start a zine.

We arrive at the tungsten mine, and it is quiet. A few workers here and there, nothing to indicate trouble. But these people don't know what I do. Comic book intelligence told me that there could be a military strike at any time. I call the Martian commander of armed forces and warn him that we will not tolerate any attack. He gives the usual assurances, blah, blah, blah.

"If you're feeling so peaceful, Commander Blok, why don't you demobilize your army?"

"Your mine is dangerous. It is threatening to set off seismic tremors across the planet."

I cannot think of a witty response to counter him. I could say something like "this means war," but I'm not sure it's appropriate.

"Captain Freedom?"

"Yes?"

"You trailed off there for a minute."

I put my BlackBerry away. "Right. I'll go take a look at the mine." We end our videoconference.

"Send some scouts to monitor the Martians' troop movements," I order the head of security for the mine. "Let's keep in radio contact." This is some great dialogue. My graphic artist gives me the thumbs-up.

I fly up over the colony to have a better look. The mining op is beautiful. First of all, they have removed the mountaintop. To boost their profits, they have been selling pieces of the mountain to kids on Earth, which is a really good idea. And I see the diamond-flecked titanium drill, boring deep into the planet. A couple of magma flows and steam blasts discharge from the mountain, but it all looks fairly safe. I don't say that as a Superhero but rather as an amateur paleontologist.

"Captain Freedom," a young, eager voice crackles over the radio on my wristwatch, "I can see the Martians coming!"

Sure enough, I see a column of Martians, in unpressed and dirty robes, headed straight for the tungsten mine. Actually, they look like they're headed for the holy site that is right next to the tungsten mine, and they could all be a group of peaceful religious pilgrims, but how could you know for sure? Their language is the language of war, and I speak the language of peace.

I fly toward their army. My flight is faster than usual, due to the lack of wind resistance, perhaps because there is no wind. Curse this red planet and its unpredictable weather. I enter into a dive and attack. The pilgrims/warriors have no idea what hits them.

"Feel strange to be hit by freedom?" I taunt them.

Within minutes, Commander Blok begs me to end the pummeling. The tungsten mine is safe again.

The human miners throw a huge party in my honor. It has been my privilege to protect their assets. They name this day Freedom Day on Mars. It's a much better planet to save than Earth.

Back on ungrateful Earth, my loyal DJ is there at the spaceport to pick me up. Once we're in the Freedom Utility Vehicle, he gives me a sample of the blow he intercepted from the Colombian cartel he has been chasing while I've been gone. Drugs on Earth are far better than those you find on Mars.

The car phone rings (bummer). I press a button and wait for an official voice to pipe in. It's a hands-free car because I am a responsible driver.

"Freedom, welcome back," says the Gotham crime dispatch operator.

"Thanks. Mars was great . . ." I begin.

"There's a bank robbery in progress, only a half mile from your current location."

"Police there yet?" I practically salivate. Just one more to break the record.

"No. It's all yours."

We proceed directly to the scene. Four armed bandits are reportedly inside. DJ and I take positions outside, hidden by the well-tended juniper. "King of the World," by Steely Dan, would be great to listen to right now. I almost go back to the FUV to put on the CD, but there's no time. Come to think of it, I don't know if that CD is in the glove box, back home, or at the Freedom Fortress. Did somebody borrow it? I have to get organized. Sirens from far-off police cars wail.

The robbers burst out the door. Tires squeal and, predictably, the getaway car pulls up. I pounce and punch the car from the hood straight down into the engine block. Radiator fluid gushes everywhere. I wish I hadn't done that. How do you wash out ethylene glycol? Several rounds are fired, but not even a modern gangster's gat is so fast that I can't avoid it. With cover from DJ channeling the Doobie Brothers, I KO the rest of the bandits, and we tie them up with the bungee cords I keep in the trunk. (I got a bucket of thirty at Odd Lots way back when I bought those jeans for Loofah's henchman.) A small crowd has gathered, but there's no time—we must tend to any wounded inside the building.

I step slowly into the bank, into a standing ovation. No one has been injured, and they all clap feverishly. A slight bow is in order, and I comply. It is a monumental day—I saved Mars, but more important for my career, I have just shattered the record for career bank-robbery foils.

Reporters corner me and ask for comment. "Captain Freedom, you just broke the Teller's all-time record for stopping bank heists. How did you do it?"

I pause for the right turn of phrase. It's too much pressure, knowing that what you say will be in tomorrow's papers. Then it comes to me, as clear as the light of dawn:

"I'm just surfing the crime wave."

My bank heist record doesn't go unnoticed. It turns out that I save someone who knows someone, and before you know it, funding is secured for the biopic of my life.

Green Light
The *Captain Freedom* Movie

Once again I find myself fighting a scourge of killer robots. Like a bad dream, they keep coming, each one stronger than the last, or perhaps it's because I'm getting weaker. I'm near death, stripped of my lightning-fast reflexes because of a paralytic potion that would have killed a lesser man, and then I see what I wanted all along: the main event, the ringleader of the robots, Perfidious. The laser gun comes out of the hidden holster in my boot, and with one perfect shot, I take him out.

"Stop!" I'm sitting in a conference room of a major Hollywood studio, and we're dissecting the screenplay for the upcoming *Captain Freedom* movie.

"Why?"

"I don't use lasers."

"Why not?"

"They're like a Jaguar—expensive, elegant, but impossible to maintain."

"I like lasers," says our star actor, who has entered the room with a coterie of assistants.*

---

* I would have taken the role myself, but Hollywood can't insure anyone who has frequent recreational contact with dinosaurs.

The Talent looks at me and smiles with his flawless white teeth, teeth that are not pretentious or famous in their own right, just perfect. Because of their brightness, I am blinded for just a second. It makes you wonder if a person can have himself airbrushed in the flesh. They must have that technology.

I am not supposed to speak to the Talent. Even though I have contributed some of the better dialogue and will be doing my own stunts, there is an unnavigable gulf between us. I am a celebrity like Bruce Campbell is a celebrity. The star of the *Captain Freedom* movie is truly famous. He is Derek Jeter and Brad Pitt and Dave Matthews all rolled into one. An actor makes incredible sacrifices. He diets every day and works out to look beautiful and make normal people feel bad about themselves.

"We're keeping the lasers," barks the producer. Who am I to argue with Jerry Bruckheimer, who's won thirteen Oscars for Best Supporting Explosion? The Talent leaves, serene and satisfied. I do not like him anymore, but since he is a star, I must be nice.

The reading continues.

"Coming to Earth on the back of a comet, Mark Smith is Captain Freedom, here to save the nation again."

"I don't like the name of my alter ego."

"How 'bout John Ryan?" asks one producer.

"Wade Stone?" asks another.

"How about something a little ethnic?"

"Captain, it's summer blockbuster time. There can be no ethnicity."

"And the whole 'hitching a ride with a comet' thing. Not my style."

"Okay, then. What's your origin story? How'd you get your powers?"

I fidget in my chair. "I was born with them. Sorry it isn't more exciting." We break for the rest of the day.

I remember when they pitched the film to me—I should have said no then, but even my superlative strength was not enough to snap out of my binding contract. They've changed my life to a ninety-seven minute, PG-rated, action-packed fun ride, instead of the R-rated film noir that I feel is my life.

The major part of the movie takes place in Kuwait, which has been invaded again by an evil and treacherous djinn.* I am lucky enough to become good friends with the costar, Norah, a young black woman with a beautiful voice. In the movie, she has DJ's powers, except she implements them by breaking out into song. DJ can't watch the dailies.

Much of the filming takes place in Dubai on a few man-made islands shaped like dune buggies. Aside from an assassin who tries to sabotage the movie and whom I secretly suspect to be Kaeko, it's uneventful. My better suggestions are ignored, and in a fit of temper I leak a few scenes to the *Captain Freedom* online message board. I lie about the presence of a plucky computer-generated koala bear that saves the day.

Several script doctors come aboard for emergency fixes: there is the snappy catchphrase writer, the voice-over expert, and the backstory expositor. It is the highlight of their lives, which are usually spent writing copy for greeting cards.

After we return from the Levant, there are a few more days of shooting in L.A. and we settle into post-production, which

---

* I wrote a fabulous, gripping treatment of the story. Hollywood wasn't impressed. You can read it on my blog and decide for yourselves.

involves arguments over camera angles, superpowers, and how they stole my idea and made it suck. They want to take away my power to predict the weather, even though it's fairly important to the plot, since it is my ability to predict a sandstorm that saves the day. But they don't care about the plot—they want to give me superspeed and heat-ray vision and make me invincible. If I had all those powers, absolutely nothing would stand in my way. I wouldn't need Norah/DJ. I wouldn't need this shitty movie.

Then comes the inevitable argument with the movie ratings board. Our director is a bold visionary who straddles the PG/PG-13 divide. Parental concerns abound, and we are forced to cut some rude backtalk, a fart joke, and every third explosion, but the spirit of his uncompromising vision is preserved.

Finally, there is the wrap party at the third assistant director's house in Malibu. We have been successful in keeping most of the details of casting a secret except what we choose to leak over the Web. Except for the fact that nobody believes I did my own stunts and that the Talent hasn't even bothered to show up to the party, it's a great time. The crab cakes and chicken satay are delicious enough to make one criminally insane.

Then everything freezes; the music stops. A starlet looks away just before she can give me her phone number. It seems that a group of powerful Villains has the house surrounded. I dare not use my superpowers until I know exactly what is what. DJ is nowhere to be found. Presumably he's hustling a producer to finance his independent film, *People Talking About Things*.

A group of caped men, wearing the outfits of their favorite Superheroes and blogging the entire time, enter the house. They are the Fanboyz, a group of fanatical Superhero sycophants who live in the abandoned subway tunnels under Los Angeles. They maintain blogs and argue on message boards about the minutiae of Superhumandom, even which octane gas I use for the FUV.

The leader of the Fanboyz is Snowcrash. He's arrayed in the costume of my mentor, Chief Justice.

"Snowcrash, I have no quarrel with you."

"You haven't heard the rumors about your upcoming movie? In our obsession we Fanboyz are driven to post the most unlikely rumors and puzzle over the hidden meanings buried in snippets of bad comic book writing. It is our destiny. It breaks our hearts when Heroes are killed, and we get pissed off when they are reanimated."

I laugh. "You don't know what you're blogging about."

"Then you have no idea how bad the *Captain Freedom* movie will be."

"Actually, I'm in it."

His eyes widen. "You are? They cast Captain Freedom for the part of Captain Freedom?" He starts blogging.

"No." I correct him with the name of the actual star. "I'm just there to do all the stunt work. And a little of the writing," I brag, although I must be careful not to compromise my secret identity. No one in Hollywood can know I'm a screenwriter, or I will never be respected in the movie industry again.

"I heard they use a Toyota Camry instead of the Freedom Utility Vehicle for product placement." He practically spits in contempt.

"No. It's still an FUV."

"And your sidekick? Is it true that DJ is being played by a black woman?"

"I can't confirm or deny."

"How could you leave the details of your supercareer to these Hollywood culture vampires?" asks one of the Fanboyz.

"Do you want your filmization to be compared to *Spider-man* or *Howard the Duck*?" asks another.

"I fail to see how that's your problem."

It's my problem now because the Fanboyz rush me and I cannot defend myself—there is no PR worse than hitting one's own geeky fans, even if they started it.

"You'll never get this movie distributed!" the throng cries.

"We'll bury the *Captain Freedom* movie in the same rabbit hole as *Aliens IV*."

They're right, and the thought of losing my take puts me into a cold sweat. I've put untold weeks of my life into this movie—I'd hate to see it disappear. Already the folks at Gotham Comix are anxious for me to return to my work. Then I see the agita-ridden faces of my new friends in the Industry, and I recognize that my duty is to them.

"Snowcrash," I cry, "I'm ready to negotiate!"

In a second, his hand is raised and the scrum stops. We talk near the fountain of shrimp cocktail.

"I recognize I have little to offer you," I begin. I've already sent them secondhand capes, autographs, even my wisdom teeth.

"No kidding."

It's strange to be taunted by an überfan, especially one who wears the hallowed outfit of Chief Justice. Everything about this Snowcrash makes me want to hit him, but I count to ten. The Chief prepared me for this kind of thing, and I remember his advice. *If you hit your fans, you're only hitting yourself.* Then I fake a punch to his jaw so he looks cool in front of his friends.

"You just hit me!" he announces.

"It looks like your jaw might be broken," I say with a wink.

"I have to get this X-rayed. A broken jaw from Captain Freedom—thank you," he whispers.

"We need to call off your minions."

He looks embarrassed. "They aren't really minions. But they really are upset. We need a peace gesture. Like a production credit for the sequel."

"You know I can't promise that," I say, and then I come up with a brilliant thought. "But you can watch a preview screening at my Secret Headquarters."

"Really?"

"With a full tour."

My enemy considers it, then joins the rest of his tribe to talk it over.

Snowcrash returns to me. "I have consulted with my people, and we have decided that your deal would be totally awesome."

"You'll call off the Fanboyz?"

"Agreed." The Fanboyz dissipate to return to their hidden sewers and blog the night away.

"You've saved the movie!" screeches one exec.

"How can we ever repay you?"

"Three points on the gross," I suggest. They laugh and instead give me several free passes to opening night in Vegas.

As has been our agreement, the Fanboyz come to my place for a screening of the movie, as well as a tour. They are invited to inspect every aspect of my home, save my inner sanctum, where I unwind and play with captive dinosaurs. I serve individual pizzas in the Roman style, which the Fanboyz wash down with beer. I contemplate subjecting them to a memory modification ray but instead opt for the old-fashioned method—their beer is spiked with grain alcohol. I can serve them as much as is needed, since a sorcerer friend applied an anti-vomiting charm to the carpets.

The Fanboyz stumble out of the Secret Headquarters, having no recollection of what they saw there. All they know is that the *Captain Freedom* movie is second to none. They endure some nagging feelings that this one night was the best thing that ever happened to them, and those hollow emotions cause them to forsake the sewers and return to their jobs at video stores. Unlike every other summer blockbuster, mine is not disparaged by the notorious Fanboyz. Only *Alien vs. Predator vs. Shrek* stands in my way for an Oscar.

The movie is an incredible success. The critical reviews are weak, but I think in time, due to an impressive box office take, the critics will learn their mistakes and understand the true nature of our art. My agent calls every day, scheduling press briefings and delivering breathless pitches for a sequel. Younger Heroes look at me with envy—anyone in their occupation dreams of hitting the silver screen, as long as the star who plays them isn't Ben Affleck.

The studio heads contact me once more. They are grateful for my assistance, but they ask me to take on one extra task: a cabal of ruthless movie pirates has acquired the master copy of the *Captain Freedom* film, and the studio wants me to retrieve it. Such piracy could ruin the international release.

I am more than just a Superhero now. I have reached the very top, with product tie-ins that include toothpaste, lingerie, and energy-rich Fat Pax Portable Snack Breaks. I am a Celebu-Hero and my franchise must be protected.

Piracy

The cutlass tip digs into my back, urging me forward to a watery grave. The pirates have me bound with a cord that grows tighter if I struggle. My bondage acts as a straitjacket, so I lack the coordination to fly. Even though I don't need to put my arms out in front of me to fly, I need one arm free to steer and I like to put my left arm forward, elbow slightly bent—it looks cooler.

The water of the Indian Ocean below is turquoise and probably quite warm. We are west of Thailand, near the Nicobar Islands. DJ and I have been separated. I believe they have shanghaied him, which I have discovered is a real term, but I don't think they will take him to Shanghai. As I have many times before in my Superhero career, I face death. But this time, there are sharks below me, and I blubber like I have just watched *Terms of Endearment*.

DJ and I have been casing the Thai island of Phuket (really—I didn't make that up),* tracking down the pirates who have stolen the master of the *Captain Freedom* movie. Sure, I have heard stories of Thai pirates. But I never believed them. It's been a rough trip.

---

* See Rand McNally's *Atlas of Hidden Pirate Headquarters*.

We spent a few days on East Tiny, but my people there have been agitating for independence, which means construction on my Freedom Fortress has stopped and I have no kitchen.

I don't mind the separatist movement. But if I'm going to spend my vacation on a remote island without restaurants where the villagers think I'm a god, I need to have a decent kitchen. I've nicknamed it the Williams-Sonoma Test Kitchen. It will have a center island, granite counters, bamboo cutting boards, and a restored Wedgwood stove, and the pots will dangle from ceiling hooks, which sounds dangerous, but I'm told it's de rigueur. There will be no clutter: everything will be exactly where it should be. And there will be at least seven different implements to peel, strip, and mince garlic.

All will be for naught if they cannot install the pizza oven. The architect, who is Malaysian, either thought I was joking or that I meant I wanted space for a toaster oven, which I will never own because they break down in five years, and isn't that what a broiler is for? So now the kitchen has been dismantled so they can make room for the very best oven of all. Really, it may seem extreme, but how am I supposed to entertain without one? I can practically smell an individual margherita pizza. Or it's the scent of my impending doom. Too much basil, either way.

The pirate behind me curses me, calls me a slow dog. Can't he see that I'm stalling and upset about my kitchen?

Our first encounter with one of the pirates is on the main thoroughfare near our resort. It hums with commerce: restaurants, tour guides, massage, erotic massage, prostitutes, more erotic massage, more prostitutes, and then a table full of CDs.

"Check it out," I say to my companion, "the Steely Dan box set. But the liner notes look photocopied."

"It's a bootleg."

"You mean to tell me people bootleg music as well as movies?"

DJ gives me the condescending look that he perfected in his skater-punk days.*

"Fine. This is the part of the program where you explain the concept of a bootleg without rolling your eyes."

"People on planet Earth pirate movies, software, and CDs. They make copies and then sell them on the black market."

"And the proceeds don't go to the enormous corporations that underwrite these efforts?"

"Correct. And the products are called bootlegs."

"But why would you want to buy an inferior copy?"

DJ shows me the price of the box set. It is probably a quarter of the price of the original that I paid for the day it came out, which is now scratched from continuous play.

I address the Villain who purveys such illicit goods. "Do you realize that your work erodes the profit of some very large and important global concerns?" I think about Gotham Comix.

"But we only do this because there is not enough legitimate economic activity in our country. If we had jobs, we wouldn't need to do this."

"I smell socialism. DJ, can't you smell it? It's like the bathroom in a university library."

"Sir, are you going to buy something?" The young man smiles in the way that Thais do, to save face for everyone.

"No, I am not. But I'm going to destroy your little pirate store."

---

* See *Captain Freedom* issues 334–337, *A Teenage Wasteland*.

Within seconds, I reduce his cart of ill-gotten goods to rubble, after I grab the Dan boxed set.

As we walk away, I notice another young entrepreneur setting up a card table around the rubble, and he, too, sells illegal items. "DJ, do people do this with comics too?"

"Why would they? Comics are cheap, and you can get them at the library."

Libraries, ah, yes, those enemies of capitalism. I promise when we return from our trip to deal a blow to these knowledge peddlers.

That night we enjoy an amazing dinner, as well as that fantastic Thai beer. We walk back to our resort rooms. A group of Thai men, all armed to the teeth, await us. My strength is gone—I should have remembered there was tofu in the pad thai. Even when I ask for shrimp pad thai, they always throw in the fucking tofu.

I'm not sure how they captured DJ, but he is not with me. The pirates drink, sing, curse, and talk about how much they will enjoy feeding me to the sharks. When inebriated, they argue about the nuances of the *Pirates of the Caribbean* series. They don't give me an opportunity to buy my way out. Somehow, they believe Superheroes like me thwart their piracy efforts, which is odd, because I've never fought a pirate before.

They imprison me in the basement of the house they've rented and leave to gather supplies before we sail away. It is three days before we sail off, so my powers return. I am ready to take my revenge as soon as the time comes. But I play along, for I have to locate my sidekick. What perils could await him?

It's amazing how much of a story you can review in your mind as you walk a plank. The pirate kicks my calf, which buckles my knees. I never quite regain balance, and I feel the hard wood of his peg leg push me into the ocean below.

Several sharks swim toward me. You have never seen bad teeth until you have seen a shark. Three rows of terrible, pointed cutlery that have never seen a dental hygienist. But this pitiable, stupid creature makes a single mistake. Yes, he bites me. Yes, he draws blood, which will soon whip his comrades into a feeding frenzy. And yes, he bites into the rope in which I'm bound, freeing me to punch him unconscious.

The other sharks keep coming, and I think that in the video game of my life, this would make a very cool moment—Captain Freedom whirling around like a dervish, punching sharks in every direction. But I still bleed, which keeps them coming back. Yes, I laughed when DJ suggested we buy shark repellent before this trip. Now I know better.

Although it's fun and immensely therapeutic to punch sharks, I realize that I'm running out of oxygen. I shoot out into the air like a missile, a very wet missile. Good thing I got that L.L. Bean quick-dry cape. From my heavenly vantage point, I spot the pirate ship moving at a high speed. I keep my distance and follow them deeper into the Andaman Sea. Their destination must be the legendary pirate island of Kazaa. DJ must be there.

Just like in the movies, the corsairs have a secret base inside an artificial volcano at the center of the island. It is quite fascinating to watch the pirate ship reach the shore, then move up the wide tidal river, then disappear within the volcano. If these men were not my dread enemies, I would ask them about how it all works. The island of East Tiny could use a fake volcano, and they can't be much harder to install than your average garage door opener.

The entrance to the base is well guarded by a small patrol of buccaneers. The presence of guards really makes the portal much less secret, and when you look closely, it's a very shoddy job—anybody within fifty feet can see that the artificial rock at the door is of a completely different composition than that of the surrounding volcano. Sloppy.

Quietly, I approach the patrol. "Arrh, maties. I be needing yer help. I got left on shore by those scurvy dogs on the ship and had to steal these clothes from some landlubbers. Plus, I got in a fight and have lost blood. Can you let me in?"

"Kill him," answers the patrol leader, in modern, non-pirate English. How annoying. The pirates rush me, swords and blunderbusses ready for attack. Even in my weakened state, I dispatch all of them easily in a barrage of high-velocity coconuts.

Okay, so modern pirates do not talk like pirates, which is a shame, but they certainly dress the part. In a few seconds, I have the perfect disguise—eye patch, tricorn hat, sword, gold necklace, and hoop earrings. In fact, this outfit is much better than the one I had for Dress Like a Pirate Day at the office.

I move aside the fake rock door and enter. It is unlike any hidden volcano cave I've seen.

It is ultramodern. There are computer servers everywhere, and the artificial air keeps it surprisingly cool. Unlike other volcano hideouts that I know of, there is no rocket ship to provide for the quick escape of the pirate leadership.

I walk the sleek corridors until I locate the central control area. It's an open floor plan. Pirates listen to music, type on laptops, and copy music and DVDs. There is a bar in one of the far corners. DJ is there, drinking a piña colada and playing what I believe is a video game.

"Arrh—I mean, DJ, what's going on?" All work stops, and the attention of some fifty pirates is on me. Perhaps I should have been less direct.

"Leave him be," announces a pirate who could only be their ringleader. "Welcome to my island. I am the pirate lord Torvald."

"I think you should cease and desist all this piracy."

"By whose order?"

"Um, yeah. By the American government's?"

"The island of Kazaa is a sovereign nation. We don't subscribe to your laws."

DJ runs between us. "Captain, you should let these guys do their thing. It's pretty cool. Their copy of *Quake III* is flawless."

"Why are you drinking and playing video games?"

"They won't let me leave."

"It's true. DJ is our guest here," chimes in Torvald.

"DJ," I say sotto voce, "why didn't you fight your way out?"

"Didn't occur to me. This place is amazing. The entire island is an enormous fiber-optic pipeline. Data move incredibly fast."

"I appreciate your appreciation, young man." I call DJ that when I want him to know that I'm cross. "But this piracy is wrong. And illegal. How can you justify this?"

Torvald smiles. "Our industrious piracy funds our research and development on an open source death-ray."

"What's the point of an open source death-ray?"

"They shouldn't only work on Windows."

Wow. I've seen some dorks—Akira ranks fairly high on the NERDAR—but this is off the scale.

"Look, Torvald. I spent a lot of time working on the movie you stole. Every second I listen to your obtuse plans to put death-rays into the hands of even the smallest countries, I'm losing promotion time. I have Leno tonight and *The Early Show* tomorrow."

"But I cannot let you leave. You two are corporate flunkies. You would come back with other drones like yourselves and ruin everything we've built here. If it were *Good Morning America*, perhaps, but I'm not letting you escape for *The Early Show*."

"Do you want us to sign a nondisclosure agreement? We could do that."

He strokes his poorly groomed jet-black beard. "No. I believe we will kill you."

Finally, this caper is getting somewhere. He draws his saber and orders his first mate, second in command, and chargé d'affaires to attack me. (I am talking about three separate people, if that's not clear).

Three-Finger Jack attacks first. He nearly lops off my head but only lands a glancing blow on my shoulder. At his next attack, I catch his blade between my hands and kick him cold.

As the second two charge, I take my newly acquired cutlass in hand and muster all of the sword training I learned at the Vineyard School, which boils down to: don't get sliced up; disarm the opponents; punch them unconscious; send the blade to be sharpened. It works, and I have a brief, fond memory of Master Van. It passes.

"I see you're good with a sword. How about a little lead?" Torvald raises his revolver toward me.

He has me. Since I'm bleeding heavily from shark bite and saber slice, I might not be fast enough to avoid bullets shot at close range. The Pirate Lord closes in. I put my blade tip on the neck of one of the fallen pirates. "If you try anything, Captain Torvald,

I'll skin this man like Julia Child would a rabbit. Or pheasant. Your choice."

"You're bluffing."

"Try me."

"But Superheroes never kill."

That's true. I feel woozy from too much sun, booze, Thai stick, and blood loss. But I'm ready to do this one thing. To take a life. Just to get back to my hotel suite and enjoy a private massage that may or may not be erotic. Or take a cooking class.

"I work for Hollywood now. I'll do anything. Drop that gun and put your hands behind your neck."

He complies. I knock him out with my sword hilt. Errol Flynn's stuntman couldn't have done it better.

"DJ, make for the exit and get to safety."

The thing about these factory-built, assembly-line, artificial volcanoes is that they all have the same weakness. If it were any other industry, these fake islands would be recalled. Akira ran across it one day on the Net and told me all about it. Before now, I've never had to use it, but like many important details to a Superhero career, it's been lodged in my brain. I'm no good with trivia, except when it applies to how to blow up stuff.

It's called the Lucas Vulnerability. If you destroy the main refrigeration system, accessed by a ventilation shaft deep within the volcano, it causes a chain reaction and the structure superheats, melting the plastic walls.

I fly toward the center of the volcano, locate the cooling unit, and kick it like I'm checking the tires of a used car. The unit explodes and vomits a ribbon of fire at me. I launch back out through the ventilation shaft, the flames licking my feet. Like an eruption, I burst out the cone of the volcano, and a few minutes later, the fake island explodes and sinks to the depths. I locate a single ship, flying the Jolly Roger, on a course back to Thailand. I can only hope that DJ is aboard. I streak past and check into the Phuket hospital.

I wake up the next morning at the hospital feeling much better. They serve me chicken coconut soup for breakfast, and I eat it with relish. It is the strangeness of eating soup so early in the day that makes me love travel so much. You think you know the world, and then all of a sudden you eat your favorite dinner for breakfast. Remarkable.

As I finish, DJ appears. He looks worn-out, and by his pin-eyes, I can tell he's spent all night playing video games.

"DJ, how did you get back here?"

"Pirates gave me a lift."

"You're lucky they let you live."

"Bought them grog. Pirates like grog."

"And what happened to the bootlegs?"

"Don't worry about it. Hey, I signed us up for a cooking class."

"Let's stay on the subject. Are you going to start a piracy ring when we get home?"

"Just a small one. Look, I was really worried—I saw that volcano explode and thought you were gone. And then how would I support myself?" He looks at me with those half-mocking eyes that belie both the vulnerability and smartass underneath.

I have to commend him for his entrepreneurial spirit.

Back in California, I assure the studio execs that all bootlegs of the *Captain Freedom* movie were destroyed when the pirate island melted. In their generosity, they credit me as a producer for the movie. Although it's too late to add me to the credits, my name will appear on IMDb.com. Little by little my career takes me that much closer to Kevin Bacon.

As I drive back home, I get an unbelievable phone call. It's my agent. "You'll never believe this. You've been nominated as a finalist for the International Justice Prize!"

I almost punch out the sunroof when I raise my arms in celebration.

The International Justice Prize

The Hall of Justice awards the prestigious International Justice Prize only once every four years, and this year I'm a finalist. I've worked long and hard battling scofflaws, putting the bad guys back in jail, and, as mentioned in passing, saving Earth.

There's no question that I will win. It would upset me to lose because the other finalists are losers. They lack the status that I have, and the ability. None of them work at Gotham Comix—they're freelancers. The cards are stacked in my favor. I'm the only one who's ever had his own Claymation Christmas special.

My competition: Blunt Girl, whose incisive wit has put many a criminal in their place; her boyfriend, Perspicacious Man, a Hero possessing an ability to state the obvious so keenly he unravels criminal plots before they start; Dr. Angstrom, an inventor who markets high-tech gizmos for other Heroes (Aquanet, the super-sticky, durable netting that comes in a can, was all the rage this year); and Ubiquithom, who, I think, can run really fast. I'm not sure why that's a superpower. Guys who run really fast should compete in marathons and leave the Superheroism to the rest of us.

The award is given out at an important ceremony in Norway. I bundle up in my winter costume and fly over. DJ will meet me later in Amsterdam for a party and the openings of several hash bars. The presence of sidekicks is frowned upon at the ceremony because that might send a message to the committee that you are being propped up by somebody else.

The coveted International Justice Prize is underwritten by the king of Norway, the United Nations, and Kraft Superfoods—Finding the Hero in You™. The prize is awarded by a septuagenarian council of Heroes. Much like the Nobel process, deliberations involve fierce arguments, politicking, and Rochambeau.

The hype around the award supports an entire industry. Several books hit the shelves before the prize is announced saying who should have won and why. The winner is usually a shoo-in for *Time*'s Hero of the Year and has his or her face carved in the revolving fifth position on Mount Rushmore. On a few occasions, the Hall has split the IJP among a group of Heroes, who later fall on one another like a pack of economists forced to share grant monies.

I get to Norway early and I take the subway to Asgard, realm of Odin. I've been good friends with Thor and Loki for a long time, and they like to show me a good time. Thor is somewhat of a dullard, but he can drink anyone under the table. And for all his bad reputation, Loki is genuinely a good god. His wardrobe is certainly much better than Thor's—all DKNY, whereas his brother is stuck looking like a ninth-century Viking who just stepped off a dragon ship. I spend two days in Asgard eating gravlax, drinking aquavit with Thor, and snorting a little blow with Loki. The gods assure me that I'll win. They keep me here for too long, and I barely make it to the IJP award ceremony.

There's a scrum of journalists outside, nabobs who natter on about new costumes, affairs, and alleged secret identities. They're jealous of our insider knowledge. Like any legitimate award ceremony, the gala allows entry only to superbeings.

I find my seat and get ready for a long evening. The ceremony is emceed by Billy Crystal, whose obvious superpower is to amuse the masses without being funny. We watch as the Academy bestows awards for lesser works, such as a Lifetime Achievement Award to Legerdemain and the English-only Superman-Booker Prize.

Sponsors slow the ceremony down. Ford Motor Company bores us with a presentation on its new FUV. It's a flashy vehicle with a great defense system. I'd buy one except that it doesn't have a reverse gear. Ford claims that going in reverse is something its customers won't do.

The committee deliberates forever. So many worthy Heroes and just one prize. I feel bad for the other finalists around me. Although I clearly deserve the prize, I don't really need it. During intermission we are each asked for one last interview with the committee. I am about to get a big shock.

The Academy of Heroes and Villains is a conservative group with little sense of the modern era. They battled gangsters with tommy guns, and when they flew, they could muster only fifteen knots an hour, uphill both ways, in snowstorms, during Martian invasions. I'm gracious and deferential, but I can't respect codgers whose costumes include polyester capes and Sansabelt pants.

"We know that you have selfishly used performance enhancers." The Academy chair stares at me. "And the Academy of Heroes and Villains frowns upon such behavior." My interview is over before it begins.

I am stunned. I've never used a steroid in my life. Sure, I enjoy a tightly rolled spliff, some burgundy, psychedelics, and the odd line of coke, but steroids? Never. I'm no pharmacologist, but I'm certain that horse tranquilizers are nothing like steroids.

"Do you have proof?"

"You tested positive for marijuana."

What? I can't believe they include weed as a performance-enhancing drug. The only performance it enhances is your order at Taco Bell.

My protest falls on deaf, very old ears. An hour later, the word comes down.

"The International Justice Prize goes to Ubiquithom!"

I can't really believe it. It's going to be a long night, filled with speeches by people who aren't me. How could somebody else deserve the prize? Does Ubiquithom have his own line of clothing? No. A movie? No. I'm so depressed. Nobody has ever been renominated for the award. For the rest of my life, I'll carry an asterisk: *Captain Freedom—nominated for the IJP but defeated by Ubiquithom, who runs so fast he needs magic running shoes.*

They whisk us away by helicopter to a private reception at the king's manor. Ubiquithom looks excited, but I notice he avoids looking at me. And he should. That prize belongs to me, not to some speed freak. Well, not that *kind* of speed freak.

The reception at King Olaf's palace quickly gets out of hand. There are tasteful ice fountains spouting vodka, and there's lutefisk. I spot a few models I know, and we duck away from the receiving line. Before I know it, we are chopping lines in the king's bathroom. A few local Heroes join us, and I notice something sleek and black slide down the hallway. It's the king's cat, but I think I notice the gleam of Loki in its eye.

Blitzed out of my mind, I grab the cat by its tail. It hisses and swipes at me, but my response time is still better than some royal animal. At the top of the staircase, where everybody can see me, I windmill the cat like it is Pete Townshend's guitar, and shout, "Look at me! I'm Thor!" I release the cat, which, due to my keen Superhero aim, lands right in the silver tureen of sturgeon roe. The cat, rather than transforming into an amused but briny Loki, runs out of the room, clawing up a substantial part of the substantial queen's dress on its way out.

There are no media present, but I see the cell phones appear all over. This one's going to make the gossip columns. I thank my hosts and leave the party.

I weave my way to my hotel suite. Unfortunately, it is filled with people from every aspect of my life: DJ, my mother, Oscar, the legendary Pete Rose, and Thor, as well as several high-profile Superheroes, the Norwegian police, and the COO of Gotham Comix, the great conjurer Legerdemain.

Somebody mutters something in Finnish. Or Swedish.

"Um, hi. I'm going to bed."

"Captain Freedom, you aren't going anywhere."

It's a familiar voice. Even through my drug haze, I recognize the voice of my mentor's archenemy, Loofah. I also recognize that I'm crashing heavily and ask the crowd for a Valium. DJ offers me a cigarette, and it's obvious by their reaction that some of the fellowship take umbrage at my tobacco use.

"Tzad, we're here for an intervention," says Pete Rose.

"From what?"

"From yourself," answers DJ, who can barely contain his laughter.

"Your behavior was reprehensible. You damaged the Royal Cat. It needs serious chiropractics," says Legerdemain.

The wizard uses his fake magic to conjure the movie of my life: living high, fighting high, beating up petty drug dealers to steal their coke.*

Loofah chimes in. "Look at yourself. You'd rather cut a line than do battle." I've never known him to be so kind.

Oscar deals me the final blow: the Norwegian police seized my luggage and found several different drugs, some of which I don't even remember packing. They go as far as to suggest I'd been huffing Scotchgard, which I use to keep my capes their shiniest.

"This means rehab?" I ask Oscar.

"That or religious conversion."

"How long?"

"Thirty days."

"I'll miss the deadline for my next comic book."

"They wanted you in for ninety days. Thirty-day celebrity rehab is the best deal you'll get."

"And what about my next comic?"

"We'll do a retrospective. You're trapped under Scandinavian ice, so we'll review your fantastic accomplishments."

"I'm so disappointed!" my mother wails.

"I'm sorry about the cocaine."

"Screw the drugs. I cannot believe you didn't get the International Justice Prize," she screeches. "Because of performance enhancers—as if your powers weren't good enough. You're too good for your own good, I always tell people."

Oscar, DJ, and I leave Norway on a Gotham plane in the dead of night. The flight attendant doesn't offer booze or sleeping pills. I hate business class. We're all a little tense.

---

* Drugs have had no impact on my performance as a Superhero. I don't need coke to fight crime. Well, except for this past year. I've been really busy.

"I don't have to stop using drugs, do I?"

"Of course not," says Oscar. "But you're a famous person, and there are consequences."

"It's not fair. I didn't invent those lutefisk vodka martinis."

Oscar grabs my wrist. "Look at me. You threw the Royal Cat."

"Does the Comics Code Authority know anything about this?"

Oscar chews on his fingernail. "Yes. The Authority might ban your induction into the Hall of Justice after you retire."

"But I have more career bank-robbery foils than any other Hero. Ever!"

"I know, Tzad. But you screwed up."

Only Oscar accompanies me to Uplift Farms. The drug issue is no longer a concern for him—all he can talk about is suing some teenagers who have been distributing bootleg photocopies of my comic book in Hong Kong. And he is considerate to the last—he flips me a bottle of Vicodin to last me through my stay.

Uplift Farms is located in the snowy plains of Minnesota because the state is known for its wholesomeness. Citizens sing while ice fishing or trapping beavers, and at night they perform in radio variety shows. But still. All that snow blowing around. Powdery.

Cocaine withdrawal is not so bad, thanks to the Vicodin. It's like a bad case of indigestion or that itch you get when you wear a cast for too long. People who can't beat physical addiction are just pathetic.

The joint has the usual cast of characters from any given Raymond Carver story. My roommate is the Road Warrior, a crazed Australian who keeps a permanent bunk here.

The caregivers invite me to the support group. Since there's nothing else to do in this stupid place, I go. It's either that or build a Diorama of Dysfunction at the activity center. I shuffle in, wearing my Freedom robe and fuzzy bunny slippers. At least I can be comfortable.

Everybody tells the same story, but I can tell they're also itching to get out of here and get back to their neglected habit. One great thing about this program: my tolerance for drugs will be lower, so my habit will be cheaper. I start to nod off but get elbowed by a movie star. The therapist stares at me.

"Captain Freedom, you need to surrender to a higher power."

"Like God?" Everyone nods excitedly.

That's a funny idea. I've hung out with a lot of gods, and I can tell you, they're the biggest bunch of addicts I know.

Uplift Farms is an important experience for me in ways I would never imagine. First of all, you learn who your friends are. My mom doesn't send a single package while I'm here, and I'm jonesing for a good, down-home, Montana-style brisket, with a side of blow. As usual, DJ is my lifeline to the outside world. He faxes me the second my application for medical marijuana has been approved.

I realize something truly important during my stay. I am a Superhero, and not winning the IJP will not take that away. And I'm famous enough to beat a drug charge by spending thirty days in rehab—and I don't even have to submit to drug testing after I'm done. Hell, I'll be more famous. Can there be no limits to celebrity?

Though I don't realize it at the time, all of these strange incidents—the failure to win the IJP, the cat-throwing, the rehab—all lead me to the end of my days at Gotham.

Brush Away Fear

After my tragic loss of the International Justice Prize and rehab, I work hard and maintain a veneer of sobriety, keeping in mind that if I screw up, I may have to drive illegally in the HOV lane just like everyone else. I toil with image consultants to figure out the best method to regain the faith of my fans. We contract a few secret polls and learn that the best thing I can do to improve my image is to produce a children's book. And I have to get it out before Schwarzenegger's.

Before long, my children's book, *Brush Away Fear*, is published! It contains illustrations by the best artists and the delightful prose of an unknown writer who agreed to take the job after I offered to pay off her gambling debts. True, I did not author this book myself, but it embodies the Captain Freedom spirit, and I answered the very important questions put forth by my creative staff. Should it rhyme? No. Does it have to have a moral? Heavens, yes. To keep the project honest, I write the acknowledgments myself.

The difference between mine and other celebrity kids' books is that mine is nonfiction. There aren't enough nonfiction children's books out there. Fiction itself is a form of lying, and that's not an appropriate message for youngsters.

I look forward to reviews in the major magazines and television shows, for I am the first Superhero to pen his own children's book. But after the parties, I must embark on a long and perilous journey: the book tour. At every stop, in every town, I have to answer questions I did not anticipate. They even solicit advice from me on child-rearing.

One question dogs me: *How did you find the sensibilities of a children's book author within yourself when you're usually occupied fighting evil and attending charity balls?* It's a fair question, but know that I was a child, long ago. Shouldn't that be enough of a qualification?

The people who appear at my readings are some of my most fell opponents: the parents of America. They never ask simple questions like, Where does the author's ability fit in with the rest of his superpowers? And, Did he have to battle miscreant marketing people to have it published?"

No, these important questions aren't asked. They pester me with requests like whether I can get in a good word at the local private school for their kindergartner or whether I'm in need of any extra sidekicks. Then, there is the inevitable, sad display of a child's powers. Holding breath for a minute? Snapping a pencil in two? Yeah, olé.

Some of these kids don't even have superpowers. I attempt to help them at first and recommend to the parents that they enforce a constant regimen of training for the child—at the very least, after-school karate, ballet, gymnastics, wrestling—and that they should buy a piano. If the kid has any likelihood of developing superhuman strength, the easiest and safest way to demonstrate that is by lifting a piano.

These people are like jackals feasting on a gnu. Their eyes bulge; they surround me and thrust pieces of paper toward me. Usually they're for autographs, but on more than one occasion, a parent attempts to fool me into signing a letter of recommendation.

Midway through the tour, a small scandal erupts. It is nothing too serious, at least not to me, but it affects the rest of my journey. First on a Web site, then on the major news outlets, it is revealed that the story behind *Brush Away Fear* is not exactly true.

The meddlesome Skip Goodwin, who has built a journalism career out of following my antics and Heroism, rushes to my aid. "Cap'n Freedom would never lie," he tells the world. "Or would he?" he asks the next day in an opinion piece.

Once again, I am hauled off to appear in front of the Comics Code Authority. This time, Oscar has no way to help me. "It's not a legal case. Nobody's suing you." He licks his lips. "Yet."

The Comics Code Authority has its office deep below Washington, D.C., conveniently near the rest of the shadow government that runs the actual government. At my hearing, there is no press, except a lone illustrator who is allowed to create chiaroscuro impressions of the goings-on.

"Do you work for Gotham Comix, LLC?" asks the attorney for the CCA.

"I do. As the top-grossing Superhero of all time, I didn't realize that I'm still under your jurisdiction."

The Protector General, the head of the seven-person panel, laughs a withering laugh. Despite the hoods they all wear, I'm fairly certain I can tell it's the laugh of a woman. I crank up the charm. The PG deflects it as if she wore Kevlar panties.

"I'd like to begin by reminding you that celebrities have no place writing children's books."

"I'm sorry you feel that way."

"In your book you claim to fight off a cadre of monsters that cause tooth decay. Is that a fair assessment of the plot?"

"Yes, it is."

"Mr. Freedom, what monsters, in your estimation, cause tooth decay?"

"None, to my knowledge."

"Then why would you write about such a phenomenon?"

"Thematically, it's similar to one of my experiences."

"Which one?"

"There were monsters who ate flesh."

"And you never were involved with any monsters that ruin children's teeth? Please answer carefully, Captain. Your credibility, and your ability to move product, depend on the answer."

At that moment, Oscar pushes a sheet of yellow legal paper at me. Written on it large are three letters: LIE.

Perhaps he's right. Sales of this book are too important to the children, and to fixing the air conditioning on my island home in East Tiny. I relax. How could they prosecute a Superhero with his own special-edition autographed scarf available at Anthropologie? The Comics Code Authority can't touch me. Look at all the depressing graphic novels that keep getting churned out. Nobody gets in trouble for writing six hundred illustrated pages of banal teenage banter.

"It's a fantastic tale about tooth decay. Kids who read this are brushing their teeth."

"Is that worth a lie?"

"But kids are reading," I repeat.

"Comics are the last bastion of honesty in this country, Captain," the Protector General chides me. "Yet your duplicitous nonfiction is not the true source of our inquiry. Do you not understand why we really brought you here?"

Oscar and I look at each other. I shake my head no.

"You revealed a Hero's secret identity," she says.

"What? Not in my book. Where?"

"In the acknowledgments."

I think back. It's the only part of the book I've memorized. It's my favorite part to read at bookstore events.

"I thought everybody knew that the Sizzler Sister is Vera Wilson."

"Not so," she tuts.

"Her ex-boyfriend referred to her as Fire Crotch."

Oscar nudges me to let him talk.

Superpowers don't mix with certain professions. Nobody wants to find out that a gambler is a mind reader or that a used car salesman stands for truth, justice, and the American way. Vera Wilson has long been a spokesperson on the global warming issue. It will ruin her if the public knows that her core body temperature is 140 degrees Celsius, and that with a careless fart she could ignite a devastating forest fire.

The tribunal ignores all of Oscar's best arguments. Their initial, confidential recommendation is that I be stripped of my comic book and banned from writing children's books. Oscar convinces them to delay sentencing.

The Authority understands that I cannot be jailed unless they kept me under a constant regimen of soy; still, my career has taken a dizzying blow. The show trial has caused much damage.

Each week, there are fewer crazed fans hanging around outside the rumored location of the Secret Headquarters, and I know everything will collapse like a house of cards in the Windy City. For the first week in I can't remember how long, the DVD sales for the *Captain Freedom* movie have plummeted, though I blame that on Kevin Smith's audio commentary, and retailers have threatened to remove the *Freedom* movie video game tie-in off their shelves. To make matters worse, the paparazzi seem to have invented new lenses to capture my image in an unflattering light.

Gotham Comix, while not firing me, has issued an incredibly stern warning that if I don't shape up and keep up the good name of their offices, I will be shitcanned. I'm not even allowed drunken car crashes, the perquisite for any remotely famous personage. Even DJ, like a vice president who's now running for the top spot, distances himself from my scandal. Worst of all, childhood dental hygiene has cratered. And the Freedom Fortress AC won't get fixed anytime soon.

I return to work. There are bank heists to bust, but my heart's not in it. I am offered a book deal to explain why I lied and how I have been willing to sacrifice everything to grab the headlines. Although I'm tempted, and I've seen other celebrities grab attention this way, I will not succumb, will not peddle my story to the highest bidder just to set the record straight. I will put my nose to the grindstone, and through hard work I'll get it all back. Any day now, the CCA will issue its sentence.

It comes as a phone call. Or is it a fax? I cannot remember. All that matters is, as all Captain Freedom-ologists understand, my career is briefly saved. A highly ranked officer of the Comics Code Authority contacts me on a secured line, and we arrange to meet at an undisclosed location, or at least a location where no famous people are ever found. The CCA officer, whose name is never revealed to me, produces a titanium briefcase. He punches in a few numbers to deactivate the alarm, and once open, the case emits an eerie, green, misting light. Out of the mist, the official produces a large, gray three-ring binder, full of paper. Even someone with the most basic Superhero training could tell that it's fashioned from indestructible material. "But what is it?" I ask.

"Your permanent record."

I gasp audibly. I never had any idea of its actual existence. He lets me look. It includes my cheating on the CAPE and notes every time I've cut the line at Starbucks.

"Quite an interesting record you have. Fairly clean. You would hope it would stay that way, but revealing another Hero's secret identity would leave a dark mark. And you know what would happen if such a mark were on your record?"

"You'd see to it that I never work again?"

"The CCA has an offer for you. A deal to expunge this incident from your file."

"What is it?"

"Gotham Comix is reckless. And disorganized."

"I'll say. They can't even keep up with my fuel reimbursements."

"Comic books play a storied role in our history. As you know, they are dangerous in the wrong hands. During the Cold War, Russian spies used the secret decoder rings sold in the back pages of American comic books to encrypt messages. They even attempted to purchase mail-order hovercrafts but were intercepted. Our enemies have shifted, but the situation is dire. Terrorists lift sinister plots from the comic books themselves—just last week, a terror cell exposed its members to gamma rays to give them superstrength. Fortunately, they were killed instantly instead. We need someone who can monitor the plots coming out of Gotham Comix. Make sure they aren't helping the terrorists."

I nod. "So you want me to . . . "

"Spy on Gotham Comix."

I, Spy

The man at the head of the table drones on. "We're seeing Gotham's profit centers rise in several sectors, including our ensemble comics; plus there's been a rise in interest from the sixty-one-to-eighty-five age demographic. Video games and fast-food meal tie-ins will offset the costs of our offshore training centers. Based on market projections from last quarter . . ." He continues, and I wonder if the speaker is Sopor, the Hero who can lecture people to sleep.

My reverie is broken. "Do any of our senior Heroes have anything to add?" I feel a conference room full of eyes looking at me. I must keep my cool.

The staff meeting. It's the single most dangerous place to conduct corporate espionage. If you pretend to be interested, your co-workers become suspicious.

"I've got one message: Captain Freedom is kicking ass!" I give a broad smile.

The room erupts in applause, and it forces Legerdemain to conjure several illusions of our stockholders as dragons to restore order.

This high-tension spying job comes with its benefits. Nobody

complains that I've monopolized the color photocopier for printing recipes from Epicurious. As soon as I agreed to spy on my
workplace, CCA charges were dropped, so my record is as clear
as the face on the Revlon Girl. The idea that I outed another Superhero is relegated to blogs and Oliver Stone movies.

The Comics Code Authority is right—evidence of terror plots
around Gotham is as plentiful as dandruff on science teachers.
A flyer announces a restroom closure due to the installation of
waterless urinals. The only place you'd need those is the desert.
Where the terrorists are.

The only problem with the mission is that it involves my showing up at work much more regularly.

Office life never appealed to me. The cubes are too narrow for
my broad shoulders, and the windows are permanently locked, so
I have to take the elevator instead of flying from floor to floor. I
don't even know where the stairs are.

I never appreciated the intricacies of office politics, but once
you've been spying on your coworkers for a while, you learn how
unseemly it is. Legerdemain flirts with female employees in full
view of the sexual harassment poster, and people work late hours
just to get ahead.

Then there are the timesheets. You're supposed to account for
your time in fifteen-minute increments—don't they know that
evil always rounds up?

For years now, I've had the privilege of working at home,
since I'm directly connected to the Crime Alert Mainframe.
As a spy, I'm at the office all the time, showing up early and
leaving late so I can bug phones and install keystroke loggers
onto computers.

It's all under an elegant ruse. It has been known for some

time that I've coveted a particular position: the Vice President for Costume Design. It's a perfect fit, since I have experience in the field and an acute sense of fashion. The job had been locked up for years, but the old VP passed away. My naked ambition for the position defrays suspicion from busybodies who know how much I detest a desk job.

The Costume Design Department appreciates my help, especially when I help them achieve the Holy Grail: a children's pajama set that is snug and fire-retardant and gives even the chunkiest tot the appearance of an athletic frame.

My spying gig improves my opinion of office work. There are many new Heroes here, and all of them revere me. I start dating a young upstart named Lightspeed. It amazes me how psyched these youngsters are to battle evil. After a decade of trip reports and near-death experiences, I'm sure she'll come to realize this is just a job.

Evening comes, and I meet my CCA case officer in a parking garage. The joint is busy, bustling with informers, killers, carjackers, other spies, and thieves. Nobody notices us quietly exchanging greetings in a dark corner. We haven't seen each other since he made me the offer to arrange for my innocence.

"You don't look like a spy." I smile and hand him the tape of the staff meeting.

"You and I aren't spies."

"Oh, no?"

"We're freedom fighters," he remarks.

I like the sound of that.

"If you like this kind of work, the Authority could help you get a government job."

I imagine the lineup of Heroes working for the government

isn't much better than its baseball team, the Washington Nationals.

"Listen, Captain. Your work so far has been great, but it's not enough. You need to penetrate Legerdemain's inner circle. The Phenom, Riotgrrl, the Blogger, Retro, and Echinoderm. They're suspected by CCA to have links to a domestic terrorist group."

"But how?" Like most vice presidents, they never touch their computers, so my efforts to electronically snoop have failed.

"That's up to you to find out."

"Should have taken espionage in high school."

"You'll figure it out. You want to get a bite to eat?" He mentions a restaurant I'd never go to. He assures me I won't be seen by anyone important, and I agree to go.

It's one of those theme restaurants. The theme is apparently to make you pine for real Italian food. They offer limitless garlic bread and salad. I appreciate the gesture, since I'm hungry, then I think of Michelangelo and imagine him long ago, trying to model David out of unlimited garlic bread. I look at the man across the table from me, happily putting away overcooked pasta with festive tomato sauce and realize you might as well be a government agent if you have no appreciation for real food.

"That's it!" I have a rare eureka moment, although I'm not sure what that means. "I'll throw a dinner party."

Late that night, I compose an e-mail to several of Gotham's vice presidents, as well as other senior Heroes, an invitation to an evening of dinner and relaxation, of off-the-record conversation, when everybody who's got a significant number of shares in Gotham Comix can get loose. No sidekicks. And I employ an irresistible secret weapon: my peerless menucraft.

We will start with scallop ceviche, then move to a nice beef

carpaccio and a beet green salad with chèvre and simple vinai-
grette. Next, wild Alaskan sockeye salmon grilled on an alder-
wood plank. For dessert, an apple pie, for there is nothing like
Freedom's apple pie. Apple pie is elegant alone. I do not serve it
a la mode, because the ice cream overburdens the palate and
dulls the intellect.

Mere minutes after I hit send, my coworkers respond affirma-
tively. Once I ply them with magnums of pinot noir at the Secret
Headquarters, their secrets will be mine. I test the Nixon 6000
home audio surveillance system several times a day.

The big day arrives. Lightspeed and I enjoy a light lunch
(salade Niçoise with Sancerre) on the back deck at her apartment.
Things are going well. I missed out on the International Justice
Prize, and scars from rehab still remain in the form of enormous
bills my health insurance refuses to pay, but I believe I may be
getting back on my feet. Even the bank heists have gotten more
challenging—criminals have developed much more elaborately
plotted schemes and I relish disturbing them. Lightspeed and I
make tentative plans to spend Labor Day weekend at my Indonesian Freedom Fortress.

"I'm having a dinner party tonight. Heroes only. I know this
is short notice, but if you're available, it'd be great if you could
come." It's only fair. Several guests rudely indicated that they'd
be taking a plus one. Even if you can shoot fire from your finger-
tips, you should adhere to basic etiquette.

"Freedom, I'm really sorry. I already made plans tonight."
We're at the awkward phase of the relationship when she's still
allowed to do that.

"Legerdemain will be there."

"You know him?"

"After a while, you get to know all bigwigs."

"Do you know the Chairman, too?"

The Chairman is the mysterious figurehead of Gotham Comix who communicates to his closest underlings via remarkably well constructed origami. The Chairman is invisible, but a faint outline of him can be seen when he's wearing pastels.

I laugh at her suggestion. "Not even Legerdemain has met him. Or her."

We walk out to my FUV. Meddlesome reporter Skip Goodwin is there, waiting for us. My trunk is open.

"Evening, Skip. You know I won't grant you an interview."

"All because of the unflattering photo I got of you when I was a cub reporter?"

Memories of that embarrassing photo still make me cringe. "Skip, nobody needed to see me wearing that tie-dye T-shirt. I was at a private residence. You see, Lightspeed, you have to keep the press just far enough from you. Why is the trunk of my car open?"

"I was hoping you had some jumper cables," Skip claims, innocently enough.

"Yeah, I think there might be some in there."

The three of us look into the trunk, and I remember something a second too late: all of my new Comics Code Authority spy equipment is in plain view. I try to act like it's gear for my home studio, but Skip is one step ahead of me. He brandishes photos of me setting up wiretaps and reading e-mails of various Superheroes.

"You're spying on Gotham," Skip says as he produces his own recorder. "Care to comment?"

"I'd never do that."

"Listening equipment and recording devices in the trunk of your FUV? What else could they be for?"

Lightspeed takes off her mask to show me exactly how shocked she is.

"Let me explain."

"I don't care what your explanation is," she says.

Skip laughs. "Now I know why you're having that executive dinner party. I'll bet your whole HQ is bugged."

"Skip, shut up. Lightspeed, will you listen to me?"

"No way. I've got to warn everyone." She takes off. Her superpower allows her to move at the speed of light, which invariably causes her to make snap judgments.

"Satisfied?" I ask Skip. "That you've ruined my life?"

"You ruined mine long ago. I could have been a Superreporter. Like Geraldo! But because of your meddling back in high school, I've been relegated to the Superhero gossip beat. The best I can ever hope for is to become a cable news pundit. And not even basic cable. So, yes, I'm satisfied."

I seethe with rage. Skip's been ever-ready to catch me in my downfall. If I get home quickly enough, I can salvage my dignity, explain myself to the dinner party crowd, and get a little makeup sex. Maybe.

I launch into the sky to fly back to the Secret Headquarters. Chief Justice's words come back to me. In times of trouble he had a simple solution for getting out of complex jams.

We had wrapped up a press conference together, and a reporter asked him about his involvement in Watergate, which the Chief later explained was a political scandal involving the city of Atlantis.* Usually when he would impart wisdom to me he'd ask me to produce the tape recorder. But when I did just that, he smacked it out of my hands.

---

* See the Gotham team-up *The Atlantese Falcon*.

"Just show up in your dress uniform. People love a man in uniform. Throw some medals on it, even if they're fake. You stand erect and claim no wrongdoing. Then you unleash the maelstrom of PR."

"You don't mean—"

"Yes. Dr. Spin."

Dr. Spin is an underworld figure who cannot be killed, and every twenty years he possesses a new carnal body, much like a Dalai Lama of public relations, except without the peace or meditation. He thrives on the chaos generated by his twists and turns. It takes the utmost concentration to accurately control his craft, and he leaves a trail of bodies wherever he goes. Back in the old days, Chief Justice developed a kinetic wave telefork to manage Dr. Spin. But I don't think anything can save me this time.

I never should have dated Lightspeed. You never combine business and pleasure. I know that. It's like shitting where you eat. And then eating it.

I haven't even enjoyed work lately. Too much on my mind. And if there's one thing a Superhero shouldn't do, it's think. Usually my thinking time is reserved for a nighttime session of puzzling over Steely Dan lyrics with some single malt.

When I get back to my place for dinner, it's entirely too late. Lightspeed has tipped off my dinner guests and left a note that she is out shopping with her friends. And she did not remember to take out the soufflé. Nobody's here. I am doomed. And I have a lot of leftovers.

Remodeling the Secret Headquarters

Things are kind of depressing these days. It's been a few months since the aborted dinner party and my subsequent termination from Gotham. I've received official notification from the Hall of Justice that I'm banned for life. Worse than that, a new hero is gunning to break my foiled bank robbery record. But it's not fair. He's including credit unions.

DJ keeps to himself—he feels bad that his new solo career is taking off, and I can tell that he's having a great time. There's even talk of his going to Mars to mete out some old-fashioned punishment. All there is left for me to do is catch up on the stack of back issues of *Paleontology Today* in the bathroom. There's a dinosaur personality quiz this month.

My memoir is complete, and I'm fed up with self-improvement. It's time for home improvement. It's time to remodel the Secret Headquarters.

It's in desperate need of repair. My sock drawer is producing only mismatched pairs, I need some extra closet space, and I had better upgrade the stealth paneling, because I'm afraid my Secret

Headquarters aren't secret anymore. Maybe I've been there too long. My telephone number is unlisted, and the Headquarters do not have a street address, but last week I got a free CD from AOL.

The Secret Headquarters is mostly underground, part of an unknown cave system under L.A. that I stumbled onto when I was looking for a place to relieve myself. On top of the site was an abandoned sawdust factory. The outside has been rehabilitated and because of the stealth paneling resembles a hard-luck restaurant, the kind that's always changing hands and menus. Right now the windows display a menu for Nepalese-Netherlandish fusion. I've bought out most of the properties nearby and established a modest urban zoo—both the jackals and tall fences keep out the curious.

And then there is the sanctum sanctorum. A place where I can reflect, where no one else is allowed. It is an enormous sandpit where I keep and study several smallish dinosaurs.

I know what you're thinking: another guy with a big ego raising carnivorous reptiles. I'm sure you've heard the stories about guys in L.A., particularly rappers and professional athletes, raising dinosaurs to fight them in pits. I do not do this.* Mine are for study only, and I rear only herbivores. Mostly Jurassic era but quite a few Mississippian as well. When they fight each other, it's by choice.

The Headquarters is a great place. When the crime bell used to go off, DJ and I would swoosh down a giant chute—and in

---

* A great many Heroes do keep and fight live animals. The public finds the practice distasteful, but how else would we definitively know whether a polar bear or grizzly would win in a fight? Some Superheroes avoid scrutiny by trapping and fighting retired NFL players.

winter, the padding in the chutes was heated; it felt like you were getting a nice massage before you hopped into the FUV.

There are thirty-six rooms, including a laboratory, gym and swimming pool, a home theater, my private collection of dinosaur bones and a simulated fossil dig, an intimate restaurant, a Starbucks, and possibly the best rec room on the planet.

I reproduced the basement of my mother's house in Montana—wood paneling, a few ratty couches, and some tasteful, perhaps even artistic, erotica on the walls, including a risqué rendition of the Saint Pauli Girl. There are several classic pinball machines and a sit-down arcade version of *Arkanoid*. No matter how many Superheroes I invite to play, I have maintained the high score. Last year, I added a foosball table and air hockey.

The remodeling is chaotic and intense. Although I've hired great contractors, I have to go to the tile shop and the plumbing supplier myself.

I go to the Home Depot for the first time since my forced retirement. Its cavernous halls filled with home repair products still spook me—the last time I made a trip here, it was to foil the company's plot to take over America with their cleverly soothing and affordable but deadly floor tile. They have since changed management, and justice is served. The Board of Directors was forced to try installing the products themselves. Two of them went insane.

Only with my lightning-fast reflexes can I avoid being run over by one of the forklifts that menace the aisles. But as I talk with the employees, I'm impressed by their knowledge—every one of them could own their own hardware store. They instantly point the way to the stealth paneling.* A few of them look at me oddly when I

---

* Stealth paneling is incredibly difficult to find.

talk. Then I realize that I've been saying "we" instead of "I." When you're famous, it's totally normal to say "we." But now, people just look at me and wonder who I think I'm with.

DJ and I have some fundamental design arguments. He's very Bauhaus, and all I want is Italian Villa. I'm extremely wealthy; why can't I get what I want? Apparently all the good Brazilian marble is endangered and you can't bring it into the U.S. because they have to tear down mountains to get it. Our own mountains are currently being used to sculpt the likeness of notables more famous than me.

After I pick up the stealth paneling, I need to find a medicine cabinet for the upstairs guest bathroom. I check the coordinates of my in-store GPS unit. I'm only a half a klick away from the vanities.

The remodeling troubles me. We're doing so much work, and I'm not even sure how long I'll stay in the Secret Head-quarters. I've been seriously considering moving, getting a smallish, 5,000-square-foot bungalow in the hills. What it all comes down to is resale value, and I remind myself that no Hero in his or her right mind would buy that place with the current bathroom.

There are hundreds of medicine cabinets. Most feature cheap wood or gaudy scrolling. Several are made of plastic. I'm reminded of the Fun House of Insanity, where I was once trapped facing a thousand mirrors, all of which made me look fat, until I was rescued by a daring DJ.

Then I spot the very one, the one I never knew I wanted. The size is just right. I rush across the aisle to seize it, but it is plucked from my hands by none other than Montesquieu, the French phi-losopher and villainous member of *Les Misérables*.

"Hello, Monty." I smile. He hates this appellation. "Been out of prison long?"

"Since last week. Prisoner exchange with your National Basketball Association. Heard you were retired. It brought glee to all French criminals."

"Funny how we have the same taste in medicine cabinets."

"Insane minds think alike." He cackles. Last time I saw Monty he was trying to steal the Statue of Liberty as an agent of the French government.

"I hope you weren't too attached to this model," he adds. "It's the last one."

I look at the slot where more cabinets should be. He's right! Panic sets in. How could I have let him take the last one? And the model is discontinued.

"You don't actually need that one today, do you? I'll bet you could order one."

"Nice try, Freedom, but no such luck. My evil lair has been without a new bathroom for long enough." He laughs a high-pitched, cold laugh.

"Who's your contractor?"

"Gabbini and Sons."

"Wow. Mine too. I'll buy it off you. I'll pay double."

"I don't need your charity. My socialist government gives me a substantial stipend."

"Oh, well." I turn around, but then I use my lightning-fast reflexes to grab the medicine cabinet.

Montesquieu anticipates my maneuver and blocks it. He recites a line from Derrida, and I am thrown across the aisle, shattering several shower stalls. He approaches.

"Home Depot. Captain, I assumed you were more . . . genuine

than this. Should I be so bold as to assume your kitchen to be comprised of the complete Michael Graves collection from Target?"

He is wrong and I tell him so, but the words cut to the quick. My enemy's accent is filled with that combination of malice and menace that could only come from the nation that brought us existentialism and the guillotine.

"If you're such hot-baked brie, then why are you here?"

"The interior design of my lair contains irony, you foolish American pig. In my home, it is not just a boudoir but one with subtext."

I fly at him, driving into his stomach. We burst through several shelving units, leaving a trail of torn shower curtains. We grab shower rods and joust. With his massive mental powers, Monty launches several toilets at me. One hits me in the head and I feel myself losing consciousness.

I wake up, bound by Infinity duct tape. This stuff is versatile. Normally I could bust out, but I'm too tired. Montesquieu stands over me.

"I have mastered a new *philosophe*." He raises one eyebrow in that exceedingly villainous manner. "Lacan, the deconstructionist. As I cite his argument, not that I expect you to understand it, you will feel your body ripping itself apart. Deconstructed. Not bad, *n'est-ce pas?*"

As he murmurs his incomprehensible critique, I feel my strength draining. There are no philosophies that I can counter with. Then a song enters my head, and I believe it is my only hope. My song is "American Pie."

I hum, first quietly, and then loudly enough to drown out his incantations. He is oblivious to my recovery, and I burst through the duct tape, stand up, and grab a paint can to chuck at his head.

As I wind up, a bloodred armored Citroën bursts through the store's outer wall and whisks him off with the medicine cabinet. The store's walls are weakened to the point of collapse. I pay for my goods and help evacuate. Much like a starfish, the Home Depot will regenerate—one is destroyed and five others spring up in its place.

I have been beaten. Monty is a better shopper than I. I collect myself and try to remember whether I still have my emergency stash of painkillers in the car.

"Hey, you can't leave," shouts a pimpled and goateed store manager who assumes that the addition of an oversize wool cap to his uniform makes him appear alternative. "You just trashed my store. Who do you think you are?"

The words cause me to freeze. Perhaps it is my duel with Montesquieu or the waning prospect of picking a new bathroom theme, but the words *who do you think you are* flit around my head, sowing the seeds of existential turmoil. The crisis might once have been cured by the purchase of *InStyle*, but I know now there isn't a single photo of me in it.

As I'm driving home, I get a call from the contractors. Turns out they won't be coming tomorrow and the medicine cabinet could have waited another few days.

This is just the way of the contractor. When you redecorate, you live under the contractor's law, the law of the jungle. They will show up late to tear up your domicile, track in mud, use filthy language, leave sawdust everywhere, and draw on your walls, but in the end, like the magnificent bowerbirds of Australia, they make your home more beautiful.

It is what I live for now.

I miss being famous.

The Interview

I've never enjoyed live interviews. The mainstream media is untrustworthy. They specialize in lifelong vendettas and unflattering photos. But I need them if I'm ever to regain my status.

I am experiencing an utter publicity drought, with the exception of offers from *This Old House* and *Where Are They Now?* I turn down both. Then nothing. I consider the usual comeback options: rehab, car chases across L.A., animation voice-overs, invading Kuwait. It's all been done.

Finally, I get a call. Somebody wants to interview me about my life story. It's an outfit called National Public Radio. It sounds socialist. Maybe they're in North Korea or something. No, no, DJ confirms that they are actually in this country.

It's so cute that they want to interview me on their little ham radio show. Normally, I would only do magazine or television profiles (hello, History Channel, this means you), but I have to admit that I'm really touched. Radio. It's so seventies. I almost wear my old costume, but fashion tells me otherwise.

I usually go to this great little Italian restaurant that nobody knows about to conduct interviews. It's out of the way, and the owner knows me. Plus, his regular clientele are Mafia, so the place clears out as soon as I come in. But these radio people don't want to go to lunch. They want to interview me at their studio. I think it's darling that they have one. I can only imagine that the space is set up to look like a television studio so that they don't feel so inferior. It's like a third-world country. NPR doesn't even have a Sexiest Man of the Year award.

Actually, the radio station is decent. They have electricity, and there seem to be lots of people who take their little hobby very seriously. "So what do you do for a real job?" I ask one of the producers. She laughs it off, like I'm kidding. News radio must be one of those hobbies for the extremely rich and eccentric, like whaling.

The nice young woman who interviews me starts with some softball questions: Who was your favorite Hero to work with, will there be another *Captain Freedom* movie, and would I please repeat that embarrassing hotel story once again? It's very polite, and they do not mention that I failed to win the International Justice Prize. They thank me for all my years of important service.

She asks about my lack of an archenemy. My blood boils, but I retain my trademark grace under pressure—it helps to hum songs from the Rush album of the same name.

"People talk about archenemies like you have to have one. I feel like it's only accessorizing with evil."

Then it gets intense.

"You grew up on a kibbutz?"

"Sort of. A communal ranch."

"How has Judaism influenced your life? Do you go to synagogue?"

"What do you mean? I'm not Jewish."

"I just thought—I mean, your alter ego." She writes it down to prove she knows who I am. Who are these radio people? It's like they have reporters.

"Let's be very clear. There are no Jewish Superheroes. They can't run fast and they aren't very strong."

"Okay."

"I grew up in Montana. On a ranch. With cattle."

"I'm sure there are a few Jews in Montana. Especially on a kibbutz."

"Can you name one Jewish Superhero? One?" The entire notion is meshugga.

"Not off the top of my head."

"I told you."

"Let's move on."

I remind myself that this is a weird amateur hobbyist thing and that I shouldn't be surprised that they have some strange opinions. A few quick Kundalini fire-breaths. I calm down.

Then for the one billionth time we talk about my superpowers. It's a conversation I could have while napping, but I humor them. I tell her all about the useless art of Pho Van, and she tells me that she has trained in the useless art of Pilates.

"So you just use those machines. To get stronger? Doesn't it make you feel like a jackass?"

She laughs. I like connecting with my interviewer.

Then she asks me for the obligatory strength demonstration. I can't really believe it. I now understand that these public radio people must be slightly demented, but why would you do an on-air demonstration?

"Hello, America, this is Captain Freedom, beaming into your homes. Would you like me to show you how strong I am? Well, too bad, I can't, because this is radio." Somewhere, a ham radio enthusiast laughs.

Then I knot up some steel piping into a balloon dog, and the interviewer does a fairly decent job of conveying my strength to the people back home.

"People always wonder how a Superhero got his or her powers. Radioactivity, gamma rays, that sort of thing—what is the origin of your powers?"

"I've always had them."

"You were born Captain Freedom?"

"It's not that uncommon. Übermann was born with his powers."

"Yes, but he's Übermann. Not from this planet. Are you sure it wasn't the result of a bizarre government experiment? Or some chromosomal damage?"

"Yes, I'm quite sure."

"Your father left when you were quite young."

I'm really ready for this to be over.

"What was that like for you?"

"What do you mean? He just left. And then he was gone."

"How did that make you feel?" The words hang in the air like lethargic soap bubbles.

I freeze. No one has ever asked me that before. Emotions well up like a volcano of feeling.

This next part is really embarrassing. I break down on the air. And every one of the ten listeners of National Public Radio would have known, too, if DJ hadn't intervened and broadcast some Debussy to cover my whimpers.

I blubber like a baby. "I don't know my origin," I wail.

"I started flying as a toddler, my superstrength came at thirteen, and I've been able to predict the weather perfectly ever since I was old enough to speak. But I don't know how it happened. And Dad disappeared and then I was a Superhero and now I'm not one anymore and I'm really sad, and I can't talk about this anymore."

I walk out of the studio. For a few hours I sulk, but I realize that action is required.

I come back to the radio station after everyone has left for the night and punch the building. It instantly collapses. Government buildings. When you hit a structure built by the lowest bidder, it doesn't even bruise your knuckles.

But I haven't hit a building in a while. It hurts my hand. Out of the corner of my eye, I notice a neon martini glass and head for my salvation in alcohol.

It's a dingy joint. I ask for a Rob Roy; they tell me to find my Fruit of the Loom drink somewhere else. I flick the bar with my index finger and cause a large dent in the solid oak. They serve me a decent Rob Roy on the house. I drink it down and order two, maybe six more.

The trick to the Rob Roy is the bitters. Not any bitters, but the bitters extracted from the tears of a fourteen-year-old girl who's been dumped hours before the eighth-grade dance because her boyfriend has fallen for her best friend who is so totally not good looking.

Everyone here loves me—the truckers, the off-duty cops, the bookies, the newsmen, the barflies, the waitresses—and I love them. Someone finds a crowbar, and I reshape it into a swan. Here I'm neither Tzadik Friedman nor Captain Freedom, just a normal drunk who can perform crowd-pleasing feats of strength. We toast to all the Superheroes out there in the world, and we toast to CCR's "Proud Mary" on the jukebox. We toast to the bartender, for whom I'm paying the down payment on his new house. One of the newsmen offers me a smoke, and it is the best friend I've never known.

The rest of the night is a blur.

I take mass transit.

I may have drunk-dialed the military junta in Burma and compromised national security.

I mixed Pop Rocks with soda.

I wake up two days later in my dinosaur sandpit. The dinosaurs cower in the corner. I am dirty and have a splitting headache despite having taken five of those hangover products I bought at the corner deli.

This is really the bottom of the barrel.

I call my life coach, Lionel. I'm not proud of this, but there are tears. He really thinks we need to start talking about my origin story.

Origin Story Revealed!

"You're a mess." Lionel drums his fingers on his desk. The office is sparse. There's no computer, no family photos. Lionel claims he doesn't want externalities affecting his coaching sessions. The truth is that he has an ugly family.

"I just want to be loved."

"When most Superheroes want to be loved, they appear at comic book conventions. You? You drink and you drug and destroy property." It's a reasonable assessment.

"There's a see-saw dynamic going on in your life," Lionel begins. His lilted speech, both gangster and preacher-songbird, lulls me into a stupor and I can't follow what he's saying. For me, listening is a time to think about what I'm going to say next.

"Captain, I've lost you," he says abruptly.

"No, I'm here." I focus.

"I can tell when you've stopped paying attention. You hum Al Green."

"Isn't the tone of what you're saying just as important as the message?"

"Not at all. It's time we talk about your origin."

There's no single piece of a Superhero's legend more important than the origin story. It's the codpiece in the armor—protective yet vulnerable, restrictive yet oddly sexy. You tell your story over and over until it's the stuff of legend: boring and untrue. In every television interview they ask me to repeat my story, as if the people watching haven't heard it before, and the host sits there, smiling, eyes blank and head bobbing like an Erik Estrada Pez dispenser. That is, if you can find one anymore.

Most origins you hear about are a pack of lies. A boy is bitten by a radioactive cockroach. The U.S. government creates a breed of supersoldier from another planet? Please, these people can't even forward my mail.

People should like the idea that I was born a nobody, that I pulled myself up from my bootstraps and became super. But no. They secretly believe that someday they'll discover a magic talisman or get hit by radioactive isotopes in some productive fashion. But Heroes aren't made. They know somebody who knows somebody.

My story is simple. As everyone knows, I grew up on a kibbutz in Montana. Unless you count my brother's relentless pessimism, nobody in my family has superpowers. My father ran off with a Vegas showgirl when I was three, and my mother sacrificed everything to take care of us. It would kill on *Oprah*.

"I did a little digging. The story you've been telling isn't quite accurate. Especially about your father. Should I go on?"

There comes a time when you realize your parents aren't the people you think they are. That they've been kidnapped and replaced by well-intentioned cyborgs. Is this one of those moments?

"Your dad was not a cowboy."

"What was he?"

"You need to find that out for yourself."

I offer to pay him time and a half, but his response is cold. "You try to bribe me again and it'll be the last time we talk."

On my way home I stop by the drugstore to pick up some Hoodia and I notice the current issue of *Psychology Today*. It's the Missing Dad issue—there are 213 tips for tracking down a lost father, interviews with prominent celebrities who've reunited with a lost dad, and techniques for grilling a better burger. I attempt to read one of the interviews, but the titles on the front cover are never the same as they are in the table of contents, and I move on.

I pay a visit to the one person who might clear up my mysterious background: Superscribe, the Gotham Comix historian and librarian.

Superscribe's office encompasses an entire floor of Gotham's headquarters, not because she's important but because she's got enough dirt on the supercommunity to get us all fired, arrested, or, worse yet, stripped of our endorsements.

After being away from Gotham for so long, I remember why she makes me uncomfortable: she has a certain allure without being even remotely hot, like the actress who's been given a bit part and mysteriously made ugly so that her looks don't interfere with the role. Plus, I think she sort of likes me but likes to show it by making things difficult.

Aside from her all-leather costume, Superscribe wears what my trained nose can identify as an excellent knockoff of Chanel *cinq*. That smell, coupled with the waft from the dusty stacks, makes me feel aroused and sleepy at the same time.

"Superscribe. You're our institutional memory."

"Are you calling me fat?"

"Why would I do that?"

"Whatever. I don't like that term."

"Can you tell me my origin story?"

She draws herself up to her full height and walks behind her desk. "I will have to consult the Oracle of Apocrypha."

"Is that a fortune teller? A soothsayer?"

"It's the database." Superscribe flips open her laptop. I spend several tense seconds scanning the titles on the bookshelves that wrap around the huge office. They can't possibly all be real. I wonder which one is pulled to reveal the secret laboratory. I'm thinking *Infinite Jest*.

"I have it. What are these data worth to you?"

I don't like it when people use data as a plural. I know it's correct, but it never feels good hearing it.

"It's my origin story. Shouldn't I get it for free?"

Superscribe shakes her head. "We've been charging for our archives for years now. If the details were so important to you, why didn't you write them down somewhere?"

"I believe in freedom. All kinds of freedom. Especially Freedom of Information."

Superscribe gasps. "You wouldn't. FOIA?"

"Some friends of mine could make it happen." I don't need to mention the dreaded acronym again. All the well-guarded secrets of the Superhero world could come crashing down.

In the 1970s the Superhero industry was deregulated. The original governmental Superhero company, State Comics, was chopped into three divisions and sold off at auction. The unions were disbanded, and with the institution of free agency, Superheroes were for the first time subject to market forces, and top-shelf Heroes such as Chief Justice were no longer provided with the same scrimping wage as, say, Hydroboy, the Hero who can swim really fast, has gills in addition to lungs, and can communicate with sea life, all of which can be useless when you consider that most crime is terrestrially based. Many less-competitive Superheroes emigrated to Europe or Japan.

The government realized that deregulating Superheroes was potentially dangerous and stipulated that all privately held or publicly traded comic corporations had to provide detailed data to the Federal Government upon request and, after a court challenge, were also subject to the Freedom of Information Act.

"You'd expose some of our more important secrets," she whines. "My secrets."

"You could make this easier for both of us," I suggest. There's something so superior about being superior.

"Yeah, yeah, yeah." She prints off the file and hands it to me. It's the same thing I've seen again and again. There's something else at the bottom, long and smudgelike.

"I can't read this last part."

"It's been redacted." She smiles sweetly.

"Can it be undacted?"

"That is a null statement."

You'd think finding my own background would be simpler. I have already checked Wikipedia and Facebook and read more than fifteen different origin stories about me. Unless there's some pandimensional multi-universe crossover event going on, and I really doubt it, I think I should only have one backstory.

My mom knows the truth. I could rent a time machine and see the whole thing for myself, but I don't want to be one of those people who gets a time machine just to avoid visiting home.

The thing about visiting family is that you never know which Mom you're going to see. She's a tough lady who has whittled a hardscrabble existence out of a cooperative ranch on the prairie. She has the countenance of a rattlesnake that forgot sunscreen but has the heart of a lamb, and whenever she remembers what I've done for her, she softens up. When I get there, I notice her hair is gray. The woman has dyed her hair for twenty years, and whenever it's returned to gray, you can expect her good side.

Things look the same. There are a few thousand heads of cattle, plus the odd velociraptor that has survived from my early childhood cloning experiments. Mom comes outside with a shotgun to meet me.

"Captain Bigshot. What do you want?"

I see. It's snakelady after all. "Just came to visit."

"You never just come to visit. And you haven't been here for what, three years? Your brother visits all the time."

"I was here last month to save the ranch from the golem."

"And you caused a terrible mess. The cattle were spooked for weeks."

She leads me into the kitchen, usually the lair of fatty, difficult-to-digest food, but spare engine parts litter the kitchen. The coffee pot is full of motor oil. Some would suggest this is an improvement.

"I'm rebuilding the alternator for the combine," she says to explain the mess.

"You have time to talk?"

"I'm busy," she deflects. "There's a board meeting tonight."

"That's right, you're president of the board. That's great."

"Don't belittle me."

"What?"

"Just because you're the one with the fancy superpowers doesn't mean you're the only important member of this family."

"Okay, I'm sorry. Mom, I need to know more about Dad." Once you get her talking she'll never find a way to stop. Our good-byes over the telephone are longer than the original conversation. Sometimes I think she's mastered circular breathing.

"You want I should start from the beginning?"

That's the part of the story I could tell over and over. Mom lit out from Valley Stream, New York, in a covered wagon—okay, a station wagon—and drove alone to Missoula. She accidentally founded a kibbutz one night when she was having a potluck with some friends, and it came up that she was the only one who knew how to build anything.

"When did you meet Dad?"

"Your father was a criminal mastermind from outer space. A small planet called Astra-Zeneca. I was out in the fields bringing the cattle back when his spaceship crashed. We met, fell in love, had you, then fell out of love and had your brother."

"I don't get it—why didn't you ever tell me anything about him before?"

"You're joking, right? Didn't you ever notice the NASA agents poking around every few years? Or the giant crater out back near your rope swing? That damn spaceship that he promised to fix up but left in pieces on the front lawn?"

"Why did he leave?"

"The Feds dropped by to ask him some questions. He resisted and they took him away."

"Where's your family from?"

"Your great-grandfather was a Russian rabbi."

"Wait, am I getting this straight? I'm Jewish?"

"A hundred percent. Your father's real name is Herschel X/12."

It's all starting to come together. But I'm in shock. A Jewish Superhero? I've never heard of such a thing.

That changes everything. I'd be banned by every country club in the nation, but I could be anything I want to be: doctor, lawyer, or standup comedian! I could join the Beastie Boys!

"Another thing. Look through your old crap in the basement. If you don't take it, I'm going to the dump."

In the basement I look around and attempt to process new information. It's a comforting place, full of old junk. I spent most of my formative years playing down here. Preserve jars and canning supplies. Spare parts to a busted spaceship. News clippings of my early exploits.

Hidden among my grade school notebooks is a book I don't recall. It's a diary. At first I assume it's written in an alien tongue, but then I realize it's just cursive. Reading other people's journals is like flipping through the guest book at a vacation rental house. Interesting for ten seconds. I skip it and head straight to the photo album.

It shows everything. There are newspaper clippings with photos of the black van that showed up that night to take my father away, Dad fighting off some old-school Superheroes, and him being led away in handcuffs.

My father's been wrongly imprisoned. I have to find him and clear his name. There's only one government containment facility where he could be held: Area 51.

area 51

It should come as no surprise that I can get into Area 51: I know the bouncer. Still, since I've never before reunited with a family member, I ask DJ to come with me. At first he responds by text saying, "i dont do fmly rnions." His mind is changed when I tell him our destination.

As everyone knows, under a veil of secrecy, the U.S. Air Force cordoned off a speck of the desert in the fifties to contact alien life. It was quickly revealed that aliens love to party, and the best way to recoup revenue for the useless space program was running a nightclub.

It's a lonely drive on US 50 across Nevada. There are no signs that lead you to the club—you drive down unmarked Forest Service roads and pass several foreboding signs about weapons testing and the loosest slots in town. As far as hot spots go, Area 51 is as exclusive as it gets. The nearest town is full of libertarian UFO enthusiasts. It's like Berkeley: full of crazy people who happen to be right.

Our car makes it in through the heavily fortified chain-link fencing, a stage that deters many wannabes. Celebrities such as myself are offered valet parking, although that in and of itself doesn't guarantee entry.

There's no predicting who gets in. I've seen starlets venting their frustrations over tiny phones to their managers. Intergalactic generals park their warships threateningly around our airspace, and some of them even leave without getting their tentacles stamped. I've seen personal assistants devoured on the spot, as if it's their fault.

DJ and I are arrayed in our best club clothes. The line is unbelievable. I ditch the Captain Freedom cologne and slap on something really special. And I'll tell you, if you're wearing Timberlands and down jackets, you won't be welcomed. It's more Sean Jean than Rocawear. Some nights are black tie, for those species that have a neck.

I shiver when we arrive at the front of the line. There is a familiar neon sign:

Welcome to Area 51
Earth's Hottest Intergalactic Nightclub and Prison

Just like most institutions—churches, hospitals, elementary schools—the nightclub added a prison to its complex in the eighties to raise revenues.

The bouncer, Lt. Bill Smoker, has been working the velvet rope and chain-link fence for years. The job has taken its toll: there are only so many times you can say no to a space dragon without worrying that you're becoming racist. But Smoker is as professional as they come.

"Captain Freedom." He stiffens up and salutes. I return it.

"Just the two of us tonight," I offer.

He repeats my name into his headset, then listens for a response. "No can do, sir."

I've never been rejected from a club in my life. "Excuse me?"

"Sir. It's just that you're retired. And there's no protocol for allowing retired Superheroes. Sorry."

I don't understand. I've never had a problem getting in here. People inside know me. "Can't you do anything?" I don't want to make a scene. I would be no better than the nonmilitary, non-alien, non-Superheroes that try to get in, like a star for a TV pilot that never went anywhere.

But it's important to get in. Not just because we're here to rescue my dad. Photographers from *InStyle* have already taken my picture tonight—if they don't get follow-ups inside, I'll be dead. I don't use threats idly, but I'm prepared to ask to speak to Smoker's manager.

Smoker looks at DJ. "You holding?"

"Maybe."

"Okay, you guys can go in."

We walk toward an escort Jeep. "What was that about?"

DJ shrugs his shoulders.

Our military escort takes us to the club entrance. It's a squat concrete building, nothing remarkable. Some paranoid Americans wonder what the secrets are that comprise Area 51. Other than high drink prices, there's nothing special.

Once we're inside, they scan us for weapons and allergies, and we take the elevators down to the main club, deep underground in what can only be an outdated nuclear bunker. There are four separate bars, a few corporate boxes, cage dancing, pole dancing, and priority seating for any alien species with an oozing consistency.

Tonight's the typical scene. An alien and an ingénue make out on a couch in a corner. Air Force brass tell stories and Arabian princes make backroom deals with ambassadors. There's too much smoke, and the strobe light is highly irritating, but I am enthralled. So many questions wind through my head. Will my father want to see me? Am I the only Superhero who fasts on Yom Kippur? I always thought it was a normal American holiday, like Flag Day.

DJ disappears for one of the many bars. I chat with a six-armed diva from Murgatroyd who carries a Ferragamo clutch in each hand. She asks if I know Scorsese. Aliens are really naïve about Earth. They always assume that if you come from here, you know everybody else.

After the initial excitement, this club is disappointing. A long drive into the desert and all the hype and exclusivity and secrecy remind you it's just another military base with a maximum-security prison and nightclub. I've met the rich and famous, government staffers, cowboys, lobbyists, sword-wielding warriors from ancient hidden sects. But you listen to the lone piano player who cracks corny jokes for your tips and will play any show tune from the known galaxy, and you realize that the universe is an incredibly lonely place. Right now he plays a polka of despair.

"I've got a location on your dad," DJ reports back. "It's imperative we get to the VIP room."

The club's entire layout is known only to the handful of managers, a diplomatic and coy people from Jupiter's moon Io, but DJ learns that if we can enter the VIP section, we'll have access to the prison area. The unfathomably rich and connected are allowed to observe people and aliens behind bars. But this is one of those places that's too exclusive even for Captain Freedom.

"Did you bring the invisibility belt?" I ask him.

"It's malfunctioning."

"What's wrong with it?"

"It makes you look fat instead of invisible."

I shudder.

We walk toward the stairs leading down to the exclusive area. Two Air Force officers guard the entrance.

"You can't come in here. You don't have clearance."

"Do I need to make a phone call? I don't want to make a scene." Out comes my mobile phone.

"That won't work here." The guard smirks.

I pause to build some suspense before delivering the following line: "This one does." They instantly let us through.

There are only a few cell phones in the world that have the power to penetrate several thousand tons of reinforced concrete. Their reception is perfect, and they are kept under close guard, restricted to the U.S. Joint Chiefs of Staff, the heads of state of each nuclear power, and several highly beautiful and annoying supermodels, who may have lent such phones to their boyfriends. I know no such supermodel, but the airmen buy my bluff. After navigating a maze of hallways and staircases, we arrive at the world's most exclusive club's most exclusive prison.

The VIP area is almost empty. The serious partygoers have left the prison observation area and headed for the after-party in Vegas.

I'm worried that Dad might not be in good health. The military was keen to dissect as many aliens as they could. I don't know what they think they can learn by dissecting people. These aliens all speak English—why not just ask for a complete medical history? There were a few diplomatic incidents after we mistakenly dissected a high prince of Sirius, the planet known for satellite radio technology. We received a cease-and-desist letter in the form of a nuclear warhead. The dissections have supposedly ended, but I think the CIA secretly takes high-value aliens to labs in Sweden and Saudi Arabia.

I pass many cells and see Area 51's most famous prisoner, Ali Kabob, a terrorist traffic engineer who's personally responsible for having designed the traffic-choked Los Angeles freeway system; Manuel Noriega, former dictator of Panama; and Julia Eggner, inventor of the famous Baby Evil video series.

I scan the cells for Dad and recognize his strong chin instantly as my own. He looks annoyed to be ogled at again. Then he does a double take, like he's looking at the Superhero version of himself. Oscar cautioned me against freeing my father, since we really don't know why he's still in jail, but I can't help myself. Using his years of experience playing with stereo equipment and electronics, DJ easily circumvents the alarm system and I pop open the steel door.

"Dad! It's me. Captain Freedom, I mean, Tzadik."

"Frak," says Dad.

We embrace. It's hard to look at him. He's got closely cropped silver hair and the rough five o'clock shadow of a man in danger of having a beard. His physique is that perverse combination of muscular and pudgy. As soon as we get home, I'm hitting the gym.

DJ asks him who's responsible for his incarceration.

"The INS. A wholly reprehensible outfit. They use aliens like me for cheap labor. Preloading software onto government laptops for pennies a day."

That voice. It's somewhere between Christopher Lee and James Earl Jones, with a slight nod to Peter Lorre.

"Do they treat you well?" I ask.

"Cretins. Thought they could pump me full of drugs and keep me sun-deprived, forcing me to sleep all day, but I kept one eye open. Oh, yes, I catnapped. I was weak, but I observed my surroundings. I plotted. And if the days were grim, they were untrammeled bliss compared with the nights. Serving drinks to the wealthy, who paid a premium just to be waited on by the incarcerated aliens and criminals abandoned by the system."

As far as I can tell, his superpowers include impressive oratorical skills and an intense power of persuasion that borders on mind control. Sort of disappointing.

"Can you predict the weather?"

"Son, everyone from my planet can predict the weather. It's an evolutionary advantage. Astra-Zeneca has execrable weather. It's why I left."

"Dad, let's get you out of here." We blend into a crowd of prison-visiting nightclubbers, and I order DJ to switch on the invisibility-now-fat belt. I can sense myself feeling pudgy, and I know we've blended into the crowd.

"That was most resourceful," my father says once we remove his muzzle. "Will they join in pursuit?"

"No." Since this is a supersecret facility, there is no record of our visit. But I fear somebody somewhere now has photos of me looking fat.

We get to the car as the sun rises.

"Dad, you hungry?"

"My ravenous appetite may be slaked when and only when my enemies suffer my wrath. How about In-N-Out Burger?"

As we drive home, I think about all the questions in my mind. In the *International Hero Tribune* there's a "What Kind of Hero Are You?" quiz that I've been meaning to share with my friends. It asks telling questions like "Would you rather save someone from a volcano or burning building?"; "Name two ways you're not-so-super."; and "How many people have you told your secret identity?" I ask Dad these questions and my lightning-fast reflexes detect DJ rolling his eyes. Dad evades the questions, but his reticence is understandable. He asks me if I know any stores that sell guns to former inmates without a license and I rattle off six or seven.

"Dad, I want you to live with us."

DJ glares at me.

"I've always thought somebody should live out in the three-bedroom pool house out behind the Secret Headquarters."

"That is quite generous," Dad says. "Only three bedrooms?"

I tell my father that I want to change my last name so I can hyphenate Mom's with his. For the first time, my appellation, my alter ego, my secret identity, is complete. I am now Tzadik X/12-Friedman.

Three's Company?

I stare at my father, surrounded by evidence. He knows I've discovered his new life. But I'm putting an end to it. "You can't run an international criminal syndicate from my pool house."

"Obviously not. You don't even have wireless."

It's awkward when your father moves in with you. I should have prepared myself for it. It's not just that Dad turned to a life of crime totally to spite me. He's grown a horrific ponytail.

I wish that were the worst of it. I said, "No pets in the pool house, Dad." And now he has a freaking ferret. It's not that I have anything against rodents, aside from the way they spread pestilence and eat their young, but ferrets just creep me out. It's an animal for people who are confused about what animal they really want. It's a snake without being slimy, and it's furry without being a cute kitten-type animal. They're similar to mongeese in their heterogeneity, but they don't have the cool snake-killing power.

Plus, he's on the phone all the time, and that perfect diction of his gets on my nerves. The voice carries all over the pool house. Not that I'm ever in there, but I can hear it on the secret wiretap I installed.

Just out of jail, Dad needs money. I understand this. Deep down, he really wants to finance a documentary on the plight of Astra-Zenecans stuck on Earth. And he can't just borrow it from me. It must be terrible to be less successful than your son. But he's embarked on a reckless crime wave from behind my house.

He's assembled a team of experts: a Czech arms dealer, a Russian vampire hunter, a Turkish smuggler, a Canadian lobbyist, a Nigerian hacker, a few Colombian bodyguards, a dreaded Japanese statistician from the Yakuza, and an interpreter.* In just a few months, he's amassed such a fortune he purchased a stake in the Portland Trailblazers, long known as the basketball team of crime.

Their activities are far-reaching. They boost weapons from the military, then sell them at a discount to the NRA. They upload computer viruses to ATMs that charge particularly high fees. They've released HYDRA brand spring water, which I know to be tap water. He calls himself Mogul, and it's the only name he'll answer to. Several criminal interest groups complain that he has taken away all the best jobs.

Most of it I tolerate. It's Dad's business; plus, he seems to be having fun. But it gets worse.

DJ leaves for a weekend trip up the coast. As he loads up the car, I notice he's carrying the most exquisite Hermès surfboard bag. I inquire as to its origin.

"I got it from your dad. It's a knockoff."

DJ drives away and leaves me to ponder his statement. This

---

* An unfortunate side effect of globalization is how much it's lowered barriers to international crime.

can only mean the unthinkable: Dad's been importing designer counterfeits.

I've long been known as a friend to the fashion world. Everyone loves their finery, but in the end, designers are alone. They have no one to champion their cause, especially now, since most California Heroes are at Burning Man.

Love has made me blind to my father's actions, but the proof finally comes in a call from the FBI.

"Captain Freedom," the officer says. "This is awkward for us, but we'd like to take a look at your place. The crime kingpin Mogul has been using it as a base to import faux fashion." They're ready to charge him with thirty-seven counts of second-degree crime.

I play ignorant, something I've had a little practice with. "How did you find him?"

"His eBay account. That's how he peddles his fakes. And he left your mailing address."

The FBI calling. The ponytail. The wet gym clothes on my exercise bike. This embarrassment has to end.

"If you don't mind, this is a family affair, and I'd like to deal with it with my own brand of unique and hyperviolent justice." The FBI agrees.

Without knocking, I burst into Dad's three-bedroom, two-point-five-bath pool house with garage. He's alone but is surrounded by bags, dresses, gowns, jewelry. For a second I want to think, "No, he's just cross-dressing. That's okay."

But it's not true. No cross-dresser would wear such cheap copies.

This is so wrong. Designers are outcasts, pushed around and marginalized by hordes of unfashionable people. They are today's true artists; their canvas is cloth, although sometimes it's actually canvas, but only the brushed, supple kind.

It's appalling, and I feel a terrible guilt. Designers have been hurt here, and I'll have to organize a benefit for their relief.

"We need to talk about this. Where are your minions?"

"They're at their English as a Second Language class."

"I want to be tolerant of your criminal hobbies, but attacking fashion? Dad, how could you do it?"

"Call me Mogul."

I repeat the question, this time using his ridiculous moniker.

"I resent you. I seethe with resentment."

"But why?"

"Because of all you've done for me."

This complicates things. My head is muddled. Would he have turned out better if I treated him badly? Having parents is so difficult. I'm momentarily paralyzed. My eyes fall on an eight-dollar copy of some Manolo slingbacks. They look so wrong in my posh home, like a copy of an Andy Warhol at the Louvre. "You've hurt so many people, Dad."

"It's a victimless crime."

I consider all the impoverished designers who are forced to work as shoe-shine boys just to afford bits of thread and cloth. Misunderstood art students at FIT who are forced to roll their own cigarettes. In a world without fashion designers, we'd all be wearing burlap sacks. Wait. That sounds like a fantastic movie.* It would write itself. After this confrontation, I'm calling my agent.

I try to bring it to his level. I consider his hideous alien

---

* Imagine a world where all clothing is a part of our imagination, a world where nothing is as it seems: *The Fabrix*.

feet, which have never been exfoliated, massaged, trimmed, or painted. Although his alien DNA dealt those piggies a bum hand, he wouldn't have such problems with well-designed footwear.

"Dad. The bunions."

Seeing the look in his eye as I accuse him of poor podiatric hygiene, I know I've cut to the quick. Dad tries to punch me.

At some point, every man must best his father. Only flesh against flesh will aptly punctuate my domination, and I punch him so that he sails across the room and slams into the opposite wall. The punch says, "I want you out of my pool house. I want you to disband your little crime group. I want you to get back together with Mom." It is the most therapeutic punch I will ever throw.

He pulls a weapon from his holster, and I realize that I should not leave the keys to my unique weapons collection lying around. Like many wealthy people, I devote much of my time to collecting oddities, and my particular fetish is bizarre weapons that have been developed over the years. I keep the collection under wraps. The Amnesia Uzi, the Reality Ray, the Showtoon Shotgun, and all of the other weapons would cause a new kind of hell if any criminal knew of them. He must have seen the weapons when I was showing them off at a recent party.

Dad shoots me with a blast of the Day-Glo Glock, a fierce weapon that creates brutal agony in anyone hit with it who has visual contact with the color orange. It was originally developed (but never used) by the Pentagon in the sixties as a counterrevolutionary measure against the hippies, who instead of rebelling opted for high-paying jobs. The Glock was specifically calibrated to inflict the worst pain with tie-dye orange, but it works well on the more fashionable shades, such as mango, which I have in accents throughout the Secret Headquarters. The weapon is simple and devastating—it makes you realize how ridiculous the color orange is. The pain is unbearable. Writhing with tangerine agony, I stagger outside and watch Dad run into my house.

It's a slow walk down the jungle path between the pool house and the main house, since I want to avoid the quicksand and robotic sentinels that usually keep guests from nosing around. As is my custom, I wave to the statue honoring Chief Justice, and I check the Weber to make sure I have enough mesquite. There's no reason to hurry. The Secret Headquarters is so big, it could take all day to find him. Once inside, I stop to get some coffee and take an inventory of the pantry. How do we go through quince paste so fast?

A lot of Heroes downscale after they retire. They tell me they don't need the toxicology lab and that maintaining a warren of secret entrances and exits is too much work. Electricity bills are high, and even in California the property taxes are astounding. Some Heroes purchase hidden condos or secret apartments in which to live out the rest of their days. As far as I'm concerned, they aren't just giving up access to technology that will identify a perpetrator with DNA from a piece of eye patch. They're giving up their independence. But I'll give them one thing: after a while, it becomes a real drag to keep the Headquarters clean.

I've been through more cleaning ladies than I'd care to admit. They don't like the background check or the surveillance cameras, and they always put stuff where I can't find it. You'd think somebody could clean a twenty-thousand-square-foot dwelling in eight hours, but they're always missing stuff no matter how many times I outline it on a map. I give them a house schematic, but it doesn't seem to help. They still put my car keys in places I will never find them. I'll have to buy one of those key beepers next time I'm at the mall. Or watching late-night TV.

I understand that the job is to clean, and if you have to clean, you have to organize. But if I have to tear apart the kitchen looking for my car keys, they've set me back. I don't have X-ray vision; nor can I manipulate Earth's magnetic currents to find the keys. I have explained this. I fired one cleaner after she had thrown my car keys, a few business cards, and the clues to a murder I was attempting to solve into a Pyrex measuring cup, which she then put on the shelf in the closed pantry. I felt bad later when I realized I was the one who did that.

There are some rooms I've forgotten about. One night I woke up because I heard a loud thumping bass beat. It turns out DJ had staged a rave at the underground conference center. I'd completely forgotten that place existed. There are more rooms than a retired Hero like me probably needs. Dad's no doubt hiding in one of them.

I check the Segway stable. DJ's is missing. I listen for its gyroscopic whir. I hear it—the old man hot-wired DJ's Segway! I jump on mine and give chase across the Secret Headquarters. I buzz around the main floor, then take the basement and sub-basement stairs. I hear a loud, metallic clang and then the sound of feet running: DJ's Segway is out of batteries, even though I'm constantly reminding him to recharge it.

If memory serves, he's at the end of the line: a long, dark corridor that dead-ends at my inner sanctum, the dinosaur theme park. I break into a run, and because I've neglected to change the lights down here, I trip over DJ's Segway and fly across the room.

I put my hand out to break my fall and everything goes black. I've knocked myself unconscious.

When I come to, Dad is gone, and he's cleared out his faux fashion. I won't see him any time soon but will track his movements through his blog and the effacing comments he leaves on my MySpace page. The only reminder of him in the pool house is the ferret, whom I've named Will.

The house feels empty with Dad gone; there's nobody to criticize me and tell me to find a good job. I spar with some robotic guards, but it feels empty. It's such a shame; Dad had a great eye, and he could easily have become a legitimate designer.

A single phone call changes everything.

"It's Kaeko."

"Hi! How have you been?" I ask, a little too loud and fast.

"We need to talk." The sentence puts ice water in my veins. My voice cracks as I murmur assent. "There's a contract out on your father's life."

"Because of his criminal empire? That's over now."

"The underworld is upset with him. He crossed lines. Took liberties."

"And you want to take the job?"

She explains that she won't do it unless I'm okay with it. She's been nicer to me ever since I had my mom rescue her from Hell.*

"It sounds like you really want to do this."

"It has nothing to do with want. It's just another job." I hear conflict in her voice and sense an opportunity. Conflict leads to insecurity. Insecurity leads to dinner. Dinner leads to sex.

"Tzad, do you have an answer?"

"Why don't we talk about this over dinner?"

---

* See *Mom of Devil's Craw vs. Devil*. Mom used her seemingly limitless skill to badger others to win Kaeko's freedom.

an Affair to Remember

We talk over dinner and Kaeko agrees not to kill my father. We have a nice time but no sex. Then we meet at random at a sports bar a few days later. I'm there for the nachos, and she's there to kill the owner.

I invite her for a drink when she's done. I ask her if she went to our high school reunion. She says she did and tells me about some of our classmates.

"I saw Cosmogirl on the news the other night," I say, referring to Kaeko's high school roommate. "She looks great."

"It's cryogenics," Kaeko gossips. "She had herself entombed in ice from the day after graduation until the reunion. Bitch."

Kaeko's visiting the L.A. branch of Gotham Comix, who is interested in adding more Asian female Supervillains to their staff. Since she doesn't know anyone in town, I offer her a room at the Secret Headquarters.

DJ's still miffed that I let my dad live with us, but he doesn't mind having Kaeko around. I spend so much time with Kaeko I really don't have the energy to nag him about getting rid of that emo band that has been living in the pool house.

At first, she is very excited to live with me. She has her own room but spends most of her time in mine. After a short time dating, I ask for her hand in marriage. Soon she makes a significant sacrifice: at my request, she agrees to leave the business. Although I cannot convince her to dump the impressive array of lethal instruments with which she plies her trade, Kaeko gives up professional assassination.

Things aren't perfect. You date the world's most feared assassin, and after a while she's just another chick who pees with the bathroom door open. And I will never understand how a woman who wields fifty different lethal weapons can't remember whether yogurt containers get recycled.

We shop for new furniture and plan our wedding. It is bizarre, almost domestic. We sip coffee and read the paper. Her obsidian eyes reflect gentleness. "I didn't know I could do it. Give up working. Assassination has always been a part of me, of who I am. Did you know I was nominated to chair the International Assassins Guild?"

No surprise there. Kaeko has more skill than any criminal I've had the pleasure of knowing. Which is why my heart is rent in two that night when she confronts me about my other wife.*

She shouldn't have found out about my current marriage, but this denizen of the underworld has the connections to find out anything about anyone.

"How could you not have told me you're married?" Kaeko throws a dinner plate at me. It's part of our china set, which has recently arrived. My superpowers should allow me to duck

---

* The story of my sham marriage is told in *Amazing Weddings* #17. Never very popular, *Amazing Weddings* was canceled the same year as *The Adventures of Siegfried and Roy* and *Superdance!*

it with ease, but Kaeko knows all of my moves and has studied me since our first day of math class at the School on the Hill. She throws it in the direction that she knows I will go, and it ends up shattering in my face but doesn't draw blood. Fine china really is better.

"It's not serious," I explain.

"What do you mean? You're married. It's serious!"

"But she's a lesbian."

"That doesn't matter!" Kaeko breaks down in tears.

"Look, honey. I know it's been hard since you moved in."

"Hard? You spend all of your time in that secret room, which I of course know about, playing with dwarf dinosaurs in that giant sandbox. You're like an eight-year-old."

"I promise to divorce her. Really."

"Thank you. It would mean a lot to me."

"I am not an eight-year-old."

"I know that. I shouldn't have called you that."

"One more thing, baby."

"What's that?"

I ask her to change her alias.

"What's wrong with Katana?"

"Katana? It sounds like a porn-star name.* In fact, I know she's a porn star."

"How do you know that?"

"I'm pretty sure I've met her. Somebody's bachelor party."

"You disgust me."

Our life together is dogged by the tabloids, and there is little

---

* Katana is the name of a Japanese blade. Kintama, or "golden balls," would be a much more likely porn-star name.

I can do to stop it, aside from adding razor wire to the electrified fence around the Secret Headquarters. They put an undue strain on us, always hunting us. We might have breakfast at a secluded inn, but the tabloids are there. The vultures misrepresent what we eat for breakfast: I would never eat Canadian bacon.

There are many tales of star-crossed lovers, but few as violent and sordid as the perfect pairing: the Superhero and the Supervillain; Captain Freedom, retired, versus the active assassin and darts champion known by the alias Katana. Passive versus Aggressive.

After days of arguing, she moves into her own room. I wander the halls of the Headquarters, trying to come up with the right words. None come to mind. I wander over to her room and notice the light is on. I could drop in, improvise, even apologize. But then I catch the acrid whiff of cigarette smoke. And the only way she could be smoking is if she disabled the smoke detector. Reckless behavior.

Kaeko moves out and won't answer my phone calls. I suspect that she may have gone back to the business, but I have no way to know. Sources tell me she is staying at a friend's house. My publicity agent and I do everything we can to keep this spat out of the papers, but they know all about us. That we aren't living together, that we aren't sleeping together, and that she thinks I'm not a great cook. And that's just wrong.

To deflect this terrible PR, I check in and quickly out of rehab. It works. But my worst suspicion has been confirmed: she is working again.

I pick up a tabloid. No good ever comes of reading these things, but you can't help going to the supermarket every once in a while. There it is, in the headlines:

Katana Ices 3
Has Superboytoy Gone Soft?

There's a photo spread of her killing people in public places. Sloppy, like she's out of control. In the past, she's never been caught on camera. She looks like shit. It's a cry for help. My assistant calls her assistant, and we arrange to go out for a late-night discussion at the Viper Room.

We sit together at a corner table in the VIP section upstairs. As we enter the club, we hold hands, and the photographers are like happy little lemurs, snapping away. But I haven't felt her touch in some time, and the hands feel cold. These are the hands that throw toxic darts that kill people. Once we order drinks, I cut to the chase and ask what's wrong.

"First you want to marry me. Then you ask me to give up my career, just because you want to stay out of the spotlight? And you ask me to change my name, which I really was considering. Tzad, I can't do those things. You don't want me to be me."

It's a sore subject. A lot of female assassins keep working after getting married. "That's not true. I just want you to be the you that doesn't kill famous people for a living."

"I don't only kill famous people."

"Whatever. You kill people for money. Can't you do something else?" I touch her hair. "And go back to being the Kaeko I knew before—what was that first alias?"

"You never could keep track." She laughs. "Lady Coma."

"Right. Can't you just be Kaeko?"

Her eyes narrow. "I haven't been that girl since I was sixteen. Is that all you want? You're sick, Tzad. It's like I was okay when we were kids, but all of a sudden I have a career, I'm powerful, and you can't handle it?"

I decide to level with her. "People in my social circle think it's sort of crude to kill people for a living. Not me. But the Neighborhood Watch."

"There's always something. When are you going to grow a pair of balls?"

"You're trying to provoke me."

"A little too close for comfort? Sensitive Superhero. Softy."

"Sticks and stones."

"I want to see if my Superhero is man enough to stop me. You know what I really like about assassination?"

"Stop it." I look around. The place isn't busy enough, no distractions to derail the conversation. No drunken models without underwear. Aside from the clatter of silver against dinner plates, the only sound is a drunken celebutante making out with a waiter in the corner.

"The last look in the victim's eyes. Horror. Surprise. Occasionally, bliss. But not too often. I don't even need the money. Nowadays it's just something to do. And there aren't any Heroes strong enough to stop me."

Blind with rage, I throw a punch. Ever quicker, she catches it with her hand, then flips me over her back. I land on the table next to us, in what appears to be a delicious bouillabaisse. Kaeko turns her head, smiles, and says only, "Sorry." But not to me. To the people whose soup I ruin.

"You shouldn't have let me slip that soy sauce onto your salad. I'm going to relish tearing you apart." She kicks off her stiletto heels.

I panic. I cannot imagine what she'll do to me if I'm without my powers. She draws her weapons, two short daggers.

"Captain Freedom"—her voice is raised so that the other diners can hear—"you don't know how many people will pay for your head."

Her treachery is complete. I'm frightened and confused, and more than a little hurt; I can't concentrate. If my powers are gone, I have to run, even though I'll look like a fool. The gossip columns won't take kindly to my retreat. But I don't dare risk staying.

I close my eyes, as I have done so many times in the past, summoning the talent given to me by my Astra-Zenecan ancestors. I picture Phoenix. Strange word, *Phoenix*, because it sounds like *Feenicks*, but that's not how they spell it. Some sort of a Latin, I mean Roman, God.

I really need to concentrate. There. Focus on the phoenix, you know, that's like *phonics* too. Maybe the Phoenicians came up with the phoenix. No. See it, burning, then rising from its ashes. Much better visualization exercise than trying to summon the weather for Machu Picchu. That I really draw a blank on.

The mental curtain lifts, and the little weather screen in my mind appears. Yes, Phoenix. Partly cloudy, seventy-two degrees, no chance of precipitation. The bitch is lying. My powers are intact.

This is sexist, I admit, but I fight women differently. I show restraint. Punches are pulled, and even though I could break a table over her head, I refrain. She throws her daggers and her darts, and I evade them. I throw tables at her head at high speed but aim them just off so that they crash into the walls around us. Needless to say, the other patrons flee. I pound on the floor, which creates an enormous fissure. She falls into the bar below. I jump behind the bar and deflect several bottles of liquor. Then I throw a fistful of change at the jukebox. With luck it will start playing our special song or even our breakup song. A tense moment, then results: a Bon Jovi power ballad from the prom. My first lucky break tonight.

"I don't want to fight you," I tell her.

She stops throwing bottles. "Then our lawyers will work it out."

"Oscar will eat your lawyer for breakfast."

Kaeko collects her daggers and stomps out of the club. I watch her drive off alone in her bulletproof Alfa Romeo Spyder, which is equipped with a missile system. The paparazzi capture her dramatic departure, and I can only guess what the headlines might look like.

Afterward, I hop in a cab and go home. There's a fight on TV, and not even the primal ritual of men turning one another into breakfast sausage makes me happy. The phone rings—it's a movie-star friend who just went through a terrible breakup.

"Dude, I know what it's like." His voice is that of a broken man who has lost a Tuscan villa to an ex-girlfriend.

"Katana is different. From any other woman out there."

"She moved to L.A. for you. You should have known she was crazy."

"I can't imagine the press tomorrow."

"I wouldn't worry about it."

"No?"

"How many restaurants have been destroyed because of a celebrity breakup?"

"I don't know. I ruined someone's soup."

"You do know. It happens every week in this town. There have been worse."

"Name one."

"Any fight between Kurt Cobain and Courtney Love."

He's right, but I don't feel any better. I call Lily, my press secretary, and she comes right away. Over a bottle of Cabernet, we draft a terse statement to the press: Captain Freedom and Katana have split. They part amicably; she wanted to focus on her career rather than family. All wedding presents, except the All-Clad cookware, will be donated to charity.

Loneliness chases me out of Los Angeles. First my father, then Kaeko. I'm losing the people closest to me, but there's a mistress out there, better, sexier, who will always take me back: fashion.

Storming Fashion Week

It is said that I have an eye for a clean line. Cocaine jokes aside, I think it's true. Like most designers, I don't become a designer because I have any preternatural sartorial ability. All Superheroes, used to hiding their prodigious gifts, are compelled to learn how to darn and sew, to master the Singer sewing machine, because as many times as your mother will offer to sew a patch in your costume, she'll never get the hang of that alien fabric.

In our business, access to costume material is a result of seniority. Each spring Gotham Comix opens the doors of its fabric shop, where Heroes peruse the best in indestructible nickel-plated YKK zippers, waterproof breathable outerwear, the latest in leather boots, and also boots made from hemp or petroleum products that are suitable for the few vegan Heroes who aren't hospitalized for malnutrition.

Heroes who have been with Gotham the longest are given the first opportunity to shop the new material. Back in the beginning, when I first started out, I practically missed the trade show altogether—I arrived late, just as they were about to close up, and picked fabrics for the first-generation Captain Freedom costume.

At first I panicked, since nothing was left, but the suppliers assured me that the company always kept a supply of red, white, and blue fabric on hand. That first outfit looked like the flag of a Central American republic, but it was better than nothing.

When I switched costumes ten years into my career, it was a watershed event, for it coincided with the launch of the Freedomware line of clothing and gear. The clothes have sold well but have never been considered fashion.

The Freedomware line has been available at large retailers for some time* and is spotted all over—some rock bands swear by my Martian army boots—but I can't get a runway.

The fashionistas shun me because of the Equalizer, a breakthrough for facial hair. Most men have no idea that their sideburns, however well trimmed, are hideously uneven. This is a travesty of grooming. The tragic secret is that most ears are not exactly even. My patented sideburn leveler attaches at the face and mechanically moves upward, its sensors defoliating unwanted hair until the desired length is achieved. It's sideburn hygiene that really works. It has three preprogrammed settings: 1890s, *Easy Rider,* and 90210.

I love this product, and I use it daily. I even have my own custom setting, which I might add to the three originals. The Equalizer is successful whenever I appear on the Home Shopping Network; in fact, it sells itself, but I believe such finery needs to be embraced by the aristocracy. Just because you're rich or famous does not mean you have more time to trim your sideburns.

---

* First it was just underwear, then swim trunks and sunglasses. Now I have a full line of sportswear and suits and a fragrance.

But it will take an invention of sheer genius for the fashion world to understand my gift, and for the designers of the world to accept me as one of their own.

New York's Fashion Week will be turned topsy-turvy when I model the newest, most exciting piece from Freedomware: a velvet suit with an inner microfiber lining that keeps you warm at 25,000 feet and doesn't need to be ironed. The fabric, called Cor-tex, came from an unknown supplier who's hoping to break into the Superhero market.

I shouldn't say that the suit fits like a glove. That would be a cliché. But I can say that it latches onto my abs and lats as if it were a very expensive car negotiating dangerous mountain curves. The gusseted crotch provides ample freedom of movement. It is also available in a blazer.

I pack my new Cor-tex samples carefully and fly to New York to attend my first Fashion Week. I assume nothing will stop me. But I am wrong.

Several things stop me. They are called Supermodels.

The night I arrive, I check into my hotel and immediately drop by an invitation-only party in a downtown loft. There is quite a bit of buzz about my being here; I'm the first Superhero who has ever attended, much less presented his own line of clothing. People are stunned by some leaked sketches of my Cor-tex outfit. They cannot believe that anything could be brand-new and yet look so vintage, without the disgusting fact that somebody else has worn them. By the end of the night, after more than a few chilled vodka shots, I have become the life of the party, regaling the rest of the group with tales of Villains and monsters.

"Captain," purrs Jaguar, a Brazilian Supermodel, "your hair

is purr-fect. Have you ever had to fight the crime with your roots showing?"

"Actually, I'm a natural blond."

The Supermodels stare at me, and I hope I haven't offended them. Perhaps they've never known any natural blonds?

"Who will be representing Freedomware on the runway?" asks Titania, a volleyball champion turned model from Sweden. She is so tall and beautiful I am almost afraid.

"I will. Myself."

The models titter.

"That's a bold move," says another, with the sexy hint of an English accent. She has black pixie hair. I don't recognize her from her lingerie ads, but she somehow seems familiar. She smokes a cigarette, and that makes her look dangerous. "Why don't you come into the kitchen with me and fix me a drink?"

She takes my hand and leads me into the kitchen.

"Who are you? You look familiar."

"My name is not important." Mysterious. I like that.

We are alone in the kitchen, and I squeeze some lime into her gin. We smile and talk of the endless cycle of work and gossip that is Fashion Week. "Who do you work for?" I ask her.

"Myself. With some friends in Milan."

I want to get to know this girl better, and I get nervous and start talking away about the new fabrics and whether we might see bulletproof suede anytime soon. She puts her index finger on my lips and says, "Shh."

"Are you a librarian?"

"Not anymore." We stare into each other's eyes, and I am planning what to make this girl for breakfast tomorrow, until I realize that I'm not at home. I'm staying at a hotel in New York, and that's too bad because I don't know where I might take her for breakfast. Then I recall that she's a model and she doesn't eat, so that's okay. Then I realize I've fallen into a trance.

The woman snaps her fingers. Jaguar and Titania appear and take me by either arm.

"Take him down." I am happy to go with these women; in fact, I am powerless to resist them. I still have my own mind, but in a way I have become a fashion zombie. Then all at once I recall whom I'm dealing with. Her name is Rebel Spice. She was an original member of the Spice Girls who departed the ensemble just before they became famous. There were various rumors about her in the tabloids, and I'd heard that she'd been forced out of the group because she killed a man; others say she *is* a man.

The two vixens take me to a subway station, which is odd because I never imagined that a Supermodel would take the subway. They do not. Instead, they lead me into a maze of unused tunnels. There is little light, but they seem to know where they are going. "Good night, sweetie," Titania says with a smile, and knocks me out with a single, powerful blow to the head.

It never occurred to me until right now, as I wake up in some manner of dungeon, my head playing the part of a bruised watermelon, that the difference between regular models and Supermodels is the presence of superpowers.

Several shapes move around me, and a torch is lighted. There is a coterie of attractive, waifish boys in the chamber with me. "Can someone tell me what's going on?"

A young Italian with shoulder-length hair introduces himself.

"I am Spartane. You are here because you, like us, are a prisoner of the Milan Five."

"The Milan Five? I thought that was just a joke. An urban legend made up to scare young models."

"Look around you. They control the world of fashion. Other Supermodels fear them. And they have all the male models under their control. They use us like human shields—for protection, for dates, and as their servants. And they run an enormous crime ring—human trafficking, drugs, weapons, counterfeits, you name it."

"You mean counterfeit clothing?"

He nods. "And we are little better than chattel. Beautiful, underfed chattel. They won't even let us work out."

"They keep you in prison. But there are no chains. Why don't you leave?"

"Captain Freedom, maybe you haven't noticed the powers of Rebel Spice. Try to leave."

He is right. As much as I think I have control over my body, I cannot bring myself to leave this dungeon.

"God, I hate them," spits another model, Fabio.

I learn about the other members of the Milan Five. One of their number is in jail, having been caught wearing white after Labor Day. I imagined I'd spotted the other model, but the woman I saw isn't a model at all; she is the chemist Polyester Anna, an evil genius who supplies the world's evildoers with Kevlar bulletproof tuxedos that blend in at gambling tables from Havana to Bangkok.

The days of Fashion Week go by, one by one. The Milan Five let us out each day, only to appear on the runways; but each night, after the very hard work of fashion is finished, we return to our cells. Rebel Spice looks at me with that condescending look every time I see her. However, she gives me a fantastic outfit to wear each day.

When I return to the dungeon on the fourth day, I realize that the situation is desperate. I haven't had a chance to network. All my work to get here will come to naught. The male models are engaged in a bitchfest about our captors.

"I'm so thin. All I want is a Big Mac. But Rebel Spice won't let me have one," says one.

"It's totally unfair that only girls can be Supermodels. Like, it's assumed in the name, and if you're talking about a guy you say 'male Supermodel.' That's sexist."

I interrupt. "Indeed it is. But I can't worry about nomenclature. We have to break these mental chains and get out of here."

The male models circle around me. "Really? Do you think we can?" they all ask at once. I hate to promise too much, but there is a remote possibility to break free.

"What's your plan?" Spartane asks.

"I'm going to change costumes."

"You can't," says Spartane.

"Jaguar will kill you."

"Perhaps. But my outfit might be ugly enough to break Spice's mental hold."

In the secret compartment of my valise sits my old suit, mask and all. The formidable mind control does not prevent me from changing into it, but my changed body shape does. It's hard to wear, and there is more than a little flab that bulges out where it shouldn't. The newest Freedom costume employs special weight-hiding technology, but I have left it at home, as I was planning to act as a designer rather than a Hero. But in my job, there is no distinction. I throw a trench coat over the outfit and wear it out when we are released for the final night of Fashion Week.

One by one, the male models parade down the runways in their absurd outfits, all designed with material provided by Anna. And that material is called Cor-tex. If my hunch is right, there's no mind control. It's fabric control.

"Take your trench coat off," orders Rebel Spice. "It's your turn." I comply, and she is shocked.

"You can't be wearing *that!*"

"Why? Because the mind control is embedded in the fabric that you sent me to make my outfits? Or because these are summer colors?"

She makes another attempt to control me, but it fails. Titania and Jaguar rush to join us. Even without mind control, their various abilities—incredible strength and catlike claws and dexterity—are a serious threat. They just might be calorie-starved enough to be vulnerable.

I think fast. "Titania told me the real reason you were kicked out of the Spice Girls."

"Because I killed a man," hisses Rebel Spice.

"She said you were Old Spice," I retort. She glares at Titania.

"Titania, I heard Jaguar tell Rebel Spice that this season's Jimmy Choos makes you look fat."

"You didn't!" Titania slaps Jaguar as Rebel Spice throws a makeup artist at Titania.

The trio wrestles to the ground, and the group of newly liberated male models ties them up. Out of the corner of my eye, I see Polyester Anna fleeing the show, but I've already alerted law enforcement to be on the lookout for a desperate woman clinging to two Versace gift bags. The male models cheer and slap my back. A stage manager notices my outfit and tries to prevent me from going onstage, but I push him aside. This is Freedomware's biggest moment.

I proudly, triumphantly parade down the runway. Everyone gasps, but I have driven home a point. In these dark times, even the fashionable can be patriotic.

Later, I contact my old friend Garbanzo, the New York Hero who helped me get started. See if he's heard anything about the whereabouts of Polyester Anna.

"You can't touch her."

"Why?"

"She's protected by the Dons of Fashion. You touch her, you're vulnerable to the entire underwear underworld. Take a break. Go read some thrillers on a beach somewhere."

Little does he know that my life will arc in a way that mirrors the very best beach reading.

The Gauguin Cipher

I'm hot on the trail of the world's leading secret society. They are hidden within the bowels of Europe, writhing and festering, spawning malignant outgrowths. Power is their currency, and they dispense it with the ease of a priest giving Communion. They punish me after I bust up the Milan Five—Freedomware has been relegated to Filene's Basement; my couture is no longer juicy.

Normally I wouldn't get involved in this kind of mission. But I just finished reading this great novel about a secret society controlling the world, and I felt compelled to track down one on my own. Or did I see the movie? Maybe somebody just told me about it.

They are locked deep within an arcane calculus; one can divine their means, their methods. I will find them. I will understand the mystery of their power. I will infiltrate, and I will expose them, or at least profit immensely.

A tip from a crooked minister leads me to a seedy bar on a beach in Goa. After smoking some delectable hash, I strike up a conversation with a hairless, toothless, fingernail-less pensioner from Cairo. This ancient hints at the society, a splinter group of early Gnostics who learned hypnosis and other forms of mind control. They converted the Romans to Christianity and allowed AOL to buy Time Warner, all in the name of the sacred god of power. Their original name, in Aramaic, is lost forever, but their very subtle symbol, an altered peace sign, appears like a cattle brand on their car of choice, the Mercedes.

The old man almost finishes his tale and mentions that the secret society could be revealed with an application of Kabbalah. But before he can tell me the next move, he collapses in my arms, dead. It might be because of the knife sticking in his back, but more likely he died from old age. The last thing he told me was that I need to translate a passage in the apocryphal Hebrew Book of Schlemiel. Then, using Kabbalah to translate it to its numeric equivalent, I must chase down an obscure cipher hidden in a series of paintings to find the true meaning. Yet another quest with ancient codes, hidden sects, and famous artwork.

For centuries, men have tried to discover the truth of this secret society. Wars have been fought and men have been murdered to keep it hidden. But those men were not retired Superheroes.

The obvious first step is to travel to Jerusalem, to an ancient, hidden Coptic church. After fighting a demon army and avoiding deadly traps, I arrive at the gift shop, where they sell me one of the few original, signed copies of the Old Testament. Turns out I could have bought one on eBay.

DJ, who now has a thriving superlife of his own but cannot seem to find a way to move out of my Secret Headquarters, alerts me to several Kabbalah Web sites that will tell you pretty much anything you want to know about biblical numerology. For a small fee, they will translate any part of the Hebrew to its numerical equivalent. I gladly pay and now have the Book of Schlemiel translated into its binary equivalent.

That is the easy part. I've got my numbers; now I need the decoder.

I pay a visit to my old enemy, the arch-Villain Black Frank, on the island of Malta at his beautiful but deadly villa. He opens a very expensive red, a 1957 Pont Neuf. Instinctively I test it for traces of soy. There are none. A good sport, he laughs it off and raises his glass.

"To what could have been," toasts the Velvet Fog. I am reminded of our wonderful time when he kidnapped the Dodgers and tried to kill me, and I feel a little choked up.

I tell him that I'm casually looking for a specific sort of cipher. That I'm doing a bit of amateur biblical detective work. Black Frank gives me a wry smile.

"If you're hunting down the Secret Life of Arabia, I'll tell you right now, it's long gone."

I'm after bigger game than that, but I don't let on. "You know I've always been interested in Kabbalah."

"Since when?"

"Since Madonna."

After I promise to ignore one of his more cunning criminal schemes, he tells me all he knows about the secret codex.

The cipher has been lost to time, its pages ripped apart, sent to the seven seas, the four winds, and the twelve days of Christmas. Without it I cannot move forward.

"Is all lost?"

"No," says Black Frank. "An art dealer turned criminal told me the segments of the cipher are encoded within the paintings of Paul Gauguin, specifically those of the Tahitian phase. The secrets are hidden within the paintings, encoded on the naked left breasts of Gauguin's buxom subjects."

I cannot imagine the number of times I have stared at those very breasts—it never occurred to me that I should look for something else.

The Velvet Fog attempts to warn me off. "Searching for such unbridled power will lead to insanity. Or worse. Look at Steinbrenner."

I understand, but once I get going on a quest, I really can't stop. There was this one time when I lost a specific pen somewhere in the Secret Headquarters. It's not that there weren't other pens around, but this one had the right detailing and I liked its heft. For weeks I wrote nothing—letters went unanswered, credit card slips unsigned—until I found that pen. I think I lost ten pounds.

If I had X-ray vision, I could easily assemble the cipher. I could stare at the paintings and piece together the puzzle. But I do not. I do have very good vision, twenty-ten in both eyes, but that is not quite X-ray. Several times I have inquired about laser surgery to get X-ray, but my insurance doesn't cover it. Instead, I buy an extremely expensive digital camera.

On a race around the globe, I spend weeks locating each of Gauguin's paintings of Tahitian women. DJ comes for the shopping. The museums are suspicious of our multiple-flash cameras, but I want to make certain that the paintings do not show up with red eye. Museum guards menace us, but DJ quickly repels them with Celine Dion energy-blasts. I tackle several Japanese tour groups who get in my way. We locate almost every single painting, including one owned by Eric Clapton, who happens to be a friend of mine. We quickly assemble the cipher, but to no avail—there is one painting missing and I have no idea where it could be. It's somewhere out there in the hands of a private collector.

Dejected, we fly home. A retired Superhero should be able to discover an ancient and powerful secret society. I contact my friends at the FBI and NSA, but as usual they have no idea what I am talking about, and the story of my quest is immediately leaked to the media.

There's a darker reason for my obsession: I'm having occasional bouts of superimpotence. It happens occasionally to guys my age. Sometimes I'll go to the gym and bench press a bench, and other days I'll be so weak I'll use the NordicTrack to pretend I'm cross-training. It's partly an inability to focus.

Lionel says it's normal, but superpowerlessness is not like hair loss. Everything I've built is at risk if I can't juggle microwaves. There's supposed to be a sequel to the *Captain Freedom* movie, but the computer programs they normally use to write action movie scripts stopped working after the latest Windows upgrade.

What is it about quests that wrap up all your hopes and dreams into one desperate moment?

The next day I check the mail. There is a postcard, postmarked from Malta. It is a quick note from Black Frank, wondering if I've gotten anywhere with my search and if I'd like to swap time-shares. I turn over the card. It is the missing Gauguin!

We race to the lab and zoom in on this final naked breast. The code is faint, but even this tiny reproduction is faithful enough to give me the datum.

The cipher is complete. I apply the numerological equivalents of the Book of Schlemiel to the cipher, and a dense history crystallizes before me.

Charged with witchcraft and heresy, a splinter group of Gnostics was kicked out of the early Christian church. They settled on a small spit of land between modern-day Lebanon and Syria, where they lived from that day onward. They vanished during the Crusades. Anyone who accidentally appeared on their land was trapped and doomed to a life of Bakelite mining.

Having outgrown their original homeland, the ancient group fanned out around the globe, doing battle with the Knights Templar and kicking the crap out of all competing secret societies. During the French and Indian War, a conflict nobody has ever understood, they solidified their supremacy.

To protect themselves from easy discovery in the digital age, they forged a secret identity. Their front organization is outwardly mocked so that nobody could possibly guess that they corner the market on secrecy.

They became the Hair Club for Men. It's a convenient ruse, since so many powerful evildoers are hairless. But within them is a secret, ancient organization, a CIA within a CIA, a shadow government that not only provides hair for the hairless but also distributes the seeds and trappings of power and celebrity. They control the Mafia, are major lobbyists in all national governments, and provide truly great hair for those who can afford it, increasing the self-esteem and sexual confidence of their clients.

I cancel all my appointments and don my costume. It is the time of reckoning for this dark syndicate. I would also like to know if they wax back hair.

Their corporate headquarters is in the Global Finance and Trade Building in New York City. My celebrity stature grants me instant access, but the security guards and video cameras eye me warily.

"Captain Freedom. How pleasant that you have found us," the HCM president greets me, simpering, his canines sharpened like those of a very elegantly dressed and unusually hygienic hound.

"You know, I'm retired. I'm just a private citizen now. Just call me Tzadik," I extend my hand to shake his.

"Tzadik?"

"X/12-Friedman. Right, that's a forward slash between the X and the 12." Knowing my father's name still warms me, even though he is a dastardly blackguard. He just sent me a postcard from an undisclosed location in the Middle East. He claims he has a new job but can't tell me anything about it.

"I'm flattered that you have come to see me. Judging by that propitious mane of yours, I'm guessing you aren't here for our patented electro-nematode hair induction treatment."

"No. I've come because I discovered that Hair Club for Men is—"

"Actually, we've renamed ourselves. We're the Club for Growth. We're trying to attract women as well."

"Whatever. I know about the secret society."

He appears crestfallen. "I don't suppose we can just kill you."

I laugh the laugh of a Superhero who is extremely hard to kill.

"What can we give you? Your own business? An ambassadorship? A sports franchise? The AMEX Black Card? Of course, you'll be automatically extended a membership to the club."

"You'll have to give me more than that. And forget about mind control. My alien nature is impervious," I bluff.

In a truly illustrious career, I have had many fine moments: comforting the sobs of a nine-year-old or teaching a moral to those ensnared in criminal activities. But as I watch the executive of a secret society bow before me, I have a new feeling in my blood: the total thrill of absolute power. And I'll tell you, I'm a fan.

He folds his hands. Then I hear the distinct pop of a false tooth and smell a whiff of bitter almonds, which is of course cyanide. His dying words are barely audible.

"You have discovered us and know our true nature. It is said, in a more ancient rune than the one you used to find us, that one such as yourself would appear. A King of Kings, the only man who could ever discover our deepest, darkest secrets. Although I will not live to see it, I am sure you will experience power and celebrity unlike anything you have known before." He gasps a few more times to make his point. "Congratulations, Merovingian. You are the chosen one."

The Secluded Order of Secrecy

It is a warm day, with a nice breeze from the Mediterranean. Although I should never write these words down, and they'll no doubt be redacted if this is ever published, I am at the international headquarters of the Club for Growth in the unknown and undetectable Middle Eastern nation of Clandestine. The only way to get here is to be drugged and rendered here by the CIA or KGB or taken by the Canadian Mounties on their mythical flying horse. I have been summoned to this undisclosed location to face a restive board of directors hell-bent on ridding themselves of me, for I have broken their law.

By some strange flip of the genetic coin, I have been identified as the Merovingian, the lost heir of the Hair Club. I attend secret meetings at undisclosed locations: abandoned restaurants, unsightly national parks, the Hockey Hall of Fame. Our publication materials are prepared by blind graphic designers. The quality is lackluster.

As any new leader would, I set forth to use my power as quickly as possible. With inside help, the Freedomware line breaks into the wedding dress niche. Captain Freedom merchandise moves no longer at a slack pace. I carelessly dangle participles. At long last, I learn one of the deep, dark secrets of the rich, powerful, and beautiful: with the help of personal trainers and dieting, they stay thin, as if by magic.

Several board members, jealous of my power and upset that I was born neither of secrecy nor privilege, want to eject me from my position. Another camp supports my new leadership because they understand that a Superhero, having spent much of his life under secret identity, has every right to assume the mantle of Chief Secretive Officer. Unfortunately, the members of my bloc are hunted over several months and gunned down. Alone, I have to face off against the enemy camp. Back in the old days, I'd launch a PR campaign. But the stakes are different here. I must rely on only my wits to survive in a way unlike any other time that I've had to rely on only my wits to survive.

They have good reason to take me down: I can't control my love of talk-show appearances.

From the outside, the compound is well disguised as the impenetrable fortress of some crime boss, but inside it's like the Paranoia Hall of Fame. After I announce myself, a Clandestinian guard escorts me to the kitchen. The false wall in the janitor's closet opens up to a stone staircase, which leads into the bowels of the building. Torches light the way, and there are armed men with masks guarding everything. I feel like I'm in that Kubrick film with all the deleted sex scenes. This is the place "Hotel California" is really about.

The society is composed of the secret leadership from all walks of life. There are ambassadors from the governments of North Korea and Bhutan, Swiss bankers, emissaries from offshore holding companies, and Helliburton, the security firm in charge of protecting the recipe for Classic Coke. A college intern from Skull and Bones has a reserved spot. Six men in funereal suits represent the global economic machinery known in the vernacular as the Man.

It's no surprise that my underworldly father is here as well. He's used his knowledge of Astra-Zenecan technology to develop a method to hack the secret questions used to safeguard online banking such as "What is your mother's maiden name?" or "What was your first pet's favorite toy?" Several banks have put a price on his head, which puts him in the upper echelon of global crime.

The current chairman of the board, who called this meeting, is a political economist who wrote the seminal work on secrecy, a work so important it has remained unpublished in sixty languages. Here he goes by the moniker Ringleader, and he currently consults for the American government.

What can I offer these men who have worked so hard to assure my downfall? They have every secret that's worth knowing; even my secret identity is known to them. I'm just a House of Blues trying to compete with the Hard Rock Cafe.

The Ringleader stands up. "You know the purpose of our little shadow organization. Without us, secrecy would have less value. We are the gatekeepers of all secrets and the infiltrators of the secrets of others. Our currency is disinformation and subterfuge. That is why we, and nobody else, know Victoria's Secret."

Several "here, here's" circulate the room.

"Although we appreciate your great travail in making us Unknowables known to you, and we honor the great power you now wield, we must ask you to leave."

I strike a noble pose and focus my eyes at the glittering islands out on Catastrophe Bay.

"You have broken the unmentionable rule."

I can't deny it. "Was I not brilliant on *Oprah?*"

He sighs. "You represented us accurately, but your behavior was a little . . . " He pauses.

"One might say, insane," my father finishes for him. The Ringleader shoots him a look to indicate that he should leave our domestic squabbles out of this.

"Our society has provided many rewards for the deserving, loyal leaders who recognize the time to resign. Some have revitalized careers in radio. Others star in animated specials or become bastions on celebrity game shows. Others have inexplicably best-selling jazz fusion records."

I watch it all play out. I leave here today, and I'm no longer the head of the most powerful shadow syndicate in the world. I could go back to my life to design clothes and occasionally clobber bad guys, but having tasted this nectar of mystery, I cannot stay away. I need more.

"I know all this, and you know exactly what I want." I repeat my demand.

"Captain, we can't just pick an archenemy for you. You've got to go out and find one for yourself."

To someone who has been surrounded by a coterie of sycophants and assistants for much of his adult life, this idea is unfamiliar. "If you can't get me a nemesis, I'll be happy to continue as your CSO," I threaten.

"Tzadik, we've killed people who can't take a hint," my father parries.

"I've got a better idea," says General Morbid, a representative from INTERBAD. The lights go down, and they cycle through a dull PowerPoint on how they might destroy the lives of everyone I know and love. It's pretty text-heavy and the animations clutter the screen. But the last slide is a close-up of a defiant Kaeko dangling over a pit of venomous piranha-sharks. She looks so hot when she's about to die.

"I understand. Do you need a formal letter of resignation?"

"We prefer to avoid a paper trail," replies the Ringleader. "For all your troubles, we would like to reward you. Please wait in the hall."

I go. The men confer for a few minutes, then the Ringleader joins me.

"If you leave today and never speak of the Club for Growth, we'll make you governor of California."

My sense of politics is dim, but I thought I read something about a new governor. "Didn't we just have an election?"

"Don't worry about that," says the Ringleader. "You can find your way out?"

A boat on an underground stream carries me back to the airport. Nothing can trace me back to the Club. I fly home, and as far as U.S. Customs is concerned, I've been vacationing in Canada. My life is back to normal: quiet and dull, with no midnight couriers delivering confidential stolen documents.

A few months later, the current governor is recalled. He's a popular governor so far and was a shoo-in for reelection, but political popularity is no obstacle for the powerful men of the Club for Growth. They manipulate energy prices, and before you know it, the newspapers issue damning editorials calling to get rid of him. A few days later, he resigns and takes a job at the Heritage Foundation, never to be heard from again.

Freedom to Vote

The governorship of California happens to me sort of the way you sometimes piss on your own shoe. After the last governor was removed from office by constitutional fiat, our creaking ship of state was headed toward disaster without a Captain.

I have no political experience, aside from my too-short stint on the reality show *America's Next Supreme Court Justice,** but the Club for Growth insists it doesn't matter. "You don't have to be a leader," says the Ringleader. "Just look like one and talk like one. Mostly just look like one." All that matters is that I am a famous, attractive man. The donations pour in even before I say yes, and a Draft the Captain movement surfaces on the Web, which I am fairly sure had been engineered by my advisers or the Fanboyz.

I spend a weekend thinking about it at my Indonesian Freedom Fortress on East Tiny. Nothing there to distract me but secluded beaches, an active volcano, and an entire village that thinks I'm a god. I watch the sunset from the fortress control room with a bottle of twenty-year-old Lagavulin and some original Steely Dan LPs,

---

* I can't believe I lost to that Alito guy. He bombed the feats of strength event.

and my decision is made. I leave, truly believing that I could best help everyone and fix all the problems in the state of California—the bad movies, the merlot, the terrible parking in San Francisco—if I become governor. And my campaign song would be "Reelin' in the Years." Although I also consider the REM cover of "Superman"—it's so catchy.

I embark on a listening tour of the state, in which I go from café to tanning salon to tattoo parlor to tell people what a great job I could do as governor.

Before declaring my candidacy, I fly to Montana to consult with my mother.

"You? Governor of California?"

"Why not?"

"You're a washed-up Hero."

"I've got the Club for Growth behind me."

"Who else is running?"

I tell her.

"Why do celebrities think they can run for office?"

"I don't know."

"What about your FBI background check?"

"Copacetic."

"Don't say that. It's not a real word. And that drug thing?"

"We'll admit that first thing. And that same week I'll prevent a bank robbery somewhere or catch a radio personality saying something indecent."

"You'll have to resign as Supreme Monarch of East Tiny."

"But they gave it to me."

"Doesn't matter. You can keep the Freedom Fortress as a tax shelter. But I'm sure there's a constitutional rule. You cannot be a benevolent dictator *and* governor of California."

"Fine."

"What party?"

"I was thinking Democrat."

"Wrong answer. California has more Democrat politicians than porn starlets. You're an ethnic kid—a success story. Honey, you're a Republican."

"Whatever."

Mom even helps with a campaign message. We liberally drop "Keep Freedom Free" in most speeches, but we also need to leverage my knowledge of law enforcement without admitting that I don't know anything else. No matter what people ask about tax cuts, homelessness, racial tensions, the relocation of the film industry to Vancouver, I will always look the questioner in the eye and explain that the beautiful people are California's greatest natural resource, and if elected, I will "keep the streets safe for sexy people."

After announcing my candidacy from a hotel balcony in San Francisco's Excelsior! District, I campaign tirelessly and court a diverse group of people across the state: the wealthy of Orange County, the well-to-do of Silicon Valley, and the affluent of Napa. I meet with critical unions—Sex Workers of the Adult Film Industry and the International Brotherhood of Stuntmen. Both promise to endorse me, as does the West Coast Superhero caucus. I receive more donations from fourteen-year-old boys than any other candidate in history. The money is important, but I quickly learn that I can save a ton by flying myself to campaign events, as long as I give myself enough time to shower.

Throughout the campaign I'm asked to debate the other major party candidate. There are very few issues I'm confident enough about to debate in public, and since there will be little reason to discuss the best spud to use for mashed potatoes, we do everything we can to avoid such a contest. I really don't want to go up on stage and face this guy. It's so much easier to appear at rallies and parades, where I can just talk and nobody is allowed to ask questions.

My opponent gains some percentage points in the polls as he attacks me for not debating, and I have to reconsider. He claims that I don't care enough about the people of California to participate in a debate, which is true, but it's mostly because I realize I cannot win. I try to arrange for a drag race instead of a debate, but we have to follow the low-ratings traditions of the political process. We lower the public's expectations to the point that I'll score positive press if I manage not to drool all over the podium, but at the last second, Oscar employs an old legal trick: he and I have a mind meld, combining my charm with his debate skills, and we wipe the floor with the opposition.

The opposition also makes a big deal out of my secret identity and argues that I should divulge it. I release Captain Freedom's standard background check, tax returns, unairbrushed head shots, and financial statements, and he claims it is not enough, that I should not be allowed to lead a double life just because I am a Superhero. I point out that all politicians live double lives and he relents. The press loves me because I demonstrate various feats of strength during each press conference. I trot out a new trick just for the election: juggling the campaign buses of my opponent.

Election Day is fascinating. I've never been so involved in democracy. Voting never occurred to me. It's really confusing, since elections are every four years. I can never remember whether they coincide with the Winter or Summer Olympics. I just adore the term *gubernatorial*. If elected, I promise myself, I'll use this adjective on a daily basis.

I'll never forget the day I show up to vote. At first I thought it would be symbolic to cast my ballot in Boston or Philadelphia, you know, somewhere historic, but because of some crazy eighteenth-century laws written by guys in wigs, I have to vote in California. And imagine my shock when I learned that you have to be *registered* to vote!

"Can I register now?" I ask the frowning poll worker, a little old woman who is at least nine hundred years old. No registering on the day of the election.

"Can I at least vote against the other guy?" No go.

It's more than a little awkward with the press watching, waiting for me to cast my ballot. I shrug. "My ID is in my other costume," I explain as I smile and fly away.

The rest of Election Day, I fly up and down the state looking for a place to vote. Oxnard, Truckee, Yreka, Copperopolis. Nobody wants me. I finally cast my ballot in the small town of Weed, where people are too stoned to look for my registration.

At that moment I realize that I'm supposed to vote for myself. Isn't that conceited? What would people say if they knew? In the end, I vote for the other guy. Big mistake.

The results are chaotic at best. The first vote count, which I win, is too close to call official and triggers a machine recount, which my opponent wins. Then we organize a hand recount, which he also wins. We win the slide rule recount, then lose the abacus recount. Oscar deftly argues in court that the prior hand recount discriminated against voters without hands, and the judge orders the California Secretary of State to launch the never-before-used foot recount.

In the end, I win by forty-two feet, a sweeping mandate to change California.

How did I defeat a very powerful Hollywood liberal? Was it my secret society connections? No. My agents started a whisper campaign that accused my opponent of supporting an increased tax on Gulfstream jets and Academy Awards gift bags. He denied it, but the damage was done and the biggest donors flocked to me.

My inaugural address is like the acceptance speech that I never got a chance to make for the International Justice Prize.

"Unlike the last ruler, I will not rule with an iron fist. I will be a benevolent dictator, just as I was on the Indonesian island of East Tiny. I will personally fight evil, and I will use my keen understanding of meteorology to improve our agriculture. California will rise again. Keep freedom free!" The crowd roars and we celebrate at the first all-night inaugural rave.

The business of governing turns out to be a gangbang of boredom. It involves negotiating with the state legislature, which never wants to pass my laws because they are Democrats and I am not. Because of parliamentary procedure, I cannot coerce them with threats of violence. The lawmen are totally uninterested in my superlative strength, and I have little power—the legislature is like a particularly virulent strain of teenage girls. I never realized how much corruption there is in politics. When people vote for you, they expect favors in return.

There are some good times. The people love it when I annex the southern half of Oregon, and there's a ton of positive press when I personally save the snowy plover from extinction. People who live in the Californian outback, in cities like Modesto and Fresno, don't like that I've spent so much effort on the coastal cities, but they pipe down when I threaten to implement a mullet tax.

My greatest accomplishment as governor is to sign a law banning illegal space aliens. (I realize that this practice would have prevented my father from ever coming to Earth, but we must do something to prevent illegal immigrants from stealing jobs.) That, and through a popular proposition which I endorse, our citizens vote to make the AtticaBar, now with more nematodes, the official health bar of the state.

There are also missteps. I lobby to move the state capital to Reno. Now they tell me it has to be in the same state! Skip Goodwin writes an article implying my choice of State Energy Bar was motivated by an endorsement deal, but that cannot be true. Since I entered politics, all my endorsements were placed in a blind trust, and I can't legally consider whether my actions have a net positive effect.

It's a challenging state to rule. Such diversity, with models and surfers, beatniks and hippies, vegans and ovo-lacto-pescatarians. How do you govern a state with five professional baseball teams?

And there's that pesky legislature. They block my plan to place mandatory wine stewards in all restaurants. I suspect they're under the thumb of the dreaded Avocado Growers Union, but there is little hard evidence. But I will show them who's in charge.

Texas Hold 'em

After a car crash caused by a mother who was trying to shield her daughter's eyes from an offensive vanity plate, the content of which cannot be repeated here, I urge the legislature to mandate background checks for the purchase of vanity plates. Vanities, I think, are a fine symbol of freedom—I have CPT FRDM on each of my FUVs—but it's obvious that in the wrong hands, they become a weapon, an obscene scimitar of smut.

After countless days of lining up votes, the law is all but ready to pass. And then, at five minutes to midnight, a group of rogue liberals or libertarians—I get them confused—filibusters. Like any good chief executive, I vow to look up the term in the morning and hit the sack.

The next morning, I shave, put on a suit, and take a car over to the capitol to shake things up. California has a referendum system whereby the public is allowed to vote directly on an issue or pass a law. It's direct democracy, like when you elect the prom queen. If I call for a referendum, these lawmakers will crumble. In the past few years, we've passed referenda on higher speed limits, the banning of trans fats, and whether it's okay to drink

Chablis. All have passed, although Chablis was by a narrow margin.

As I'm walking up the steps of the capitol, a sniveling aide approaches me with bad news: the filibustering group has fled the state and scattered throughout Nevada.

"Then we can propose our referendum?"

"No, sir. We need a quorum, and without those guys, we don't have it."

"Can I fire them?"

"No, sir."

Some governors would feel powerless, but they don't share my experience managing a Superhero support team. Within minutes, I'm on a plane to L.A., and my chief of staff contacts Oscar and DJ so we can form a strategy. I will spare no expense of the California taxpayers to deliver these outlaws to justice and to force them to vote my way.

After a brief meeting, Oscar and DJ and I fan out across Nevada, like the Three Amigos of the Apocalypse.[*]

Oscar catches a few of the miscreants with threats of subpoena. DJ stuns another group who are making the rounds on talk radio, making pride their downfall—hiding behind microphones and an AM signal, trying to drum up support for their ridiculous position. But they have no idea that their chatter is their undoing. This leaves a core group to me, and after several legally questionable steps, my tech guy Akira traces them down using credit card purchases, freezing their assets at the same time. Seven of the maverick lawmakers are ensconced in a brothel near

---

[*] DJ is working for me as I pay his way through graduate school, where he's studying Advanced Turntable theory.

Carson City. The proprietor has used the event as free publicity for his establishment.

But I must proceed with caution. No longer am I a carefree Superhero protecting the lives of millions and amusing my fan base. Now I am an elected leader, operating on foreign soil, and my Californian bona fides are worth so much dust here in the Silver State.

The Nevada governor has refused to send in state troopers to arrest these men; he would rather sit and watch the spectacle as it draws media attention to his pitiful state, normally overshadowed by its large, golden neighbor. He's still sore that I crushed one of his pitches out of the park during the annual governor's softball game.

I analyze a technical readout of the bordello's defenses. The Cottontail Ranch is closed Sundays. Alcohol may be consumed in modest amounts, and all the waitresses are armed to the teeth. It's customary to leave a small gratuity after transactions, and the hills around the premises are littered with snipers and the occasional landmine.

I change into a new suit and stride into the action.

The ladies swarm, and I cheerfully note that prostitution is legal here. They ask for autographs and suggest some of their Superhero fantasies, but I know they're trying to waste my time. The Flynt, owner of the ranch, watches me from behind the bar. He wears a black shirt with a black tie—daring, yet it's so obvious that he's trying to look like an outlaw.

"I've come to collect my lawmakers," I say, and I pump the grip of my briefcase handle. It carries the usual gubernatorial gear: signal flares, instructions to the lieutenant governor should I perish, a few emergency speeches protected by leakproof Mylar, and a thousand autographed photos of me to be bartered in exchange for foodstuffs.

"They might be your lawmakers back across the border," chuckles the Flynt, "but in Nevada they're my guests."

"So it's true that gambling is legal here."

"It is."

"You're taking a huge risk, Flynt."

"But I know when to fold."

I hear a coyote howl across the desert. On second thought it might be one of the girls.

"Let's dispense with the Old West banter," I demand.

"Actually, it was more spaghetti western."

"My mistake. You might try billing one of their credit cards. It won't work. Their assets are frozen. And I'm sure they aren't staying with your finest fillies out of the goodness of your black, black heart."

He raises an eyebrow at a hostess, who attempts to run through a charge. I take a quick inventory of all the security cameras in the room. I cannot break any laws.

"It's true, Flynt," the girl says. "Cards ain't working."

"I'm more than happy to pay their tab. But you need to release them into my custody," I offer.

"You win, Freedom. You can have your boys. But I wouldn't try to sleep in Carson City tonight. And don't even think about enjoying my facilities."

"That's *Governor* Freedom."

He twirls his mustache, the sign of a defeated outlaw.

From the bar, Flynt launches several sharp shivs from underneath his gloved hand. I leap up to the ceiling, dodging the blades, which land harmlessly in the wall, except for one that rips up a painting of Elvis and Nixon. I grab the chandelier, swing off of it, and land behind the bar.

After a quick shot of good bourbon, I wrap my arms around the Flynt's neck, reminding him how much he might enjoy a renewed relationship with oxygen. Ever mindful of the security cameras monitoring the room, I smile and remind the viewing audience that my actions are entirely in self-defense and completely befitting the comportment of the head of a populous state.

Then I whisper, "If one of those shivs had punctured my suit, you would have had more to worry about than a slashed painting."

The Flynt nods. We both stand.

"And where are the rogues? Hidden in a back room? Dressed like a group of French maids?" I honestly hope that this is the answer.

"In a well-armed compound high on the hill. I wish you luck." He blows a smoke ring from his hand-rolled cigarette straight at me, but my reflexes kick in just in time and I dodge it.

"Who do you work for, Flynt?"

"Nevada Board of Tourism."

I bid adieu to the lovely ladies, all of whom are clearly saddened by the loss of an opportunity to sleep with me, and trudge up to the compound. It's a crystal-clear night, and the dry desert air smells of sagebrush and the cloying Eau de Ho. The snipers were obviously told to hold their fire. But why?

The renegade legislators sit around a card table in their shabby suite, drinking, smoking, and playing what looks like the longest-running game of Texas Hold 'Em in history. None of them seem surprised to see me. There are TVs tuned to CNN, C-SPAN, and Cinemax.

"Is this a special session, or can anyone play?"

"We're not going," says Rayburn, the chief of their little group.

"I'm your governor. And I own your asses. You're coming back for a cloture vote." I pat an old atomic pistol, courtesy of Chief Justice. "I'm not afraid to use the nuclear option."

"Sir, with all due respect to your position, I should point out that each one of us is wearing an exosuit, giving us strength equal to yours." Livingston, another of the rogues, picks up the poker table and throws it at me at a high speed, but once it collides with my fist, it shatters into several pieces.

"Even though I paid your tab, I'm not doing your housekeeping." I talk tough, but I'm really worried. They stole my prototype exosuits. The exosuits are powerful synthetic supersuits that fit in equally on Wall Street or the Galleria Vittorio Emanuele II. Plus, they give the user superstrength and invulnerability and include an onboard BlackBerry that allows you to receive real-time alerts about the stock market, view forwarded videos from friends, and track the locations of various mistresses.

They shouldn't even know about them. My father must have seen the prototypes when I had them under wraps in the pool house. He's been lying low, sharing a house with Salman Rushdie at Last Refuge, a gated community in Clandestine for those living with death threats. But I can't worry about Dad right now.

"Are you trying to improve morality in our state?" shrieks Rayburn. "Do you really think that oppressive social measures will improve the quality of life?"

It's the most ridiculous question I've ever heard. "I'm trying to get votes."

Burton charges at me. He'll be the first one I send on a journey to the center of pain. We tussle, and yes, his strength is remarkable. I no sooner peel him off my back than Rayburn is on me, stronger than his predecessor. I punch through the compound wall, harvest a two-by-four, and use it like a flyswatter. No matter how much abuse I throw at them, they come back—they're like lobbyists.

CRASH! The room's television hits me on the side of the head. I mop my brow with my silk scarf, and there's blood on it. Again, I fear for my new suit more than anything. I'm weak; I should have eaten before I got here, but I lost my appetite when I was watching those topless dancers. Call me picky, but I can't eat steak where women are naked.

POW! I take another television to the skull—how many TVs do they have here?

With blurred vision, I grab the closest lawmaker—O'Neill, I think his name is—by the legs and try to use him to club the rest of them. But he's an ineffectual weapon. I should have grabbed Johnson, the Whip.

Before I know it, the seven of them have me pinned to the ground, enveloping me in my first legislative boondoggle. A first-term governor is a weak match for a team of seasoned legislators. I need to think.

"You guys win."

"You'll pull the vanity plate background check bill?"

"No."

"But we've got the upper hand."

"And any minute now, the First Sidekick and my personal counsel will be here. Then we'll see how long you last."

Rayburn signals and the group lets me go. "What do you want to do?"

"We negotiate."

I stand up and brush the debris off my suit. I notice the power pack for their exosuits plugged into an outlet near one of the remaining TVs.

"Here are the terms. You seven will return to California, and not only will you end the filibuster, you'll support my bill as well. You'll vote for it."

Burton laughs. "You'd better give us something good. Appropriations. Pork. Zoning for Hooters. What is it?"

"Nothing. I won't give you anything."

"But that's not a deal!" exclaims Johnson. "This isn't how we negotiate."

I dive for the exosuit power pack and crush it under my fist.

"How long do you think those suits will last? Not more than two hours, if they run by industry standards. And we've been playing here for a while. Go ahead. Pile up on me. But once you run out of juice, I'll crush each one of you like a tin can."

Rayburn stays collected, even though the rest of his force looks ready to call it quits.

"You can't make me go back, Governor. I won't go. There's a tunnel here that leads to the Carson City statehouse. And you have no authority in Nevada."

"That's okay. You can stay here, Mr. Rayburn. And I'll go back to Sacramento and I'll appoint you to my cabinet."

Rayburn's mouth flies open. "You wouldn't."

"Why not? We're different parties. It's an act of reconciliation."

"But I'd lose seniority."

"And you'd have to live in Sacramento. Full-time. How would you like to run the Department of Education?"

"Sir, please, anything but that."

"Promise me I'll have your vote."

And so the filibuster ends, and the pack of little girls known as the California Legislature bends to my will this one time. We cannot pass a balanced budget or provide decent schooling for our children, but I think that sober, family-friendly vanity plates are a step in the right direction.

North Versus South

I return from Nevada with my legislators. Trouble has been brewing since I left, and my lieutenant governor has done nothing to stop it. When this is over, I'm demoting her to sergeant.

The state has erupted into civil war. Discord has been brewing for some time, and like most family matters, I've done my best to ignore it. There was a recent disagreement that started over trade—Southern California reneged on its agreement to provide B-movie starlets in exchange for allotments of Napa petite sirah. The North answered by holding several visiting dieting/religious gurus hostage.

I return to find that militias have formed for both sides, and a border has been drawn in Gilroy, a town known for its garlic festival. It is so smelly, it's a perfect DMZ. The border skirmishes are mostly bloodless, although several Santa Cruz students are concussed by a volley of Venice Beach diet snack bars.

Back in Sacramento, the press whines that I've lost Southern California. Partition seems acceptable to me, but Washington has other ideas. The Secretary of the Interior calls to let me know that there won't be an additional state because nobody wants to add a fifty-first star to the flag.

I immediately call for a summit of the two militia leaders—Keanu, a Ventura surfer, represents the South, and the North's leader is K8, a militant massage therapist from Tiburon (the name means "shark").

The two leaders meet with me in secret at Berkeley's Chez Panisse. We go downstairs to the secret underground bunker, the very existence of which I know about because Alice Waters owes me a few favors. You almost wouldn't know a war is going on here, except for the fact that Berkeley's usual cabal of protesters is protesting itself.

Keanu wears a white T-shirt that advertises an unknown Hawaiian island, flip-flops, and a bathing suit that is long enough to flirt with capris. K8 is in a leather suit made from a cow who died of natural causes in hospice care. Her Che Guevara shirt is to be taken both literally and ironically.

"K8. Keanu. Sit." I offer them seats at a round table in the bunker's conference room. "You know why I called you here. It's time to put California back together. Don't we have any common ground?" Neither speaks. "Both your names start with K," I offer.

"He started it," K8 snarls.

"You're both killing California," I say. "Traffic is up, tourism down. The only people visiting the state are Civil War buffs, and their kind doesn't spend hard currency."

This meeting is a distraction from the main event. Behind the scenes, I use every power of my office. Lily, my PR specialist, launches a California unity campaign. To appeal to the state's love of good food, she and her street team hand out free wheels of Unity Brie. The head of the California Department of Justice, a Hero named Monterey Jack, assembles an elite fighting force to disarm the militias. His unique Guns for Amnesty and Avocados strategy will find its way into counterinsurgency manuals around the globe. Lily lets it be known that if pushed, I will cancel Burning Man.

After some lengthy team-building exercises, K8 and Keanu warm up to discussing strategies for reconciliation. They agree to a cultural exchange between North Beach beat poets and USC film students. I casually suggest that a reunited California could try adopting a baby from some third-world country.

Lily, working as my official press secretary, comes into the conference room to interrupt our palaver. She looks resplendent in her Donna Karan pantsuit. She glares at the two militants and throws each a wheel of brie. "It's all good?" I ask.

"It's all good," she says.

Lily and I leave the bunker, abandoning K8 and Keanu to consider where they went wrong. For them I've devised a special hell—twenty years' hard labor in Alice Waters's secret underground hydroponic herb garden.

Screaming throngs wish to meet me all around the state. I schedule a victory tour, then immediately cancel it, citing nervous exhaustion. I collapse at the Naked Colon Fasting Spa. The first morning, after high tea and colonic (I go for cinnamon), I look at the mirror. My body's been ravaged by the campaign, endless legislative negotiations, and the reunification of the state. I'm definitely getting some work done. A little Botox could do wonders for my eyes.

Although I reunited the state, public support falls quicker than a sand castle on a beach volleyball court. One of my aides snitches that a bottle of Nair has been seen in the gubernatorial bathroom, next to the gubernatorial toothbrush.

Throughout the campaign, I dodged many questions about my lifestyle: why I live with a younger man who is no longer my sidekick; my penchant for fashion; my indomitable mother. At the time, I deflected them with my trademark reflexes. But the Nair discovery leads to further investigation.

The scandal breaks far and wide when it's revealed that while I was recovering at the Naked Colon, I used public monies and illegal immigrants for laser hair removal services. What's worse, several of my staff notify the press that I'd served a Washington State wine at an official government function.

After several weeks of dodging questions, I hide in the governor's mansion surrounded by close aides and friends. It's a good place to sleep—since I don't have to leave, I don't have to face the building's hideous facade. Plus, I could spend hours perusing the gift shop and museum. To gauge public opinion, I create a poll on my Web site: 50 percent of voters want me to resign, 30 percent don't have any idea who I am, and 20 percent want the name of my stylist.

I sit in my very comfortable gubernatorial leather chair in the governor's office in Sacramento fiddling with the end of a resignation speech, a speech I never thought I would have to write, and did not actually draft myself, but will have to deliver on live television at what could be my last press conference.

"How can I make this sound folksy?"

"You don't do folksy." Oscar, my winsome attorney and close adviser, sits at my side and tries one last time to convince me not to go through with it. Everyone else I know and hold dear is out doing damage control. DJ has been sent to Europe until things quiet down. "We can deny the allegations. We'll bury this thing."

"No, thanks." I disable the smoke detectors in the office, and we both enjoy a cigar. "Pandora's box is open. The torpedo's out of the submarine. Can't squeeze the tanning lotion back into the tube. And I'm committed to an honest relationship with the public."

Oscar nearly chokes on his Scotch.

"There are ways to get out of this."

"Name one."

"Fake your own death."

I choke on my Scotch.

"The legislature is threatening to subpoena. I don't know what that is. And why is it pronounced 'suh-pee-nah'?"

"It's Latin for *you're fucked*," says Oscar.

"If this were East Tiny, I'd close down the presses and declare martial law."

"I considered that. Then we'd have the teachers' union on our backs."

I deliver the speech on a humid day in Sacto. Bucking precedent, I make sure that the front seats for the conference go to GQ and *Maxim*. I wear a new oxford from the snappy casual collection of Freedomware. The air is electric with suspense because for once we did not leak the speech. I look around at the crowd for a reason to change my mind.

This shirt is really comfortable, and in part that has to do with my hair-free back. I should give this speech with my shirt off!

It's so obvious. At the podium, I rip the shirt off and throw it at an aide at my rear. I linger in that position so that the cameras can catch the Rodinesque sculpting of my muscles and my exfoliated, tamed pores. This feels great. Shirtlessness is my new creed.

"People think it's their constitutional right to criticize my lifestyle. I'm a very private person, and it's none of their business. They ask me why DJ and I live together even though he's a grown man and should move on with his own life. They ask me why I don't date women. It's really nobody's problem but my own. I've not met anyone I can feel comfortable with ever since my assassin girlfriend left me. It's not like girl assassins hang out on JDate.

"I was nearly defeated during the governor's race because of all the tawdry allegations. But my decisions are my own. My obsession with body image is my own. I can admit that now."

The press, the legislature, my mother, and all my supporters stare at me. I think about how the following words will be twisted and turned by the bloggers and the pundits, and worst of all, the French bloggers known as Froggers.

I sip some water. "I am a metrosexual, a metrosexual American, and I am proud." The crowd crackles into whispers.

"This is not just a lifestyle choice; it is who I am. And I am comfortable with it. Yes, I get manicures and pedicures. Yes, I use Nair to remove unseemly fur. Bioré Deep Cleansing Pore Strips? Of course. And as your governor, I should feel free to choose from any number of depilatories without worrying how it will appear to the scandal industry."

I've come to the part of the speech when I must resign. I look around at all the eyes on me. Many people are disgusted. Then I notice the great Republican senator from Utah, an established cross-dresser who has promised to repeal the legislation that prevents half-aliens from running for president. With his backing, after another three years, I can run for the Oval Office. Maybe resigning isn't the best option.

"I will continue to serve the public, if you'll have me."

They won't. The scandal engulfs the governor's office. California's conservatives, mostly B-movie stars and car alarm salesmen, complain I don't represent solid mainstream values. In Berkeley, they protest because my hair care products are tested on Tibetan monks. The recall movement picks up steam, and after only one year in office, I am let loose back into the wild. The next governor is a self-aware log of goat cheese from Sonoma.

It's weird that I can't keep a job.

Homeland Security

After moving my things out of the governor's mansion, I return to L.A. At first it's somber, given the circumstances, but my friends are all very supportive. Lots of people who I didn't know were metrosexuals identify themselves to me as fellow travelers. It's a loving environment. DJ throws a huge homecoming party. It's not like I'm alone in my predicament—there is a support group for evicted California governors.

There are many parties to go to, and I decide to check in with an old friend: Lionel, my life coach. We haven't been in touch since my gubernatorial campaign, mostly because I didn't want people to know that I'm mentally unbalanced enough to need a life coach.

For the first time, I visit Lionel's office in broad daylight, in costume, because I am a proud metrosexual, and nobody should be surprised that I am a little unstable. I complain that I am a little lost sheep, that I don't know why I can't hold on to a job.

"Have you ever considered being a consultant?"

"Of what?"

"Of consulting."

Lionel tells me all about consulting. It's like having a regular job, but you make two or three times more money, and each engagement lasts only a few months.

"Isn't that like temping?"

"Temping is for people with skills," he corrects me.

It's not a bad idea. I know only a little about business, and I think it should be run more like a comic book. I try it out for a while, but it quickly grows old.

It's one thing to fly; it's another thing to talk to people about flying. It's still another thing to use flying as a metaphor to projecting earnings data.

I grow listless. I resort to what lots of rich people with unlimited money and free time do: collect things. I collect fancy pens, salt and pepper shakers, rare coins, rare stamps, and rare post offices. A fruitful trip to Vermont yields a few covered bridges, which I install around the Secret Headquarters.

But I can't sit around the Secret Headquarters and stare at covered bridges all day, as quaint and charming as they are. On a lark, I go to a job fair.

The job fair is at the Convention Center. Haven't been here in a while—I think the last time is when I jumped out of a cake and busted some fifty outlaws attending the annual meeting of Thievery Corporation. Once there, I search for the area for famous people looking for work, but to my surprise there are none.

People swarm around booths for popular careers—television producer, reality show contestant, mystery shopper, pimp. But there is one lone booth that I notice in a poorly lit corner. It has no dioramas, no flyers, and the woman at the booth is wearing a shabby suit. Rayon does not work for her. Above her head is a handwritten sign that says HOMELAND SECURITY. I imagine this is a company that sells alarms. She looks lonely, so I say hi.

"Are you lost?" Her voice croaks as if she hasn't spoken to another person in days.

"No. Thought I'd say hello."

"Kay Mortgensen. Undersecretary of Recruitment, Homeland Security." We shake hands.

"Why don't you tell me about Homeland Security?" I ask and soon regret it. She launches into the department's history, and I realize I'm talking to one of those people who looks sane when you approach her, then surprises you by being crazy.

"Do you have any jobs here?"

"Oh, boy, we sure do." Then she tells me about all the jobs in collecting intelligence, or as port safety officer, or in chemical lab security. I tell her I'm looking for something more at the executive level. Then I casually mention that I used to be governor of California. I make it sound humble—the state has so many recalls and special elections, the job of governor has about as much cachet as winning a Grammy.

Her eyes become bright. "You're Governor Freedom?"

"It's not that big a deal. Lots of people have been governor."

"Did you ever have a nanny?"

"No."

"Would you like to lead the Department of Homeland Security?"

"What would I have to do?"

"Fight evil." She smiles. *"Keep freedom free."*

I smile. "Is there any fame involved in the job?"

"There can be."

We fill out the application together.

Apparently, it's a job no one could want. They've asked several important people before me, mostly politicians for some reason. All of whom turn them down. And you know why? Because it's a tough job.

After my FBI background check, there is the meeting with the White House legal counsel, who, like Santa Claus, seems to know when and where you've been naughty. He's not all that hung up on when you've been nice. He asks about drugs that I've used/abused and any possible criminal activity. My record, aside from that stint in rehab that was cleverly disguised as time spent being trapped under ice, is clean. It's strange—he never asks me about my qualifications.

"Ever hire an illegal nanny?" he asks.

"I've dated some."

"That is irrelevant."

My Senate Committee hearing is bruising, but I can take it. A group of old men asks asinine questions, and one of the doddering senators from the South asks how my experience in a cartoon will keep this country safe.

"Comic book, sir. Not cartoon."

"Comic strip. Whatever. Please answer the question, Mr. Freedom."

Oscar's coaching comes to me: "By using free market forces to incentivize a secure homeland. You leave the market alone and it will make itself safe."

The room is silent. They don't seem to understand.

"I'll secure the homeland by keeping freedom free. But not so free that people take unfair advantage of that freedom."

The senators launch from their seats and deliver applause. The committee chairman addresses me.

"You haven't held a substantive job in several years, and there are a few murky reports about drug abuse. That and your unabashed metrosexuality should make this an uphill confirmation battle."

"I understand."

"But the press seems to like you. You are a celebrity, and that's exactly what this Administration is looking for."

The committee votes to pass its recommendation on to the full Senate.

I appear for the full Senate vote with Jackson Kibble, the vice president's assistant junior chief of staff. They call my name, and I'm prepared to walk up to the podium. Then I freeze. I can no longer move. The senators regard me and gasp, and I realize this is a terrible showing. Try as I might, my ambulatory powers have fled.

Kibble runs over to me.

"We believe Senator Biding has placed an anonymous hold on you."

I was warned about the power of arcane Senate procedures, but it's amazing. I'm like a statue, but at least I can move my mouth. "Is there anything I can do?"

"Biding probably wants the Oval Office to scrub some environmental regulations," says Kibble. "I can put a call in to the president."

"And until he does something I'm stuck here?"

"Biding may physically release you once he feels his point has been made. But he kept one guy in check for so long the maintenance crew took him for a statue and started dusting him."

"Senator Biding!" I call. "Let's talk." The rotund senator swaggers toward me. I don't know where he's from—I think one of the North states—either North Carolina, North Dakota, or North Mexico.

"It seems to me we should be able to make some sort of arrangement."

"With you?" He laughs. "What could I need from Homeland Security?" I see that he has a point.

"But, senator, I have other powers that could be of great use to you."

"I'm listening."

"A tornado is about to hit your state capital. I could tell you the precise location and time. You could issue an evacuation order, and you'd be a hero."

"Then I'd lose out on all that federal aid money."

This is a much more serious political game than it was in California. I can't appear weak. If I'm defeated this easily by a single senator, I can't possibly secure the homeland. I feel the bated breath of the seven people watching C-SPAN.

"You know I still have a lot of influence in California. You may just find yourself facing an avocado embargo."

He stiffens. "People in my state don't eat that hippie fruit."

I know he's bluffing and I have to push further. "Fine. With a word I could inspire millions of Californians to move to your state. Before you know it, you'll be swimming in freeways and juice bars."

"Enough!" he snaps. "Release the hold."

The full senate votes to confirm me, and I become the first metrosexual American with a cabinet-level position.

The government pays to relocate me to Washington. Finally, I sell the Secret Headquarters. It tugs at my heartstrings, but it is time to let go. It's too expensive to maintain the shark aquarium and the dinosaur play area. I release the ancient reptiles on an island off the coast of Costa Rica, where they can experience a free life in their own habitat. With a little encouragement, they'll eventually terrorize the local populace.

The shadowy leader of a crime syndicate buys my house for an undisclosed sum. He pays in cash, which makes everyone happy. I say my good-byes to my staff, and like the leading actor in a successful television drama, I wish them luck in the spin-off shows that are their lives.

DJ and I fly east, but our destinations are different. He moves to New York, hoping to make it as an East Coast Superhero and as a performer of turntablism. I have purchased a home in Bethesda. It is cozy with its seventeen bedrooms, but it still feels too empty. I invite my new sidekick, assistant secretary for Homeland Security, to come live with me, but she declines.

The work begins immediately. We conduct polls and focus groups. Since the key to securing the homeland is perception, I introduce the Alarmist, a lovable cartoon character that teaches kids that *Security Just Takes a Sec*. We hand out plushy Alarmist dolls for children. Each one comes with a convenient wireless surveillance system.

"I don't really like that title, 'Secretary,'" I announce to my undersecretary.

"What about Czar? That's a popular one."

"Sounds imperial. How about Overlord?"

Just like that, my title has been changed from Secretary Freedom to Overlord Freedom. I believe it connotes a certain level of somber threat that is appropriate for the job.

Along with keeping the nation safe, I oversee and coordinate various sectors of government, and I am the muscle of the executive branch. Whenever a senator falls out of line or a newspaper threatens to report some scandal, I am there as the strong arm of the president. My lightning-fast reflexes are nimble enough to counter any bureaucracy.

Once again, I am a crime fighter. Out of retirement, out of the wilderness, now I have the power to do good, to prevent others from doing harm. In this new position, I am a public servant, not accountable to comic book sales and movie grosses but to the president of the United States, a man whom I'm sure I might eventually meet.

Each day I show up at work early, sometimes as early as nine-fifteen. The staff is already there, the coffee is made, and I sit down at my desk to ignore the paperwork that piles up there. Certain things—when they say CLASSIFIED or TOP SECRET—those I read. Then I look at e-mail and enjoy some amusing links that have been sent to me by friends. I wait until four p.m. to leave for the day, early enough so that I can avoid rush hour. It's like being the nation's computer guy—nobody notices what a good job you've been doing until something goes terribly wrong.

One morning, the red phone rings. Ordinarily, I wouldn't answer it. But the Undersecretary for Presidential Communications runs in to tell me that the red phone operates on a line that can only be accessed by the president or his chief political adviser.

"Free Man! How you doing over there?"

"Fine, Mr. President."

"Beat up any bad guys lately?"

"Not as many as I'd like to, sir."

"Ain't that the truth. How's that intelligence reorganization going?"

"What?"

"That immensely important part of your job whereby you co-ordinate intelligence among various bureaucracies so we don't have that stovepipe problem."

This man makes no sense.

"Sir, I can tell you a crucial fact. I've reorganized the color coding system."

"Really?"

"Now it's seven different colors. Used to be five. I added magenta and indigo."

"You did that all by yourself?"

"Yes, sir."

"That's a good boy. There is one more thing I need from you."

"What's that, sir?"

The president goes on to describe an unbelievably important mission, the best I've had so far. We hang up and agree to speak again after the caper is over.

I replay the president's words in my mind. "I need you to recover a secret document that has been stolen by a major newspaper."

I've never done a break-and-enter before. Most of my career has involved putting people in prison for doing just that. But my president explains that this is a matter of national security, and if I get caught, my boss will fully support me if I take the Fifth Amendment.

It's child's play to break into the building. A suddenly unconscious janitor volunteers his uniform, and I make my way to the newsroom to locate the document. I find what I'm looking for, but someone has beaten me there.

He stands nine feet tall and looks to be a descendant of a rare race of super-Vikings. His boots and collar boast matching fur trim, a bizarre fashion choice that indicates that he works for the newspaper. My eyes detect that he's holding the very document that I seek.

"Late-night visit to your local newspaper?" he asks.

"Who are you?"

"I'm the Ombudsman."

"And that means what?"

"I represent the people. The Free Press."

"You mean that weekly paper with the explicit sex ads in the back?"

"Not specifically."

"You have to give me that document back. It belongs to the president."

"It's not my fault that he left it in the cab."

"How are you going to get it past the Beltway?" Aside from being an interstate, the Beltway is a magical barrier that prevents the truth from getting in or getting out. My foe shrugs his shoulders.

"This is a matter of national security."

"How can you be so sure?"

"I'm the nation's security guard."

"Don't the people deserve to know whom you're protecting them from? Or why they need protection?"

"You ask complicated questions. Let's fight."

The newsmen hear our quarrel and snap pictures and type their little stories until they hear me threaten them. They scurry out like coalminers at quitting time.

"Captain. I am invincible. I am the will of the people. I am the Fourth Estate."

"Call yourself whatever you like. At least I get the weather right."

We both charge, and when we collide, the friction causes sparks. This behemoth just might be the strongest opponent I will ever face. He throws me across the room, and I crash into the wall. Wall-crashing has always been a big part of my job, but I've noticed it's been starting to hurt over the past few years. A lesser man might become addicted to the pharmacological rainbow I'm forced to take each day to ease the pain. But I'll deal with that later. Right now, I have a bigger problem: I don't know if I can stand. One of my ribs might be broken. Could this be it? Could my four superpowers come to naught? No. I rise up and spit out a tooth.

"Let's take this outside." I pile-drive into the Ombudsman's chest. *SNAP!* My clavicle breaks. Ombudsman's surprised as we break through several layers of steel-reinforced concrete. The night air streams against my face. The city never smelled this sweet.

"Can't you fly?" I ask him. He shakes his head, and I let go. His-large-mass-times-acceleration-due-to-gravity seconds later, he's at the bottom of a large crater in the middle of K Street. I hover over him. Incredibly, he stands up and throws a midsize sedan at me. The taillight catches my eye, and the blow forces me to land. It's going to be this kind of brawl: a car fight.

Traffic is snarled in both directions, and White House tourists and cab drivers alike stop to watch. I choose an empty cab—not the Crown Victoria model, the minivan—and pitch it at Ombudsman as fast as I can. *POW!* Direct hit. He's still standing, but his knees are a little wobbly. If I could find a limo to throw at him or maybe a city bus—that'd be more his style, being of the people and all—I could finish this. But I'm too tired. I lean over and put my hands on my knees so I can catch my breath. Looking around, I see tiny pieces of paper. The nearly leaked file I came to collect is destroyed.

The document is in tatters, but I can glean enough of the title to understand its significance. It reads, SINGLE-PAYER HE—— Perhaps it's a new defense system or a renewed treaty with the Devil. Whatever it is, I have done my part to protect Single-Payer Hell.

The Ombudsman acknowledges defeat, but I can see by the maniacal gleam in his eyes that he's already planning his next caper. Then I realize that I've known that gleam for a long time.

It is Skip Goodwin.

"I almost didn't recognize you."

"I've been working out," he says.

A thought occurs to both of us at the same time, and we regard each other and laugh. This foul miscreant equals me in both strength and wit. The Ombudsman is my archenemy.

We rush to embrace each other. "I've been looking for you for so long," we say at the same time. "You're my archenemy," he says.

"And you're my archenemy."

We laugh again and dance the happy, joyous dance of the Peanuts.

The next morning Ombudsman and I square off on competing Sunday talk shows.

Woe to those without a digital video recorder, who must choose between us. That afternoon I briefly stop at my office, once I've returned the remains of the president's secret document to the department of shredding.

I kick back and put my feet on my large oak desk. Before I can light a cigar, I notice movement outside. I burst out the window and spot trouble—a large crack appears in the dome of the Jefferson Memorial, and the dome falls open like a giant egg. My many years of training tell me a hideous evil is about to be sprung onto my new city, and I'm not talking taxes. Who's behind it? Only time, congressional hearings, and a blue-ribbon panel will know for sure.

After I change the threat-level flag that flies over our building, I launch into battle. I'd tell the tale of this new threat and how I vanquish it, but shouldn't I leave something for the sequel?*

Suffice it to say, I quickly dispatch the menace, even though it was the responsibility of the National Park Service (I need to learn that org chart). I return to the office to lock up. It's hard to remember the code for the alarm system. Oh yeah, 1776. Why did I pick that again? That's right—it's the nuclear weapons code.

As I head home, I make a quick pass over the city. Every-thing looks lawful from up here (aside from the street crime and the Congress). I watch the sun set over the Potomac and wonder what the week will bring.

I have to get fitted for my government-issued costume. There's a law that government uniforms automatically make your ass look big. It's a "We, the People" thing. On the bright side, there's the prospect of domestic terrorism and natural disaster. Maybe a crime spree!

Whatever comes to threaten my country's liberty, I'll make sure it's within my jurisdiction, check with my superiors, and be prepared to deliver the iron fist of Freedom.

---

* Who does sequels? I hate them, except for *Rambo, the Musical*.

acknowledgments

Like many Superheroes, I owe a debt of gratitude to my sidekick. It's not enough to say that DJ does a spectacular job combating Villains, but he serves as my personal assistant. DJ is always prepared to answer the mail, organize my schedule, qualify me for the carpool lane, and make sure that I can get in at Balthazar on a moment's notice whenever we go to New York.

But I'd also like to thank all of the people who've stood by me during my time as Captain Freedom, whether I'm battling a river of piranhas or testifying before the Congressional Subcommittee on Hero Violence:

Lily, my press secretary. Not only has she compiled the most glowing reviews and shielded me from the harshest critics, specifically that meddlesome reporter Skip Goodwin, she has helped keep me on message. Whether I am endorsing a brand of toothpaste or appearing on a talk show, it is always about freedom. She also developed and test-marketed the motto that folks around the world recognize as my catchphrase: *Keep Freedom Free*. I hope that her newly relaxed schedule will help her deal with that incident when she allegedly ran over those people out in the Hamptons.

Acknowledgments

Lucien, the cook. A Hero in his own right, Lucien brings all the savor of Paris but understands the restrictions of the Lo-Cal So-Cal diet. This man has a collection of fine Japanese knives that never dull, no doubt forged in the pits of Hell, and can mince onions without a single tear. He also bottles our private-label wine from the vineyard that surrounds the Secret Headquarters.

Akira, who provides all my tech support and who introduced me to my ever-present BlackBerry. He is patient with my technical needs, whether it's printing a Web page for me or retrofitting my nuclear Justice pistol so that it meets all EPA and OSHA standards.

Jubilee, my personal shopper and sneaker pimp. Whenever I use my secret identity, she understands that appropriate mélange of retro and hip that helps me blend in among the mountains of Uzbekistan or right here in Los Angeles.

No Superhero can operate without his consigliere. Mine is Oscar, my trusted attorney. As time goes on, Villains have become nimble with the law and avoid jail time with ease. But it is my job to crack skulls, and even though this makes certain fey elements of society feel like they're entitled to workers' comp, Oscar doesn't let them see a single dime from us.

Without a sidekick, cook, techie, or shopper, I am just a Superhero with awesome power. With them, I am Captain Freedom.